ULTRAVIOLET

THE NOVELIZATION

YVONNE NAVARRO

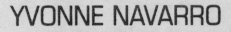

Based on the screenplay by Kurt Wimmer

CONTRA COSTA COUNTY LIBRARY

WARNER BOOKS

NEW YORK   BOSTON

Warner Books

Time Warner Book Group
1271 Avenue of the Americas
New York, NY 10020
Visit our Web site at www.twbookmark.com

Printed in the United States of America

First Printing: March 2006

10 9 8 7 6 5 4 3 2 1

FORCED ESCAPE

Violet and the doctor each had a hand on the titanium briefcase. She slammed the knife edge of her other hand across his forearm. He let go of the case, screaming, and she spun to meet the instant reaction of the Armored Medical Techs. She punched one with enough force to shatter his bullet-resistant glass chest plate; the second, she put her fist through the face visor on his helmet. Another half dozen leapt forward in unison. She took care of their little circle with a double spinning crescent kick that turned her body into a blur of energy. It took all of fifteen seconds for her to decimate every single one of them, and never once did she let go of that white titanium briefcase. Of course, its lovely, pearly white covering was a lot more red by the time Violet stood, the only upright person . . . no, the only *vampire*—in the center of the inner vault.

For My Dad

Thanks for all the things
you've done and continue
to do, and for trying
to understand me.

Thank you to:

Devi Pillai

Weston Ochse

My Dad,
Marty Cochran

Toni Emmons

Jason Erskine

ULTRAVIOLET

AFTER THE BEGINNING . . .

The Earth is a big, multi-toned ball floating in the sparkling, endless expanse of space. One side of the planet is periodically shrouded in darkness and sleep, the other is brilliant with the blues of water, the white and grays of clouds, the essence of energy. From an omnipotent viewpoint, it looks exquisite and peaceful, a world of peace and happiness, without hunger or pain.

"Mommy, is there such a thing as vampires?"

A world where nothing goes wrong and no one has to struggle just for the simple right to exist.

But for a lot of people, it's a world that no matter how hard they try, they cannot understand.

Because appearances can be so very, very deceiving.

ONE

The black helicopter cut through the air above the sky-scrapers of Chicago, moving as swiftly and silently as a deadly eel in calm ocean waters. The buildings below it were simple and beautiful, tall lines of elegant silver steel, concealed concrete and alloy that blended well with the natural beauty of the surrounding landscape and contributed rather than detracted from the environment. There was still concrete aplenty—there will always be concrete—but the heavy, ornate stone and gothic architecture of previous centuries was gone, steel and most of the older, cracked concrete had been swept away by the sleeker, cleaner structures of modern day. The shorelines of Lake Michigan and the Chicago River were lined with green-soaked city parks sporting lush grass and spectacular gardens filled with brilliant landscaping. No smoke or other pollutants threatened the purity of the air, no unnatural clouds marred the crystalline loveliness of the blue sky above the citizens who drank their coffee beneath brightly colored umbrellas and mosaic-covered tables. For as far as the eye could see, nothing disturbed the seamless, balanced blend of mankind and its surroundings—

Except for that dark, windowless helicopter.

Inside its cockpit, the pilot and copilot worked single-mindedly at the controls, navigating via a bank of liquid crystal screens, watching as the display followed the changing terrain and constantly updated the information about altitude, airspeed, and distance. Dressed in black from head to toe, they were sleek and featureless behind helmets with fitted black visors. Their gloved fingers moved over the buttons and controls with impressive speed and efficiency.

"Coming up," the pilot said suddenly. The screen to his right rapid-fired coordinates and a directional grid in a blazing display of red, green, and blue, and his voice was clear over the microphones built into the helmets. "Holding airspeed."

"Echo altitude," the copilot responded immediately. "Forward and lateral drift, numbers falling fast from here."

"On my mark," the pilot said crisply. "Three, two, one—" He jerked his head. *"Mark!"*

The copilot, whose forefinger had been holding over a red-labeled button slightly off center on the control panel, pressed it firmly. There was a muffled thump behind the two men as the locking mechanism on the back cargo bay door released, then the hydraulics kicked in and the door dropped open. The interior of the slim helicopter filled with the scream of wind and speed. Then, triggered by the opening of the door, seven two-meter black steel balls spun out of recesses in the side walls like oversized bowling balls; following the track set into the floor of the helicopter, they rolled smoothly out the open door and dropped into the sky.

The helicopter spun up and away, then disappeared into the distance as the seven spheres plummeted toward a spot just outside the southwest corner of the city, falling into a perfect line as they descended. Direction, descent speed, and wind velocity had all been precalculated, and they hit their target with unfailing precision. While the huge white building would have been difficult to miss, even the strike point itself was predetermined—low on the southernmost corner of one specific building, hitting in a precisely spaced horizontal line running left to right. They punctured the outer walls without even slowing; their momentum kept them going, barreling through metal, wood, plaster, and wallboard, never losing speed and guided by a preprogrammed internal navigation system. Anything in their way was obliterated—furniture reduced to splinters, copiers and high-tech equipment crushed into pieces of fluid-leaking twisted metal, cubicles smashed to kindling. Several puny flesh-and-blood office workers were flattened to little more than wet, red puddles that resembled man-sized blots of dropped gelatin. Finally the spheres reeled to a stop in that same, razor-straight line, dead center in the middle of their target: an enormous laboratory.

Too shocked to move, a couple dozen lab workers and scientists gaped as the first of the shining metal spheres suddenly unraveled, opening like a huge steel seed pod. In the next instant a black-clad figure vaulted out of the leftover bands of metal and yanked a three-foot sword from a scabbard at his waistband that was no more than an inch deep; no one within twenty feet had time to decide whether their attacker was a man or woman, and

they certainly couldn't call for help or finger an alarm—
every last one of them was eviscerated before finishing
useless mental questions about gender or spontaneous
impulses regarding sirens. By then the other six spheres
had split open and spilled their deadly occupants, and
within seconds there was no one alive in the room except
the seven dark arrivals.

The seven figures exchanged glances, their eyes hidden behind day-vision goggles that transformed the sunlight streaming through the skylights overhead to a more
bearable night view. Moving in perfect synchrony, they
streamed across the room like liquid oil, nimbly avoiding
the splayed, red-splattered corpses, aiming for the door at
the far end.

The high-pitched alarms were going off in every direction, but it took nearly no time at all to negotiate the
corridors and get to their main target location—they'd all
studied the computer floor plans until, if it had been necessary, any one of them could have found anything in the
building from memory right down to a specific floor outlet. The only thing that now stood between them and what
they wanted most was the vault door, but the leader's
laser pistol beam ate through the metal alloy like it was
nothing more than slightly stubborn wax. When the starting and ending edges of the laser wound met, the door
seemed to float in place for a long, breathless second;
then gravity took over and it tumbled outward with a reverberating *clank!*

The seven figures stepped nimbly over the threshold,
then they couldn't help pausing. They had been briefed
on what to expect, of course, but what they were
facing . . . it was more than big, more than huge. It was
monstrous, the stepping stone to an industrial complex

the likes of which they'd tried but never been successful at imagining.

The outside of the complex gave no clue about the interior, the way the floor dropped down more than a hundred feet to conceal and protect the endless rows of unbreakable ten-story-tall glass tanks. The blood—millions upon millions of gallons of it—within the refinery tanks glistened in stark crimson relief against the noncolor of the sterile white-washed walls and pristine tile floor, the blistering contrast enough to make a normal person's eyes throb with the effort to focus. If it hadn't been for the fact that the silos contained purified human blood, they might have been raiding one of the ancient oil refineries at the height of the long-ago world oil crisis.

The leader of the group was code-named BF-1. He stepped forward, on the verge of ordering the group to fan out—

Then froze.

The rest of his team stopped abruptly, holding their breath and waiting for his next move. BF-1 raised one clenched fist, holding them in position at the foot of one of the huge silos of liquid scarlet. He leaned forward slightly, inhaling and testing the air, straining to be sure he'd heard what he thought he had—

"Trap!" he suddenly bellowed inside his helmet. His hand snapped toward the minigun on his belt, but it was already too late. Shadows slid from behind the silos all around them—fifty or more Command Security Marines, all packing full automatic weapons. There was nowhere for BF-1 and his team to run, no time to so much as draw against the storm of lead cross-fire that enveloped them.

In mere seconds, all seven were nothing but dead, red mist and body fluids leaking all over the floor.

The gunshots finally faded, leaving the blood storage room full of silence and the stink of smoke and gunpowder. "Clear!" the leader of the Marine group finally barked; there were no more shots but none of the servicemen lowered their weapons, just in case. And, of course, they would never dare remove their helmets, gloves, or filter masks.

After a moment, another team, this time from the police and headed by three detectives, trotted from around one of the silos a bit farther back. The most senior of the trio stepped confidently forward, striding up to the stack of bodies while at the same time snapping on a pair of latex gloves, then yanking a rebreather from the pocket of his jacket and jamming it into place over his mouth and nose. The plastic-coated identification card tagging him as DET. E. CROSS clipped to his lapel twinkled in the room's stark light as he sent a practiced, slightly sardonic gaze in the direction of his men. "Touch nothing," he reminded them. "Obviously."

He bent next to the body of the guy he'd pegged as the invading team's leader, then slipped his finger beneath the edge of the face mask on the dead man's helmet. When he tugged it free, the face beneath the helmet was young and Asian, a good-looking kid whose expression was now permanently serene, the look of a man forever sleeping in death's arms. Cross tilted his head, then curiously peeled back the corpse's upper lip, revealing the guy's canines. They were at least a half inch longer than the "eyeteeth" of a normal person. That, of course, could only mean one thing.

"Frickin' vampires," one of his men, Breeder, muttered from a few feet away.

Detective Cross heaved himself to his feet as he sent

the other man an annoyed but exaggerated glare. " 'He-mophages,' please." He yanked off his gloves and jammed them into his pocket as he stepped away from the cadaver. His tone turned more serious as he regarded each of them. "This is sensitive business," he said shortly. "We're doing everything we can to avoid the appearance of a witch hunt and inflammatory epithets like that don't help."

Breeder shrugged apologetically and tried to look appropriately chastised. Before he could say anything aloud, however, Pedro Endera, the third detective in the group, stepped past him and used a gloved hand to pull a katana halfway out of a tiny scabbard affixed to the belt of one of the dead bodies. He had it out at least eighteen inches before he reversed direction and settled it back into the one-inch-deep scabbard. "Flat-space technology," he said with undisguised admiration. "Dimension compression—very rare, very pricey. The Archdiocese is going to shit when they hear the vam—" He glanced quickly at Cross and choked off the word under the pretext of clearing his throat, but his breathing apparatus did little to hide his mistake. "The, uh, Hemophages have it." He made sure the katana was snug in the scabbard, then crossed his arms. His face was puzzled. "This is almost identical to the attempt they made at the bank in Mid-Delhi last week," he said.

"Not to mention the one in Sub-Ankara," Cross added.

Breeder looked at the pile of bodies, then at his boss. Above his face mask, his eyes widened. "Raul," he said, then hesitated. "We're . . . we're really at war, aren't we?"

Cross let the remark go. It was easier to ignore the comment than say the bitter answer outright, easier to act as though it weren't an issue than admit the massive, ugly truth. He had learned decades ago that words had *power,* and power could bring out the worst in people. Besides, he thought as he frowned and surveyed the seemingly endless lines of blood-filled tanks, something was wrong here, even though he just couldn't quite wrap his head around it. With a little time, though, he would work it out. He always did. He was good that way with mysteries.

"That's queer," Detective Cross finally said. Breeder and Endera said nothing, but their gazes followed Cross's as it slid across the red glass rows. "How did they expect to transport the blood out of here? What kind of exit strategy did they think they had?" Were they bringing in reinforcements? Expecting a sudden arrival of transport equipment? Doubtful—not in broad daylight, not like this. His frown deepened into a fierce scowl as he turned back to face his two men. "Get people on all levels," he ordered. "They must've had a way out. Find it."

"Unless . . ." Endera had started to walk away, but now he hesitated and turned back. "Unless there *was* no exit strategy," he finished almost breathlessly. "We couldn't find one in Ankara." Above his rebreather, Endera's gaze brightened with sudden realization as he met his superior's eyes. "Maybe there's not one here, either."

Cross's lips pressed together and he shoved his hands inside his pockets, absently rubbing a stingy spot on one thumb. He took another hard look around the huge room. "Then what's the point?" he demanded.

Endera's throat worked, as though he were having a hard time actually verbalizing his next words. When they finally did come out, he spoke so secretively that his two companions were forced to lean forward to hear him. "Well, what if they didn't come to get the blood *out*?" He gave them a moment to digest this before adding, "What if they came to *infect* it?"

Cross and Breeder stopped, then slowly turned their heads toward him and stared. "Ad Sul," Breeder finally managed. "You mean like . . . creating a bomb? An H.P.V. *bomb*?"

Detective Endera nodded starkly. "One that would go off inside our population," he said hoarsely. "Creating thousands more just like them—"

"Ad Rasul!" Cross cut him off and spun toward the hazard teams that were waiting for orders. "I want a containment brigade on this facility instantly!" The team members leaped to obey, scurrying toward the exits to secure them and babbling instructions into their mouthmics.

Endera grabbed his boss's elbow and Cross pulled his arm away in irritation as he tried to think. "But . . . *Jesus.* What about that Mid-Delhi blood?" he asked urgently. "And Ankara? That stuff's already out!"

Detective Breeder suddenly gasped. "Oh, my God—*Cross*!"

Breeder jerked toward Endera, then followed his coworker's gaze to Cross's thumb, the one the man had used to pull back the dead vampire's lip and expose his canines. Cross was staring at it, too, stunned to see the bright, thin line of blood oozing from a tiny break in the skin—the super sharp edge of the Hemophage's tooth must've sliced right through the protective latex. Their superior's gaze cut to Breeder and his eyes widened, but he already knew it was too late. Before he could bother to protest, Breeder snapped his pistol up and shot Cross right between the eyes.

≈

Six dozen Lockheed F-48s ringed the blood refinery at pre-specified altitudes, circling the facility in a combat pattern to ensure no other aircraft violated the now-prohibited airspace. After the evacuation and sanitization of all personnel, the containment brigade had gone through the building a final time to ensure that all personnel were removed and all potentially hazardous machinery had been shut down and disabled. Then the team had carefully positioned its equipment: sensors throughout the facility, the radio detonator, and finally the explosive device. Only one F-48 flew within the actual range of the coming nuclear blast; this one would drop the laser-targeted FAE—fuel air explosive—at precisely the moment necessary to contain the radiation blowing outward. There was a backup fighter in case something happened to make the lead F-48 fail its mission, but that was a far-fetched and, if it happened, deadly scenario. Failure of the FAE to drop and/or hit the target at the precise moment would mean that most of Chicago—and its residents—would end up nothing more than a nuclear wasteland.

From the ground, the circling military planes looked like a tornado speckled with glittering black and silver triangles. They held their pattern for a good twenty minutes, then there was a sudden, dull *WHUMP* at ground zero. The refinery and everything inside and around it simply . . . disintegrated in a ball of molten light. The F-48s shot upward, engines screaming as the pilots pushed to stay above the blast zone. Only the lead one lagged slightly so he could release the FAE immediately after the detonation of the mini-nuclear device. As he turned the nose of his jet upward and pulled back on the throttle, the thirty-five-year-old pilot was more concerned about the success of his explosive device than escaping the blossoming cloud. His family was down there, his wife and three kids probably eating lunch right about now in their house in Des Plaines. His two boys and toddler daughter loved peanut butter and jelly sandwiches, and if something went wrong, all three and his wife would end up drenched in radiation poisoning, nothing but walking dead.

But no—

The FAE dropped into place and detonated precisely when it was supposed to, right to the millisecond. There was another sound, deeper and more condensed, and suddenly the burgeoning mushroom-shaped cloud collapsed into itself, layer after layer folding in as though an immense, unseen vacuum cleaner was sucking every bit of the poisonous matter out of the air. It took a total of twenty-eight seconds for both the nuclear bomb to obliterate the refinery and the specialized FAE to eliminate the remains of the nuclear bomb.

And then nothing was left except a gigantic, blackened scar on the Illinois soil that the government would surround with twelve-foot electrified fencing and let lie fallow for the next seven decades.

TWO

Sometimes, right before some especially important event in her life, Violet would stand at the window and stare at the seemingly endless ocean of buildings outside. It was an impressive thing to view, particularly because of the way mankind's architecture and design had evolved to blend itself with nature. So much effort had gone into ensuring that what man created would harmonize perfectly with the sky and the earth and everything else built around it.

Harmony.

Such a small word.

Had there ever been a word more overused by hypocrites?

The world into which Violet had been born was one that some people found difficult to understand, her included . . . yet in other ways it was all too sadly familiar. It was interesting that only the scholars seemed able to appreciate the mistakes that mankind continued to make again and again, despite their best intentions and their perpetual and sincere belief that they were wiser than the previous generations. Those in power, the elected officials and the people's representatives, were apparently doomed to repeat the errors of the past, each action masked by their oblivious claims to a wisdom they didn't have now and had never possessed.

The root of their difficulties, Violet supposed, lay in the fact that the twenty-first century had been, for all intents and purposes, the last era of any kind of mystery. Mankind had experienced such a sudden upsurge in knowledge and discovery that by the end of the twenty-first century, nearly all riddles had been unraveled, all problems had been solved—even the common cold had been cured. String theory had been unified, the secrets of space revealed, nearly everything that could be known, was. Or at least that's what everyone liked to believe. So if someone had a question, someone else, somewhere, now knew the answer—

Santa Claus? Nope. Loch Ness Monster? Definitely not. Chupacabra? Actually, yes. Will parsley really kill parakeets? Sometimes. Oh, and the one question people had always had:

"Mommy, is there really such a thing as vampires?"

Like the discovery of some previously unknown stinkbug on the Asian subcontinent, the answer turned out to be *"Yes."* And strangely, many didn't even know what they really were.

The records archives, the older ones, still held the story—apparently no one saw any reason to soften the ugly facts of how everything had started so long ago, how mankind's terror and prejudice had changed and unified and multiplied. Violet knew the facts and figures by heart, had gone over them a thousand times in her stud-

ies. For some, that's all it was—statistics, history, a part
of the past to be learned about but not actually learned
from. The *past*. But the things that happened before had a
nasty way of coming back to haunt what was going on in
the here and now.

It was kind of fitting that it would all come down to
business here in Chicago. After all, for her the end of
everything had started here, with a young woman who'd
been a nurse at Loyola Medical Center for three years
before she'd gotten pregnant. She and her husband had
been trying for a child for quite some time—long before
she'd gotten her nursing certificate—and they were overjoyed. Everything went wonderfully the first four
months: she didn't have even a hint of morning sickness,
she gained weight at a reasonable rate, she even glowed
in that elusive, special way that people sometimes say ex-
pectant mothers do.

In her fifth month, however, the woman had started
feeling a little on the down side. While her husband
teased her by calling her "Plumpy," her skin went a little
paler than it should have been and she felt more tired than
normal given the stage of her pregnancy. Worst of all,
after having been an outdoors person all her life, she developed a really annoying allergy to sunlight. All a bit
odd, but probably nothing to worry about; even so, she
and her doctor decided to do a few routine blood tests,
just to be on the safe side.

Every avalanche has to start somewhere, and with this
one it had been in a blood analysis lab at Loyola . . . and
Northwestern University Hospital . . . and Cook County . . .
and a thousand others across the country, nearly simulta-
neously. An untold number of lab technicians bent over

blood spectrograph results and stared at numbers that simply couldn't be true.

But they were.

At ten after six on a Tuesday morning, she was dressed and almost ready to leave for her morning shift when the doorbell rang. Even now she remembered how for no discernible reason her stomach had performed a nasty roll, the kind a person gets when she nearly drops some particularly treasured piece of antique family crystal. For the next few seconds she was left feeling sick and slightly disoriented, then she gathered herself and headed to the front hallway; by the time she got there, she'd already put that feeling—premonition?—out of her mind. When she opened the door and shaded her oversensitive eyes against the morning sunlight, the nurse fully expected to find the paper girl (her husband had forgotten to leave out the monthly check the day before), so she was more than startled to find a pair of federal agents flashing badges at her while a white-coated, thin-faced doctor hovered nervously behind them. Instead of clocking in at seven A.M., she found herself hustled to a stand-alone outbuilding on the Loyola grounds. There she stood, until her back ached and her feet hurt, in a line that was long enough to curve around and out of sight. Like her, no one else in the strangely silent line had a clue as to why they were here beyond some anonymous doctor's terse statement that they were "sick" and the government required them to register because of it. They were told that the armed military men and women patrolling the area were for their safety. That, of course, was a bald-faced lie, just one more added to more incidents of deception than she would ever be able to count.

Really, to use the term "vampire" was nothing short of

sensationalism. The condition was nothing more spectacular than a blood anomaly that had probably been around for centuries but never been detected before the latest and greatest improvement in medical equipment. The phrase "blood condition" just didn't pack enough punch for the news, though. VAMPIRES ROAM OUR STREETS! sold a lot more papers and sponsor slots on the expensive satellite television stations. The masses just loved "true" journalism.

In the end, it didn't matter what they were called, although prisoners would have definitely been a far more accurate title. They were all discovered, all documented. All *studied*.

She didn't know why it was necessary, but she suspected that the rest of the people who'd stood in line with her on registration day had ended up with their heads shaved, too. The medical and military people hadn't given her a choice, just leaned her back on an examining chair, strapped her in before she realized what was going on, and done it. By then, when she was told to shut up, she obeyed. She wasn't allowed to look in a mirror afterward, but the sight of her hair—at the time it was long and dark—dropping to the white floor in clumps had outright terrified her. This was America—no one just got yanked out of their homes, shaved, and held against their will.

Did they?

She cooperated as best she could. Again, she didn't have much of a choice—any at all, as a matter of fact—but she'd always been an optimistic person and she couldn't let go of the hope that if she did everything they asked, submitted to each and every one of the dizzying and inexplicable array of medical tests without protesting, they—that omnipotent, royal *They*—would let her, and of course her unborn child, go free.

From her, the feds definitely got their money's worth in terms of interesting information. As it turned out, in some ways the old legends that had grown up around the disease over the years were true . . . well, in a warped, slightly ghoulish sort of way. Most, of course, were not, and more than a few of the government's scientists looked the fool as a result of their silly assumptions. One of those prime times had been when she'd looked puzzled and clearly sardonic as a team of analysts marched into the examination room and showed her, of all things, a gold crucifix.

The disease was ultimately called Hemophagia, and its primary symptom was detrimental to no one but the carrier—that unfortunate man or woman who soon discovered that he or she possessed an aggressively accelerated metabolism. The medical team was intrigued to find her average body temperature was one hundred seven, even though she insisted she felt fine and her pregnancy was advancing normally. Electrocardiogram tapes consistently recorded a strong and steady resting heart rate of an unheard-of hundred fifty beats a minute.

It all seemed good, but as the old saying went, nothing really good comes without a price. All this cellular activity took an unwanted toll on the carrier's body. With their metabolisms speeding along at unprecedented rates, the victims of Hemophagia could expect to survive, if they were lucky, no more than ten years after their first exposure to the disease.

Appearance-wise, well, there wasn't much to see. Yes, they had slightly elongated canines, but certainly not the wolflike teeth of legend, and even these were easily at-

tributed to the massively increased density of bone and
dentin throughout the body. On a physical level, they
were simply stronger, and if you checked the skeletal
X-rays of any carrier, you could see right on the films that
Hemophagia accelerated healing. Some of the deeper
wounds inflicted on the young woman at the height of her
"testing" healed in only a matter of hours.

As the disease progressed, its symptoms became more
pronounced. No, its victims didn't suck blood . . . but it
did cripple the body's ability to regenerate blood
platelets. As a result, Hemophages were pale and anemic,
and they required frequent blood transfusions to stay
alive. The longer they were afflicted with the disease, the
more sensitive they became to daylight. The pregnant
young woman was a prime example of that—full term in
her pregnancy, every time she walked in the hospital gardens she had to use a cane and carry a heavy black um-
brella to protect herself against the glare of the noonday
sun.

All that stuff about silver bullets and stakes? Total,
ridiculous fantasy. Yes, the Hemophages were a little
faster and a little stronger than an uninfected human, but
they died just like everyone else.

And just to be sure, the feds tried out that theory on
their "guests" in a number of unsavory ways.

Her belly was flat now, bisected by a cesarean scar
where they'd taken her unborn child out of her belly and
disappeared with it—she didn't even know if it had been
a boy or a girl. Were they experimenting on the baby just
like they continued to experiment on her? Her mind
screamed with need and rage, but physically she was too
drained of will to protest, too weak and sedated to fight.
Her child was gone and she was outnumbered—she

could never escape. There was nothing to do but submit to the straps and the chair and the endless parade of medical personnel and military guards—

—even when they killed her.

She was surrounded by monitors and screens, but she still didn't know enough to see the inevitable coming, she was still too innocent. The electric shock was . . . unexpected. Indescribably painful. And, of course, utterly lethal. What the smug scientists discovered, adding another interest point to their charts and their records and their graphs, was that Hemophages were like anyone else: if you killed them, they stayed dead. Unless, like this young woman, you needed them for just a little while longer. In that case, a nice pair of paddles, a bit of lubricant, and a portable defibrillator would work just fine, and so they could continue their experiments.

But the world didn't end at the locked doors of the laboratories. Outside it was chaos, first one—the discovery of the disease—then another transnational conflict. The second one was the more devastating—wars fueled by religion usually are. It wasn't long before the protests and the marches mutated into full civil war, and the catalyst for *that* was the government, doing what governments have done since the beginning of time: trying to make a bigger, better, faster, stronger weapon.

By the time the federal doctors started withdrawing enough daily vials of her blood to see if they could alter it to make a better and faster soldier, the woman was numb, someone who'd lost everything of value and was now barely anything above a still-breathing zombie. In another part of the medical complex, in a laboratory marked CLASSIFIED ACCESS ONLY—IDENTIFICATION REQUIRED, a group of high-ranking men in military uniforms—lots of shoulder stars and bars—were given a detailed tour by a distinguished-looking doctor. Even though the doctor had salt and pepper hair and carried himself well, it wasn't lost on his guests just how eager he was to please them—after all, federal money was always a boon to any contractor project.

There are some things in the universe that always turn out the same way . . . the *wrong* way. Some folks call it "Murphy's Law"—whatever can go wrong, will. Others just label it plain old stupidity, the hunt for power, the never-ending greed inherent in the DNA of those mere mortals who can never seem to control or stop their own repetitious mistakes.

They didn't make a better soldier, or a faster one, or a braver one. As he watched the generals and the lab supervisor move across to the other end of the facility, one of the lab technicians frowned, then pressed his forehead back up to the eyepiece of his microscope. What he was seeing was anything but good—the original strain of virus had been devastating to its victims, yes, but only over time. The virus was just an anomaly, an oddity of nature that could doubtlessly be contracted by some as-yet unknown method, but it wasn't even contagious—a carrier couldn't give it to a noninfected person, even with blood-to-blood exposure. And like smallpox, there was a segment of the population—in this instance, most of it—that was simply immune.

But this strain, the new one born of DNA modification and laboratory processing and which they'd dubbed "H.P.V."—HemoPhagic Virus . . .

This was more virulent, extremely fast-moving, highly contagious, and just like its predecessor, incurable.

The technician sighed and looked up again, then rolled

his stool away from the lab table. He couldn't wait any longer—this had to be brought to the attention of not only his supervisor, but those higher up the chain of command. His supervisor was a nobody, a brown-nosing guy who looked more distinguished and intelligent than he actually was. The higher-ups had to know the dangers inherent with this kind of DNA modification, and if the lab tech himself had to take a little bit of heat for being the one to precipitate the closure of the project, then so be it. Med and lab techs were a high-demand field nowadays, and he could always find another job.

He reached forward with his left hand and spun the coarse adjustment knob on his Meiji microscope until the stage lowered, then tugged the glass slide out of the stage clips and lifted it from the stage. He started to turn toward a sterilized petri dish, then realized that for some reason, his thumb was stinging. When he glanced down at his hand, everything he saw registered in his eyes but didn't want to feed into his brain. Time changed, went into a sort of slow-motion crawl as his knees went weak and his breath stuttered with terror. It was a damned good thing he wasn't standing far away from his stool.

His first mistake had been not removing the slide more carefully from the stage—he'd cut the pad of his thumb, ever so slightly, on the bottom corner of it. It was nothing, really, no more than a prick, like the tiny wounds that were the result of the glass shards they'd used in blood testing back in the twentieth century. A minute drop of his own blood was smeared across the skin's surface, barely noticeable. Like sticking your finger with a needle when you try to sew on a button, and hadn't his mom always said that a button wouldn't stay on if you didn't add a little blood?

But the second mistake—oh, that was the killer, all right. Literally.

He'd put a bit too much solution on the slide, only a half drop over the recommended amount, but it was enough to make what was on the slide squeeze out the edges. And the edge, of course, was exactly what had punctured his skin . . .

He was infected.

The technician barely held in his gasp, then abruptly plunked back onto his stool. His heart was thundering in his chest—he could hear the strong and steady rush of blood in his ears, see his vision throb around the outside edges of his eyes the way it did when he sometimes had a migraine and he didn't have the migraine-suppressant inhaler handy. But he didn't want his heart to be doing that right now, because every involuntary contraction of that muscle in his chest pushed the HemoPhagic Virus farther and faster into his system—

Who was he kidding?

He was infected. Period. If they found out . . .

He folded his thumb into the palm of his hand along with the slide and made a loose fist, then slid his hand nonchalantly into the pocket of his lab coat. He had a single, nearly panicked moment when a glance in his supervisor's direction made him think the hawk-eyed man was staring at him, but no . . . the man's gaze went back to the general who was yap-yap-yapping at his side. He spent a long, *very* long, ninety seconds bent over his microscope and acting like he was studying his work; then, when he was sure the bleeding had stopped, he calmly walked to the bathroom and washed his thumb. After that he wrapped the slide in a wad of toilet paper and smashed it under the heel of his shoe. Then, when his hands finally stopped shaking, he flushed the evidence down the toilet, and he and his destructive little secret went back to work.

And that, as they say, was that.

THREE

Things changed even more after the mutated version of the HemoPhagic Virus got out of the lab and insinuated itself among the ranks of the uninfected. The disease established itself so rapidly in a new building that a man who'd gone to work that morning feeling just fine might easily come out at lunchtime to discover that the sunbeams felt like lasers on the surface of his eyes. It went rapidly out of control—common sense and extreme sanitary habits could have gone a long way toward keeping the numbers on the reasonable side—and spiraled rapidly into the realm of panic. Mankind has always leaned toward sensationalism and exaggeration. After all, where's the excitement in not blowing everything out of proportion?

VAMPIRISM EPIDEMIC!

The words were splashed across the newspaper headlines and the news programs. At first, victims of the contagion were required only to register, the logic being that this would enable medical workers and facilities to easily identify them in case of sickness or accident. After all, hadn't that same system worked for diabetics and HIV victims before the diseases had been eradicated? But there were different things involved here, different stakes—no pun intended—and then the clerks refused to work unless they were issued nose and mouth masks, and no amount of pointing out that it was a blood-borne pathogen, not airborne, would make them change their minds.

When the news footage showed the long lines of H.P.V. victims being registered by heavily protected admin personnel, the public became even more mistrustful of not only those who had the virus, but the information they were getting from the authorities. The rumors began and grew, and your average Mr. and Mrs. John Doe insisted that *they,* the carriers, be more readily identifiable. The human rights organizations fought but the government sided with the uninfected—those voters who were the majority and who would live *longer*—and so the H.P.V. carriers were ordered to wear identifying armbands, bloodred swatches of material bearing an ominous-looking three-syringe symbol. It became a common sight to see entire families traveling together while huddling beneath semi-sheer black veils that protected their oversensitive eyes from the sun. It also became just as familiar to see them pass by shop windows on which signs had been posted showing the three-syringe symbol within a red circle and slash. Human rights activists screamed, but in the end things moved much too quickly for them to even so much as plead their case in court.

Then came the concentration camps.

Publicly the government called them "containment facilities," but the people forced inside them knew what they really were. History, it seemed, really *was* doomed to repeat itself, although this time it was much quieter and more insidious. The camps of previous world wars had been tragically honest about their purpose, but these new camps, the ones for H.P.V. victims, started out under the guise of innocence. Despite the governmental promises, it wasn't long before no one heard from any of the thousands of people who were locked inside. It started with the single people, the men and women whose registration clearly showed there was no one to contact in the event of an emergency, no one to miss them if they weren't around. Then it spread to the rest of them, entire families and communities, all those men, women, and children who were so expensive to house and feed and clothe and, of course, provide with medical care. Ultimately they, and the pathetic belongings they'd been able to carry with them, simply . . .

Disappeared.

But the soldiers and the barbed wire remained.

Ready.

Waiting.

Because there were still plenty more of the Hemophages—*vampires*—on the outside. The number of infected had gone from a few thousand to tens of thousands, so they weren't gathered up all that easily or quickly. As for themselves, the Hemophages saw the proverbial writing on the wall . . . they saw their *fate*. And when that same fate had seen fit to take your life and reduce it to only ten years, why would any intelligent man or woman simply stand passively and let the government—or anyone else—steal away what little you had left?

The Hemophages had one chance, and they took it.

They went underground, melting easily into the darkness their uninfected brothers and sisters now abhorred. It wasn't as though the night as a subculture didn't already exist anyway—the goth clubs, the nightclubs, the entire economy of those who had already preferred the starlight to the daylight, who hated the sound of an alarm clock in the morning and the morning to night routine. Besides, they were tired of the looks of loathing, the sneers of aversion, and the snide comments—how easy it was to simply take the H.P.V. armbands off in private and be rid of them. Those same armbands began turning up in waste facilities around the world at the same time the number of newly infected registrations dropped drastically—they would not be singled out anymore. They would not be discriminated against and despised. They would not be secretly . . . or openly . . . *exterminated.*

They began fighting back.

There were open battles on the street, with H.P.V. victims blatantly ignoring police orders and the police retaliating by trying to take them with force. Seemingly overnight the cities were filled with blood. With *infection.* The virus went from a blood-borne pathogen to something that could be caught from nearly anything, and the people of the world went from free to prisoners of their own paranoia. Fashion was lost in favor of head-to-toe anticontamination suits, vanity was sacrificed for the sake of breathing masks. Beauty disappeared behind a shield of safety that turned out to be faulty. Everything changed.

It was the age of contagion, and the great uninfected masses weren't pleased with the new, uncompliant breed of disease carrier. Things went from bad to worse really, *really* fast. A new unit of governmental and military con-

trol was invented almost overnight; called the Special
Hazards Teams, they went through the ranks of the registered Hemophages and eliminated them, sometimes at
home, sometimes in public—

*The middle-aged woman forces herself out of the hos-
pital bed only because her doctor demands she walk daily
on the hip he worked so hard at reconstructing four days
ago. She used to be a dancer and while the degenerative
arthritis took that career, she's found new purpose in
teaching the skills she spent her life learning. The walking hurts, a lot, but she forgets the pain when the door to
her hospital room crashes open and four heavily armed
men clad completely in black stamp inside. They're wearing a kind of uniform she's never seen before, with red
biohazard symbols on one sleeve and a strange logo with
a styled "SH" on the other. Her pulse jumps but there is
nowhere to run to, nothing to do but face them and see
what happens.*

*She's closed the blinds because her eyes are so sensi-
tive, but she can still see the lead man point a weapon at
her, something long and dark and heavy. The kids to
whom she teaches class are at the elementary school
level, first grade, so she has no idea what kind of a gun it
is. "Are you Elizabeth P. Watkins?" one of them demands
in a voice that's probably loud enough to be heard all the
way down at the nurses' station. It's so sadly clear that
they know she has H.P.V., but perhaps he thinks her deaf,
too.*

*She blinks and tries to think of a way to stall, a way to
reason with the insanity that this soldier represents.
"I . . ."*

*"Are you Elizabeth P. Watkins?" he practically
screams.*

She swallows. "Well ... yes. But I—"

Whatever else she was going to say is lost in the thunder of gunfire. The nearly pulverized remains of her body are taken care of by the white-clad members of the Fumigation Team that streams in after the Special Hazards men back out of the room. And, finally, all that's left of Elizabeth P. Watkins, onetime winner of the Best Yearly Performance award at the Ruth Page Foundation School of Dance, is the slowly dissipating clouds of poison gas used to sanitize the bits of bone and flesh splattered across the walls, floor, and furniture.

And so began the Blood Wars with which Violet was so sadly, bitterly familiar.

The battles were fought in the streets, in homes, in office buildings, even in hospital operating rooms, where the Special Hazard Teams were ordered not to stop at eliminating only the patient. Any person, no matter their rank or position, who had been exposed to the blood of a Hemophage had to be exterminated, no matter the cost. Doctors, lawyers, political leaders—after all, the politicians didn't rule the day anymore. They'd proved to be helpless in the face of the epidemic, and few people in the private sector had ever believed them to be trustworthy anyway. The newly emerged power was a hybrid, a religious-medical-political structure that would take the drastic countermeasures demanded by the uninfected and clearly necessary to stop the spread of the disease, and it would not be influenced by petty things like human rights and the United States Constitution. Now it was survival of the fittest, and the members of that organization knew without a doubt that only the fittest were H.P.V. free.

FOUR

The armored escort car pulled up in front of the main entrance to the enormous ArchMinistry of Medical Policy complex, and like a cat coming to a halt after a full run, settled back on its tires as the driver braked and cut the engine. The building in front was impressive and heavily fortified—bioterrorism, or blood terrorism as some people were now calling it, had risen dramatically in the last couple of years and they could take no chances here. Just going in and out required sanitation and extreme identification measures, even for the most powerful. The car's occupants, the Vice-Cardinal and the Chief of Staff, would be no exception.

Even though they were inside the perimeter of the gated compound and had already gone through the first round of identification and the armed entry guards, the driver made a quick, suspicious scan of the surrounding grounds as soon as he stepped out of the car. Only when he felt sure it was safe did the veteran security officer press a lock releasing device that was keyed to his body heat, pulse, and thumbprint—should something happen to alter any one of those things beyond a pre-set range of accepted variables, the only other person who could unlock the armored car's doors was inside the vehicle itself.

The heavy door opened and the first thing out of the car was an impeccable designer shoe hermetically attached to a suit by one of the world's more expensive couturiers. A voice floated out of the opened door, slightly muffled by the fortified interior and more than a bit on the high side of anger. "As you're aware, Doctor, there's no definitive test for the virus." The speaker's words grew louder, clearly following the first occupant as he brought his other foot around. "For all we know, they've infected every blood storage facility in the country!"

The sturdily built Vice-Cardinal was out of the vehicle now and the Chief of Staff came out behind him in quick, jerky movements that made him look like a small, worried dog. He opened his mouth to continue but the Vice-Cardinal held up his hand, waving it impatiently in the air. Even though the Chief wasn't sure whether it meant he should shut up or it was just the prelude to sanitization, just that movement was enough to silence him—at least for now.

Richard Daxus, the Vice-Cardinal, was only forty-eight, but he had made a good name and position for himself. He carried himself well, dressed well, exuded the confidence of a wealthy and successful executive. He was an out-of-the-ashes kind of man who'd parlayed his humble beginnings as a young veterinarian first into marketing, then marketing medicine, then eventually into medical management. It had been a long highway—or at least it had seemed like it at the time—from obtaining his animal husbandry license to Chief of Staff at Chicago's foremost teaching hospital and then, finally, to his position here at the ArchMinistry, but he'd made it.

Daxus brought up his other hand and held it next to the first; his fingers wavered in the air for only a moment before a pair of attendants, themselves wearing protective gear, hurried out of the sliding glass and metal entrance and quickly stripped off the pair of rings Daxus had slipped over the surgical gloves covering his skin. The first set of attendants were followed by a second pair whose job it was to peel away the gloves themselves and reveal the second set of gloves beneath, these hermetically sealed to the cuff of his suit in the same fashion as his shoes. With their hands contaminated by the dirty gloves, the four attendants stepped back respectfully as the third and final pair arrived with a pair of fresh gloves and snapped these over the Vice-Cardinal's already surgically gloved hands. In this day and age, layers did more than just keep a person warm.

It took another five minutes to get through the pre-sanitization and pre-identification areas, but finally the two men were walking rapidly down the hallway that led to Daxus's office deep in the heart of the building. Actually, walking didn't quite cover it—Daxus was striding, and the Chief of Staff was struggling to keep his pudgy body from falling more than three steps behind. Daxus had neither patience nor sympathy for the other man; he had a public image to maintain and it was necessary that he look good and radiate health. Everything in his daily life was engineered to ensure that he did just that; he needed to look sleek and fashionable and so he had his hair done at the same salon that handled the Mayor's family and visiting Washington dignitaries. He was a model for the people, the embodiment of everything that American life should be, of everything *they* wanted to be.

His Chief of Staff was outright puffing now, and his face was turning purple at the edges from exertion. That would teach him to overindulge in the bagels, lox, and cream cheese in the mornings. From the looks of the gut around his middle, the man had probably been following his daily breakfasts with a coffee and double Danish. "Doctor, sir—" The man coughed, then managed to make his legs move faster so he could at least be at Daxus's side. "What I'm trying to say is that these circumstances leave us with no choice but to destroy all standing blood supplies." He paused and Daxus wasn't sure if it was for effect or just because it was a little amazing that the situation had actually come to this. "And anyone who may have been transfused or come in contact with it."

Daxus stopped in midstride and turned to stare at his Chief of Staff. He sucked in his breath, then let it out. His mind tried to do the calculation but the numbers didn't want to display in his brain. All he came up with was a mental image of blackness with way too many zeros added. "So how many deaths are we looking at?" he finally asked.

The plump man's mouth thinned out as he ground his teeth. The muscles in his jaw ticked. "We don't have a final number yet," he admitted. "In the thousands . . . at least."

Daxus shook his head in disgust, then pulled off the heavy ring he always wore on the outside of his gloves. It was a black and yellow diamond rendition of the hazard symbol; at its centerpiece was a drop of his blood, pristine and uninfected, encased in polyurethane. "What we don't understand," the Chief continued, "is why now? Why are they escalating all of a sudden?"

Daxus shrugged as he passed the ring beneath a DNA scanner. "It's simply population geometics," he finally answered. An instant later he was finally stepping through the hermetic doors that separated his office from the rest of the building. The other man stayed respectfully back as Daxus walked through a bath of green gamma rays that killed the last of any microbes he might have picked up during his travels outside the building. The heavy glass doors slid shut behind him; now the Chief, as well as the aide who had come up to join them, would have to communicate via the speakers embedded here and there in the barrier. On the surface it was an annoyance, but there were added benefits. Every time he came in here and left someone behind, psychologically this placed him in the ultimate position of power: he was a man who was so important that he did not have to breathe the same air as those around him.

It had other effects, too. In here, Daxus felt that he was finally safe, and now the Vice-Cardinal stripped off the outer gloves with a pleased expression. "There's a minimum critical number that any population must maintain in order to propagate and survive," he explained. "Very plainly, we've been so effective in exterminating them that we've reduced them *past* that number." Daxus walked behind his desk, then settled comfortably on his chair and let his gaze scan the desktop critically. Nice and clean, dust-free—the cleaning crew had done their job, right on schedule. "They're on the verge of extinction and they know it."

On the other side of the sanitary barrier, his Chief of Staff stood up straighter. "Then we have to capitalize," he said excitedly. He was practically bouncing up and down. "We have to take this opportunity to deliver a knockout punch!"

Keeping his face carefully expressionless, Daxus reached behind him and retrieved a cup of coffee from the tray waiting on his credenza. He took his time pulling off the sterilized wrapper, enjoying the impatience of the two men, relishing the fact that neither dared say anything to voice it. When he finally spoke, he did so slowly and very clearly, as if he'd waited for this moment for a long, long time and wanted to savor every second. "For the last ten years, in partnership with the Laboratories for Latter Day Defense, I've overseen the development of a weapon that can locate and kill every Hemophage on the planet." Daxus paused and watched their expressions as this information sank in, then he smiled vaguely. "In a matter of *days*."

The two men staring at him through the glass exchanged surprised glances, then the Chief managed to say, "That's . . . *extraordinary*. What's the ETA?"

Daxus took a slow sip of his sanitized coffee, and he had to work hard at not allowing his face to grimace as the blatantly burned taste of the liquid dribbled down his throat. It was awful stuff, but at least he knew it was safe. So much of the world had been ruined by the Hemophages, but soon, very soon . . .

This time when he smiled at the Chief of Staff and the aide, Daxus's smile was bold and wide, as close to genuine happiness as either of the two men had ever seen. "Now. A courier has been dispatched to bring it here to the ArchMinistry as we speak."

FIVE

From the air, the L.L.D.D.—Laboratories for Latter Day Defense—looked like a miniature city. In reality that's exactly what it was, with all the modern conveniences in one place and residences for all tiers of the personnel who worked inside. It wasn't difficult to find similarities between the L.L.D.D. and the Army posts and Air Force bases of the previous centuries, with everything from shopping exchanges, grocery stores, minimalls, and movie theaters to the more pertinent medical and testing facilities and proving grounds set apart from the rest of the carefully monitored populace. The majority of employees never left the premises, and most of them had families. That meant schools, stores, parks, gymnasiums, all maintained by crews that included everything from landscapers to waterless latrine service persons . . . all of whom had at least a Top Secret Security Clearance. It wouldn't be far off to estimate the daily headcount at five thousand plus.

It wasn't until a person arrived at the main gate that it

became apparent just how difficult it could be to get in there if you weren't an actual L.L.D.D. employee. But the girl on the sleek light green Ninja motorcycle (Hondasaki's latest model and the fastest one to date) had been expecting a hard road of it, and she had all her papers in order and, so to speak, her ducks in a row. Her high confidence showed—she was wearing a shimmering LCD overcoat capable of reflecting any color or image. In keeping with the latest fashion trends in Hollywood and Paris, this one was set to reflect her mood; right now, it was a bright, optimistic yellow.

The guard at the gate didn't even notice, or if he did, he certainly didn't care. He was heavily armored around his sidearms, and his eyes were small and dark, difficult to see behind the vision guards of the military breather mask covering most of his face. What she could see of his gaze was narrow and suspicious. He didn't bother to speak when she pulled up and cut off the engine. He didn't have to—the rider knew what was coming next.

"XPD-154," she said calmly, then passed him a laminated identification card with a gloved hand. "Clearance classified courier. I'm expected." There were at least a dozen other people milling around the entrance, civilians and guards coming and going, and none of them paid any attention to her.

He wasn't impressed by her identification and she didn't expect him to be—he probably saw a dozen couriers like her every day. He plucked her ID from her fingers and she saw that he was also wearing gloves—of course—but his were much heavier and more industrial. It looked like they made it hard for him to work, but he still managed. She watched as he slid the card into a computer scanner and the virtual centrifuge registered the drop of blood sealed inside the ID. A moment later a line of light went left to right across the surface of the computer monitor, leaving a clear image behind.

"Remove your head covering," the guard ordered.

She unsnapped her chin strap without comment, then reached up with both hands and lifted her helmet off her head. Before it fell against the shoulders of her plasticene coat, the young woman's hair, purple neon and fine, sprang free and waved in the breeze, moving back and forth like a minifield of bright lavender-colored wheat. Protecting the soft skin of her face from the helmet's inner fabric was a softer, almost sheer lamé veil; when she unclasped that, she revealed finely honed features and bright, clear brown eyes, full lips barely brushed with a touch of cherry-colored lip gloss. To match her coat, each strand of her hair was coated in a microsheen of optical polyurethane so she could change her hair color at will to any one of more than seven million colors.

Score one for the guard's professionalism: if he noticed she was beautiful, he gave absolutely no sign. He simply took her card and held it up next to the screen, very carefully comparing the digital photograph on the card to the computer image. Finally he handed it back to her and stepped to the side at the same time he pressed a button on the inside of the guard shack. In front of her, the heavy gate slid open without a sound. "Stage one clearance," he said in an utterly emotionless voice. "Proceed for verification and sterilization."

Sterilization, she thought wryly. That word had meant something entirely different in centuries past, and even now it made her pause. Could the government—or whatever the ArchMinistry of Medical Policy called itself— ever *really* be trusted? In the nineteen hundreds, the government had enacted laws enabling involuntary sterilization of women who were, at the best of times, victims of their own social limitations. While "sterilization" supposedly meant something different here, who *really* knew what was being done to their bodies on a molecular level in these chambers? A beam of light, a change in the atmosphere, and that could be that. Just by stepping into them, a woman—or for that matter a man—might be bringing their entire future family lineage to a grinding halt.

But even so . . .

She pulled on her helmet, fired up the motorcycle's engine, and headed to the L.L.D.D. Medical Certification Checkpoint. This was a smaller building made of gray metal—probably some kind of super-strong alloy—which guarded the entrance to the main facility. It was a little disconcerting that its style, a kind of corrugated tin-looking facade, bore a strong resemblance to many of the buildings she'd seen in the old history photographs, the ones that went along with those sterilization procedures she'd been thinking of only a few minutes before.

Nevertheless, she steered the motorcycle into an open slot along a parking line marked VISITORS ONLY, then climbed off and pulled off her helmet for the second time with a sigh of relief. She absolutely hated wearing head gear, and why bother?

It was usually pretty crappy protection anyway.

⚡

Being inside the checkpoint building only intensified the bad feelings. It was so much like a prison, with guards posted evenly along some security grid known only to them and raw fluorescent lighting overhead that amplified the generic coloring on the walls. Some people might have found being the only splash of color enticing, but now she felt that her purple hair and zingy-looking yellow overcoat made her little beyond a target, someone on whom all these bored and killer-trained guards could focus. Even so, she steadfastly took the route the entry guard had indicated—no doubt monitored at every turn by video cameras—until she ended up at an elevator door at the end of a short, harshly lit hallway. A glance around told her that there was nowhere else to go, so when the elevator doors opened, she stepped inside without hesitation. Inside the elevator, there were also no buttons to press—the luxury of choice had been eliminated the instant she'd pulled up to the main gate. She went dutifully into the elevator, it moved, and she stepped out of it when the door opened. End of options.

The room revealed before her was white, large, and mostly featureless. Lab technicians moved like ants among the equipment and along the walls; like the walls and floor—and pretty much everything she'd seen so far—they were also dressed in white. None of them paid her a bit of attention, and the only thing jarring were the sidearms everyone carried, dark splotches of metal against the starkness of their work garb. One of the techs was waiting for her and he gestured toward a lone chair—also white—directly in her line of passage. She really hadn't needed any help in deducing that's where she was expected to go. She settled herself on it without comment, watching dispassionately as several more technicians hurried up to help fasten the white Kevlar bindings around her forearms, hands, and ankles.

Finally, she couldn't resist trying to open a little dialogue. He was an average-looking guy with dark hair and eyes, average build. He probably had average thoughts, and those were the easiest ones of all to play. She gave him her sweetest smile and blinked a couple of times, letting her gaze hold his just slightly longer than necessary. "Mind if I ask what's on the menu?"

Predictably—weren't they always?—he smiled back. Just a small one, because he wouldn't want the video-tapes to show his boss that he was responding to a test subject, but it was there nonetheless. "Just have to make sure you're human," he said quietly. While she thought briefly about that statement, he glanced at the guards around them, then reached up and grabbed hold of a piece of equipment that looked more like a mechanical spider than anything else. When he brought it down, she could see an impressive array of stainless-steel arms; she didn't have much time to study it because within seconds each arm had pinned her back against the chair, prying open her mouth and eyes, stretching her lips and eyelids wide until her face was grotesquely out of proportion. So much for using her beauty to score points.

She couldn't say anything—with her mouth held open like this, she couldn't even swallow—but the lab technician clearly knew what she would ask if she could. "Retinal testing," he said. His voice was calm and soothing, as though he'd done this a thousand times and honed his explanatory and bedside manner to perfection. He sounded like a dentist—*This won't hurt a bit. Just relax, and the tooth'll be out before you realize it.* Next to lawyers and politicians, she considered dentists to be the biggest liars in the universe. "To detect the presence of contacts or dyes."

The eye scan was no big deal, but as she had suspected, his practiced words weren't nearly enough to prepare her for the needles that suddenly thrust into precise spots of the exposed whites of her eyes. For a moment she felt like there was liquid fire across both eyes, or maybe a lightning bolt that would meet in the middle and permanently fry her brain; her fists balled up but she refused to cry out. Struggling against the bindings was unthinkable and even though her back wanted to arch and every muscle in her body tried to spasm, she was absolutely, *rigidly* still.

The tech raised one eyebrow to show how impressed he was, but he didn't dare vocalize a compliment. "Metabolic sensing," he continued blandly. "To make certain your metabolism is within human range." A new set of needles suddenly appeared, this time plunging into the sensitive expanse of exposed gums above her eyeteeth. Again, she refused to move, to show how much it stung. Instead, she just kept hearing that imaginary dentist's voice—*Just relax and it'll be over before you know it.* Again, the tech nodded appreciatively. "Pulse, respiration," he said. He stood back and watched, counting off on his fingers as the machine did its work. Then his voice softened—even he couldn't mask his pity—and she sucked in her breath. She'd heard about this next part but never endured it until now. "Regenerative capability."

A double set of previously hidden arms twisted around in front of her face, the blades at the ends of each whining as they spun down and out of her range of vision. She ground her back teeth as the razored edges bit into the flesh of each wrist, parting the skin like a knife cutting into rare steak. Two more techs rushed up, one on each side, and inspected the wounds with microsonic scans;

they were finished and nodding their approvals almost before the cuts had begun to ooze blood.

The head lab technician waved them away, then watched the blood slide down her wrists and collect into small glass reservoirs positioned at the end of each arm of the chair. "If you were a Hemophage," he said, "we would already be detecting the immediate tissue repair at a microcellular level." She had to strain to see it, but as he talked she could see her blood being spray-misted into a second glass chamber off to her left, where it was exposed to several wavelengths of spectral light. Abruptly the needles retracted from her eyes and gums, leaving a vaguely nasty throbbing in each previous spot of penetration; just as quickly, double laser beams from another set of metal arms spit sudden fire onto both wrists and sealed the gashes, leaving only a thin red line that would disappear in a couple of days.

She blinked to moisten her eyes at the same time her lips, stretched dry by the metal extenders, snapped back into shape. Finally she could breathe and swallow normally again. She cleared her throat and squashed the resentment and anger that wanted to boil through her voice; when she spoke, she sounded calm and nonchalant, as if she'd gone through this a thousand times and it was just another day in the life of her work. "What would happen if one were to fail any of these tests?"

This time the medical technician's smile was blatantly smug as his eyebrows arched high enough to show his arrogance. He watched as the semimetal bindings around her arms and ankles snapped apart, then retracted into slots on the chair; from the faraway look in his eyes, she had to wonder if he regretted being able to let her go. Sometimes the smallest of expressions could tell volumes about someone without them even realizing it. The minute amounts of her blood in the two containers drained away, filtering through tubes toward unseen sanitized drains while the containers themselves were instantly steamed and sterilized. "Nothing good," was all he said, but she could tell he wished he could go into the lurid details of it all. The young guy made a few notations on an oversized medical PDA, then glanced at her. "Please remove all articles of clothing and proceed into the scanner."

So typical. So *degrading.*

And she did exactly as she was told.

Why? Because there was no such thing as modesty anymore—with the explosion of the HemoPhagic Virus into the public realm, the medical profession (which hadn't cared a bit about bodily privacy in centuries, anyway) had lost its last bit of patience with such mundane concerns. The federal government had been too pressed and overrun with problems concerning the virus to care whether a woman had to undress in front of a soldier or a man had to try to urinate into a jar overseen by a female nurse while standing in line with four dozen others who'd been ordered to do the same. And protesting on the grounds of religious beliefs? That only made the politicians wave away the complaints in impatience, the medical personnel roll their eyes, and the military men and women sneer.

Paying no attention to the appreciative glances of the men around her, she left her clothes folded neatly on a chair next to the entrance to the U.V. chamber, then stepped inside. The tunnel itself stretched in front of her like one of the sewer tunnels of a previous century—it was long and dark, and there was no way she could judge its length. The technician had told her to walk, but he hadn't actually said she'd be *moving* while she did. The darkness gave her a feeling of vertigo and her balance was odd; for all she knew, she might be stepping along on the surface of a treadmill, one of the moving walkways that are so common in the airports. That was doubtful, but there was no way to be sure.

After a few moments a light appeared on either side of her, tracking her as though she were a piece of paper on a flatbed scanner. It did nothing to illuminate her feet, but that didn't matter anyway. She thought she felt the thin beam of light as heat against her skin, but again, there was no way to be sure. It was vaguely purple and it bounced off her naked body, outlining it in an attractive glow. She could see her legs and arms as she walked, head automatically looking down at the darkness where her feet were—yes, now that her eyes had grown accustomed to the dimness she could finally glimpse them, stepping along in perfect time to the slow and steady beat of her heart. The bright lines of purple light emanated from translucent walls that went completely over her head; she could just make out vague circuitry and the dull gleam of metal parts beyond, see an occasional blink of red electrical indicator lights following the wiring. She kept her eyes downcast and her concentration focused, and it became almost a game to ensure that her stride was perfectly spaced and she never made the scanning light hitch or pause. This was just one more step in getting the job done.

Without warning the light beams shut down, leaving her in utter blackness. For a long moment everything was still, lightless, and heavy, and she felt like she shouldn't even try to breathe. Then the area in front of her was washed in muted gray light and she realized she was standing only inches away from the front of a heavy steel security door. She knew to identify herself without waiting to be told—after all, this was the way the world was now.

"XPD-154 Clearance Classified Courier," she said flatly, directing her voice into a mini-speaker at mouth height. Maybe there was a person on the other side of the door, and maybe not; that she might be addressing no one bothered her not a bit. "Here on retrieval for transfer to the C.P.M."

Data displays suddenly lit up on either side of the door as her voice was analyzed for stress, the graph lines etching irregular patterns across the LCD screens. She had no way of knowing whether or not she was passing these tests, but she'd certainly know soon enough. Her nerves screamed for a second as all the displays paused, the lines suddenly freezing, then the screens blacked out and the door slid open, making a sound that was a strange cross between the old hydraulic message tubes and a sucking vacuum cleaner. The chamber beyond was another study in darkness, but there was enough illumination for her to see that it was shaped like an octagon. What there was of light came from the glass cages lining the walls, where she could see the softly lit shapes of strangely sedate monkeys. She could feel them watching her but all their eyes were black and flat, like stones barely seen through a layer of dark river water.

"Your clothing and personal items have been sterilized, XPD-154. You will find them on the tray to your left."

She looked automatically toward the voice and saw a man standing off to the side. Instead of the white outfit that had been so prevalent elsewhere in the complex, this gentleman was clad in black—shirt, slacks, and shoes, even his lab coat. His white face seemed to float between the collar of his black shirt and his dark hair. She knew who he was from the photos she'd seen of him, although the photographs had clearly been "made nice" for promotional purposes. This guy was the Chief of Research here at the L.L.D.D., and he was pretty pallid and spooky-looking. In any case, if he was conscious of her nakedness, he gave no sign; she waited for him to turn away but he didn't. Her lips tightened with irritation, but she finally redressed while he stood there with an impassive expression. It was more than creepy—he almost seemed blind to the fact that a naked beautiful woman was only a few feet away.

When she was done, he finally turned his back and said, "Follow me, please."

He didn't bother to check if she'd done what he ordered, assuming she would. Obediently, she fell in step behind him as he led the way out of the octagon room and down a long corridor that echoed with every footstep. Embedded into the tile floor at three-foot intervals was the international black and yellow symbol for hazardous materials. The triple broken black circle on the screamingly yellow background played odd tricks with her eyes as she walked, bringing back a slightly different version of the sensation of vertigo she'd had a little while ago in the scanning chamber.

The man in front of her suddenly spoke, but he didn't turn around to look at her. "May I ask you a question?"

One eyebrow raised but she didn't miss a beat in her answer. "Feel free," she said. She kept her voice carefully bland.

"Do you know what this is about?"

"Should I?" she countered. Parents throughout the ages had told children not to answer a question with a question, but in the adult world and the era of avoidance methods, that tactic was always good for buying time.

"No." She could almost hear the sneer that crept into his voice, an *I'm so much better than you* attitude that he could barely conceal. "It's highly classified. But I've been cleared to debrief you because your consciousness of the gravity of this situation may increase your motivation to complete."

"I've *never* failed to complete." This time she made sure the irritation was clear in her voice. They needed to know that even the implication of her failing was an insult.

"And that is no doubt a significant factor in why you were chosen," he said in an almost soothing tone of voice. Apparently he had decided it was worth it not to piss her off. "However, it's of critical importance to every uninfected human on earth that you not fail *this* time, either." He slowed his pace so that he fell into step at her side; she risked a glance in his direction, but so far he was impossible to read. He was just a white face, as emotionless as a marble statue, floating on the air above a moving black suit.

"The Hemophages are a dying species, on the verge of nonexistence," he told her. There might have been the faintest trace of triumph in his tone. "Under the supervision of Vice-Cardinal Daxus at the ArchMinistry, we've developed a weapon that will push them past that verge . . . and into extinction."

This was finally interesting, and she raised one eyebrow as she kept up the pace alongside him. "If this weapon's so important, why not have it delivered by armored convoy?"

"The armored convoy to which you refer is leaving the facility as we speak," he said. A self-satisfied smile tugged at the corner of his mouth. Still, despite his lecture about the importance of this mission, the Chief of Research sounded about as excited over this as a bored computer science teacher in front of a roomful of sleepy students. "The Hemophages will do everything in their power to stop and immobilize it." For the first time, she saw his smile widen to where it was actually noticeable. "It is, of course, a decoy. Our statisticians have calculated that our best chance of delivery lies in reliance on a single person . . . such as yourself."

She nodded but said nothing. The corridor, with its row after row of biohazard tiles, was beginning to seem endless.

"May I ask you another question?" the Chief asked again, Without waiting for her to answer, he threw out the next query. "What is your opinion of the Hemophages?"

"I'm apolitical," she said flatly.

"Recoiling at the sight of a cockroach is also apolitical."

Now she did turn her head in his direction. Her brow furrowed as she tried to understand what he meant. "I'm sorry?"

"A cock—" He paused. "Never mind." When she still looked bewildered, he shrugged. "Extinct insect," he explained. "We wiped them out, too. Severely damaged the ecosystem, but . . ." He waved off the rest of his words and finally paused at a door on his right. Without bothering to finish his tale, he pulled a keycard from his pocket and swiped it through the scan box on the wall. The door opened with the same odd *swoosh* that the one back at the scanner had made, but he made no move to step forward. "My clearance ends here," he told her instead, and extended his arm in a go-ahead gesture.

She didn't bother to say good-bye as she started to step over the threshold, but before she could do so, the Chief of Research had snapped on a latex glove and grabbed her by the arm. "XPD-154." Something in the way he said it made her pause and look back at him. "You'll be receiving a case containing the weapon. I don't have to tell you that under no circumstances should you open it."

She looked at him blankly for a moment. "You're right," she said in a voice just as emotionless as his. A vaguely pleased smile slipped across his lips—she knew he could guess what she was going to say. "You *don't* have to tell me." She brushed off his hand and walked through the doorway.

SIX

At last, there was a splash of color in the midst of the white, gray, and black expanse that was the Laboratories for Latter Day Defense.

The room into which she'd stepped was tiny, but at least it was red, a gloriously deep scarlet that seared the eyes, tickled the adrenal glands, and made her heart pump with excitement. Really, there was way too little in the world today that had color to it—the ArchMinistry had made sure of that. For an organization that claimed to have come into existence specifically to care for and protect the people, it had effectively sucked the life out of nearly everything in its path and left a trail of dust and death as its aftermath. This tiny room—really, not much more than a hallway entrance into something else she had yet to see—was a reminder of how it felt to be alive, of the vibrancy that had once been the right of every living person on this planet.

She crossed the small expanse of space to where another door waited, marveling that even the floor, a smooth expanse of easily sterilized tile and dark-colored grout, was crimson. Next to the door on the opposite wall was another card reader, and she wasn't pleased to see that when she raised her ID to insert it into the slot, the flesh on the back of her hand was shiny, the skin covered in a thin sheet of perspiration. Even worse, her fingers were visibly shaking—not good.

Stopping her hand from shaking took an iron act of will and the grim mental reminder that somewhere, certainly, she was being watched and videotaped. She concentrated for the barest of moments and watched her hand steady itself, then pushed her identification card into the slot and spoke. "XPD-154 Clearance Classified Courier." She'd said it so often it felt like her name. One thing was good, at least: this was the last door.

The response over the digital speaker was immediate. *"Copy, XPD-154. We've been expecting you."*

Now this final door slid open, and finally she was walking into the inner vault of the L.L.D.D.

By the time she was taking her third step, she had a massive, heavily armored Medical Commando on each side of her, the kind who'd once populated the rings of the now banned blood sports like boxing and wrestling. These two fell into sync like impeccably programmed robots, matching her footsteps right down to length and timing, never missing a beat. She couldn't help wondering: if she were taking mincing little steps, would they be forced to do the same? There were at least a dozen more of the Commandos stationed evenly around the room, and while the glare of the overhead lights on their visors made it impossible for her to see their eyes, she could feel each one of them tracking her movement, automatically analyzing her, preplanning how to kill her if the need arose.

But she forgot all that when she saw the briefcase.

The white alloy container waited on a tall, simple white podium in the center of the vault. The case was about the size of a medium pizza box and no more than an inch thick, and it looked like nothing more than a briefcase a businessman might use to take his papers to work. She walked up to it without asking anyone's permission and the Commandos broke off and stepped back about three feet; for a moment she couldn't believe that she had finally, *finally*, been able to come this far. Then without warning she staggered slightly.

On one side of the podium was a Combat Reserve Doctor, and he looked at her curiously. With her heart pounding, she made a show of glancing down at the floor and frowning, as if she'd tripped over her own feet. A nice effort, but it didn't stop him from asking about the stumble. "Everything in order, XPD-154?"

She glanced once more at the floor to hide it when she swallowed, but she managed to keep her voice flat and clear. "One hundred percent, Comrade Doctor."

He stared at her critically for a moment, then turned his attention to a trio of keypads on the front of the podium. Until she'd gotten right up in front of it, she hadn't realized the briefcase was actually set into a locking station. Working from memory, the doctor began rapidly keying in the series of complex codes that would release it.

It felt like he was taking forever. The room seemed to throb around her, another damnable white box that wanted to mess with her sense of equilibrium. Her fingers wanted desperately to flex, and she finally nonchalantly slid her hands inside the pocket of her overcoat so she could clench her fists. The coat itself—a stupid, *stupid* choice of outer attire for this mission because of its damnable mood fabric—was beginning to shift its color. Had they noticed? Probably not—the men in this room had never seen it while it had radiated that ridiculous aura of sunshine, the visible evidence of how positive she'd been when she'd started on her way this morning. Now, however, it was a sort of muddy gold, steadily working its way down the color scale to brown. If she was lucky they wouldn't pay attention to such stupid things as the latest available fashion fabric; then again, they *were* trained to monitor people and every indication of a threat, no matter how minute. Beneath her hair, at the junction where her hairline met the skin beneath her temple, a bead of sweat broke free of her increasingly too-hot skin and suddenly slid down and into her ear.

Her hand was shaking—she could feel it—but she would not let it show as she casually pulled a pair of sunglasses out of her pocket and slipped them on. Her breathing steadied as the glare of the fluorescent lights lessened from laser-beam quality to the not-so-average but bearable intensity of automobile high-beams.

The Combat Reserve Doctor stopped his code execution and looked at her strangely. "You're quite certain everything is in order?" he finally asked. He sounded uncertain if he should proceed and that was the last thing she needed right now. Getting him to release that briefcase was an absolute *necessity*.

She stared back at him, unmoving and outwardly cool, hiding behind the safety of her dark lenses. Her fingers were stiff and on the verge of spasming but she'd slipped them back into her pockets. "Positively."

Again the doctor studied her, and it took every single ounce of determination she had not to move. At last he shrugged, then entered a final set of numbers into the last keypad. The titanium levers holding the briefcase in place released with a *snap!* but he made no move to pick up the case and hand it to her. Instead, he pulled a small, clipboard-mounted hemoglobin reader from one of his oversized pockets. He glanced first at it, then her; frowning slightly, he turned the clipboard around and held it out so she could touch it. "Enter your DNA to confirm receipt," he said. Despite his uncertain expression, he sounded bored, as though this was just one more task in a series that he had to do to get him through to his waiting lunch hour.

She opened her mouth to reply, then had to lick her lips. Her mouth was dry as dust and her lips felt wrinkled and cracked. She found the rehearsed words and ground them out. "I can only confirm receipt of the container, not its contents."

He nodded and his gaze sharpened, as though he was finally remembering the importance of this particular task. "That's acceptable. Opening the case is strictly forbidden. You understand this?"

"Perfectly," she said as she withdrew one hand from her pocket. She reached up and fussily brushed an invisible strand of hair off her forehead. His gaze tracked the movement and she could see him process and dismiss it as nothing more than vanity. By doing so, he completely missed the hand she casually rested on the edge of the podium to steady herself.

The Combat Reserve Doctor nodded slightly and turned his attention back to the white briefcase. "The contents are set to self-destruct in the event of nondeliv-

ery in . . ." He made a show of glancing at his watch.
"Exactly nine hours from now." To punctuate his words,
the doctor reached out and pressed a button on the
podium. On the briefcase, a set of black LCD numbers on
a nearly invisible side panel lit up and began counting
down. Her pulse jumped as the man finally lifted the case
from the podium and handed it to her. Her hand closed
around the handle, then she looked up sharply when he
didn't release it. He was studying her, a frown deepening
across his forehead as he focused on her too-pale skin. It
would be a devastating error to underestimate this man,
to assume that because he was less than enthusiastic
about his job duties he was also less than competent. He
was probably as highly trained as the deadly Commandos
who were strategically placed around the room and
whose gazes had never strayed from her back.

Giving credence to her thoughts, the doctor asked,
"What is your condition, XPD-154? Are you functional?"

She forced back a wave of nausea and kept her face utterly blank of expression despite the anxiety burgeoning
inside her. By her estimate, the real Classified Courier
would be pulling up to the guardhouse any minute. A
woman with long blond hair, she'd be driving the same
model Ninja motorcycle, but hers would be black—the
color of death. It was easy to mentally play out what
would happen then—

*She would cut the motor to the bike and lower the kick-
stand, then pull out her papers, papers that would identify her using the same words—"XPD-154 Clearance
Classified Courier." At first it would be no big deal—no
doubt there were plenty of classified couriers who came
in and out of the L.L.D.D. every day. She would wait, hiding her impatience as any good little government em-*

*ployee was expected to, while the guard typed in the
codes that were on her ID. The computer would take
about two milliseconds to process the fact that this person was there to pick up something already assumed to
have been given over to a different courier, then the monitor on his desk would go an obnoxious red with the blinking words* Security Violation! Duplicate Classified
Courier! Code 99! *and all hell would break loose.*

*The guard's eyes would widen, then he would yank his
rifle off his shoulder and train it on the unsuspecting
courier. There were four robotic machine guns at the
gate, one at each corner of the square in which she
waited, and all of them were IR-tied to the movement of
his rifle, so they, too, would instantly rise into position
and home in on her. The guard would scream,* "On the
ground! On the ground!" *and she would comply instantly
by dropping to her knees and raising her hands. She
would be too smart to protest, and even if she did and was
shot, it would all end up the same, anyway. Her eyes
would narrow and she would demand to know what the
hell was going on. The guard would approach her cautiously, watching for any offensive movement, and tell her*
"You came through this gate fifteen minutes ago!"

And the real *XPD-154 Clearance Classified Courier
would sneer at him and say,* "Then it wasn't me you dumb
son of a bitch. Check my ID—you've got a Mite!"

Any minute now . . .

Both she and the doctor each had a hand on the titanium briefcase, and neither was inclined to release it. Her
nostrils flared slightly as she tried to take a calming
breath without him noticing. She gave him an arch look
and put a heavy note of impatience into her voice. "I

really don't know what you're talking about, Comrade Doctor. I'm one hundred percent functional."

But his grip only tightened—he'd gone beyond the vaguely concerned to the outright suspicious. Damn. "Then you won't mind if I perform an examination."

Her mouth tightened. "I've already submitted to every test required for entry," she reminded him tersely. She could feel heavy lines of sweat gathering beneath her breasts, pooling beneath the layers of fabric. "Now, as you've made clear, I have a timetable. So if you don't mind, I'll just—"

Blaaaaah! Blaaaaah! Blaaaaah! Blaaaaah! Blaaaaah!

Across the small width of the white briefcase, the doctor's body jerked in surprise at the scream of the alarms. His gaze snapped back to hers just in time to see the dark lenses on her reflective sunglasses clear. Her eyes blazed into his at the same time the color of her coat morphed into a deep, fiery red.

Showing more courage than she would have expected from a medical sector employee—most of the time, these private sector techno-nerds never paid a bit of attention to their tactical training—the Combat Reserve Doctor actually snarled at her and tried to jerk the briefcase free. She yanked it toward her with the hand still holding it at the same time that she slammed the knife edge of her other hand across his forearm. She—and everyone else in the room—clearly heard the radius bone in his arm fracture.

He let go of the case and careened backward, screaming like a baby as he cradled his arm, and before they could get hold of her, she spun to meet the instant reaction of the Armored Medical Techs. She punched the one closest to her with enough force to shatter his bullet-resistant glass chest plate; before the second one could reassess his approach, she put her fist completely through the face visor on his helmet. When she pulled it back and he collapsed at her feet, her gloved knuckles were covered with blood and bits of flesh. Another half dozen had leaped forward in unison, intending to box her inside the ring of their rifle barrels; she took care of their little circle with a double spinning crescent kick that turned her body into a blur of energy in their center. As the side of her boot struck the barrels, the rifles snapped to the right with enough force to yank them from the Med Techs' hands and send them tumbling. She kept the kick going, twice more, then thrice, and let the black, metal-encased fighting boot do the dirty work of smashing cheekbones and jaws, crushing the delicate bones of the hands reaching for her.

It took all of fifteen seconds for her to decimate every single one of the other Armored Med Techs lining the walls, and never once did she let go of that white titanium briefcase.

Of course, its lovely, pearly white covering was a lot more red by the time Violet stood, the only upright person—no, the only *vampire*—in the center of the L.L.D.D. inner vault.

SEVEN

In contrast to the approaching thumps of the boots of the security force, the heels of the Chief of Research's shoes made sharp, almost bulletlike sounds as he marched toward the main corridor. When he turned the corner, he nearly ran face first into the Security Commando who was leading the group; the soldier spun but didn't slow down, and the Chief fell into step beside him, now moving at a slow jog.

"She's a Hemophage, sir!"

The Chief couldn't see the man's eyes behind his visor, but he could hear the shock in his voice. It matched the level he'd felt when he'd first heard the alarm—a Hemophage, *inside* the L.L.D.D.! It was unthinkable, sacrilege . . . *filthy*. "How did she get past the screens?" he demanded. He was so furious that he wanted to stop, grab this soldier, and shake him as hard as he could. A foolish, immature reaction—this soldier had nothing to do with the problem. He was just within range, the closest target available on whom the Chief could vent his anger. And what was the Vice-Cardinal going to say? It wasn't hard to guess. There would be repercussions here, *serious* repercussions. And here was this man, part of an elite security force that was supposed to be the best in the world, the *only* ones trained to deal with this. They alone were supposed to be trained to recognize this kind of threat, this *specific* kind of threat . . . and yet they had let her through, let her not only get all the way into their most sacred inner area, but had given her—

The Chief's face was china-white and his gaze was fiercely accusing; he was positive he actually *heard* the sound of the Commando's throat working as he swallowed.

"We don't know, sir. Maybe meta-suppressants to subordinate her blood characteristics and healing capability . . . We just don't know!" Panic made the guy's voice overly loud and high, climbing toward the edge of strident.

But the Chief's black glare was steady, with no patience or sympathy. What a stupid, *stupid* man—he had no idea how his ignorance and that of his peers was going to so terribly affect the entire project.

But there was no time for admonitions right now. He had a new goal: to not let this . . . setback actually *destroy* everything they'd worked so hard to accomplish. His face set, the Chief kept his silence and followed the Commando team in the direction of the inner vault.

⚡

Violet leaped across the juncture of one corridor with another, then skidded to a stop and paused where the wall jutted outward before turning again—the perfect spot to pause and try to catch her breath. She couldn't recall the last time she'd felt this horrible, and when she looked down at her hands, the skin was the color of old ash, mottled with gray spots like a hundred-year-old cadaver. Just that simple movement—looking downward—made perspiration splash from her forehead onto her fingers. She saw the droplets—there were three of them—fall like they were on slow-motion film, saw them leave a pattern in the whitish-looking powder that had formed over her skin. Her LCD overcoat, so vibrant and colorful only minutes ago, had morphed into a swirl of oily-looking gray and brown.

Her hands were shaking so badly she almost couldn't grasp the right button on her coat, and it took three precious seconds to get a good hold on it so she could retract the syringe from the flat-space receptacle just inside the seam. She had another heart-stuttering moment when she nearly dropped it to the ceramic tiled floor—she mustn't contaminate the needle, and breaking it would be disastrous—then she managed to twist it around and get it into position so she could jam it into her thigh.

One knee buckled and she went down, thwacking her kneecap viciously on the floor. Then, without warning, she leaned over and vomited, her belly and lungs working in tandem to expel the contents of her stomach. There wasn't much in her belly but bile and water, but her body's reaction to the high dose of suppressants she'd ingested this morning made the small, black-looking puddle just putrid enough to make her retch all over again. Gasping, she twisted away, scuttling backward like an injured crab with one knee still down. Time was an extravagance she didn't have here, and she could stay there and rest for only a few precious seconds; as the neutralizers did their work her breathing quickly slowed from panting to normal, her heart rate sped up to where it should be, and she could feel the ugly brown over-color on one of her irises—they felt like too-thick contact lenses—being eaten away as her natural clear blue temporarily re-asserted itself. She didn't need to look in a mirror to know that the unnatural violet and evanescent sheen of a vampire would just as quickly obliterate the blue.

By the time the doors at the far end of the hallway burst open and the security forces spilled through, the neutralizers had done their work and Violet was more than ready for action. She yanked the syringe out of her thigh and tossed it aside, not even registering the tinkle of shattering glass as she pressed a concealed button on her belt. What had looked like nothing more than one of a se-ries of ornamental disks along the leather suddenly bulged outward as a small, four-dimensional gyroscope activated. The security forces realized she was right there at the same time she sprang to her feet and charged di-rectly at them. By now her overcoat was a deep burnt or-ange and she looked like a ball of flame headed right for the group of Commandos. Their leader bellowed out an order and they raised their weapons on cue and opened fire. The roar of gunfire filled the corridor and Violet dove—

—straight up.

There was an astonished pause as the soldiers blinked at the empty spot where she'd stood only a second before, and that moment of hesitation was enough to seal their doom. Before they could change tactics, she spun two machine pistols from flat-space holsters sewn against the fabric of her slacks on both hips; a millisecond later the barrels of both her guns belched fire and death down on their heads.

From the safety of the compound's surveillance room, the Chief of Research and several Commando supervisors and security technicians stood frozen in front of a bank of surveillance screens. The Chief could feel the stress and anxiety building inside his skull like a massive migraine headache, the kind he'd gotten as a child before Beltane Pharmaceuticals had come up with the medication, an inoculation much like the smallpox shots of the old centuries that had ended migraines forever. His stomach churned with sudden nausea and little yellow lights sparkled at the edges of his vision. Yep, just like a migraine.

Gripping the edge of the counter, the Chief finally found his voice. It came out raspy and low, almost a whisper. "Christ—how did she *do* that?"

"She must have some kind of gravity leveler," offered one of the techs nervously. He slapped his fingers against his face and wiped roughly at the corners of his mouth, the movement betraying his own fear. "Or—"

The Chief waved him away impatiently; he'd neither expected nor wanted an answer right now—explanations could wait for later. Right now, they had to think *forward*. "Well, whatever it is, it's ours now." He glared at the monitor that showed Violet scuttling along the ceiling of a corridor like some sort of oversized spider. God, how he wished he could reach right through the screen and pluck her through it. He'd throttle the bitch himself. "Because she is *not* going to make it out of this complex alive."

Violet found the door to the emergency exit staircase almost immediately, but when she tugged it open she could already hear the security forces rushing up from the lower floors. Their boots clapped against the rubberized metal stairs, giving her a decent idea of their numbers. Clearly they weren't concerned that she could hear them—they had plenty of confidence that they could best her by sheer numbers. It didn't matter. Her gyroscope was still engaged and she saw them long before they saw her. The ignorant soldiers were, of course, looking forward and up—that was how the world in which they had been trained operated. Violet, on the other hand, was looking *down* at them from the rear, at an almost negative, Escher-like image of the staircase. Once you knew how this dimension worked, it was absurdly easy to walk across the ceiling over their heads and mow them down with machine-gun fire like the images in the old twenty-first-century video games.

She left the bodies behind with barely a glance, and the next corridor she stepped into was empty . . . but of course, it wouldn't be for long. She kept her pace brisk and her gaze darted in every direction as she reloaded her guns from magazines stored in flat-space reservoirs on the inside of her coat, all the while never loosening her iron-tight hold on that priceless white briefcase. Even so, she damn near dropped it when the familiar voice of the Chief of Research came thundering out of a set of speakers hidden in the wall almost directly above her head.

"Violet Song jat Sharif! Tell me I'm wrong!"

Without looking up from her task, Violet snapped back, "You're wrong." It was a stupid thing for the idiot to say, so she gave him a stupid answer. Sometimes, the little things balanced out just right.

"Taking a break from blowing up government buildings?" When she didn't bother to answer, he continued in a more frustrated tone of voice, *"Why are you doing this?"*

His voice was loud enough so that she could feel the vibrations through the soles of her boots. Of course, she was extrasensitive to most things that the so-called normal people missed on a daily basis—hearing, smell, taste. Wasn't that funny, considering the public's impression of "vampires" was still Bram Stoker and Bela Lugosi, neither of whom had been presumed to have any predilection toward real food.

But wait—he'd asked another stupid question, hadn't he? And, of course, she was expected to answer. Just in case there were video cameras hidden in the walls as a companion to the speakers, she lifted her head so that her face could clearly be seen. Then she drew her mouth back in something that was part snarl, part derision, and the rest an exaggerated caricature of innocence. "Because I hate humans with every fiber of my being?" She widened her eyes and blinked, then her mouth twisted of its own accord. "And I'll kill every one I see almost as quickly as they'll try to kill *me*."

"Listen to yourself," he came back immediately. *"You used to be human."* He sounded absurdly like a parent trying to admonish a teenaged girl for doing something he couldn't quite explain was wrong.

Unfortunately, his words—*"You* used *to be"*—had only validated her rage. Her expression was thunderous. "But not anymore, right?" She tossed her head and, with the briefcase tucked beneath her arm, spun the guns expertly in each hand. "I got *sick* . . . and now I'm something *less* than human." Her voice slid down until it was nearly a hiss. "Something worthy of *extermination*."

"It's academic now, isn't it?" She could almost picture the man shrugging carelessly. He'd been running scared for a few moments there, but now he would be reenergized, confident that the abundant security forces had strategically repositioned themselves for her capture. Her *demise*. Yes, he had the same disregard for her and her race that the rest of them did; sometimes she felt that the noninfected looked at her and saw the word "DISPOSABLE" tattooed across her forehead. Then the Chief spoke again and her renewed anger wiped out the rest of Violet's musing. *"You won't make it out of here with that case."*

She snapped her wrists, then brought the weapons up to bear and lengthened her stride. "Watch me!" Before he could answer she turned a corner, paused to get her bearings, then spotted a ventilation grate high on the wall by the ceiling juncture. Without hesitating, she scuttled up the wall like a crab and pulled on the cover; when it resisted, she grimaced and forced her fingers through the slots, then yanked backward. The screws gave out and the metal screeched as she forced it free. When Violet peered inside, it was all clear. The security forces hadn't thought about this route yet. She clambered inside and tried to put the grate covering back, but it was useless—too strong for her own good, not only had she sheared off every one of the screws when she'd pulled it free, she'd mangled it so badly that there was no way to bend the metal back into shape so she could at least fake it. She pulled it inside and let it drop noisily to the floor of the metal duct in which she was crouching. The sound was like thunder, reverberating along the metal pathway and bouncing back on itself. It didn't matter; they were going to find her anyway.

There wasn't much light inside the ventilation duct, just what bled in from the gratings every so many feet. Violet's eyes adjusted to the lower light immediately but everything looked the same in every direction and she had to allow herself a precious few seconds to orient herself. Being in here at least gave her several choices, although predictably most of those would already be compromised—the security forces might not be as quick as she was, but they weren't dummies either. They also had access to computer blueprint imagery showing every last space in this building, including all the ductwork, ingress and egress. There was nothing to do but charge ahead and let her instincts guide her toward her outside rendezvous and freedom. And she was *not* leaving this installation without this briefcase.

Violet nearly fell when she came to the intersection of another part of the ductwork, this one a vertical air shaft. With its drop-off only an inch or two in front of her feet, it fell away into muted silver shadows, backlit periodically by workers' tube lights set into the metal every four yards or so. When she looked up the shaft, she could just spot the Medical Commandos getting ready to drop toward her.

She grinned, checked the integrity of the small gyroscope at her belt, then jumped into the air shaft and fell upward.

The Commandos writhed on their drop ropes and tried to get out of the way of her bullets, but there was simply no escaping the barrage of gunfire as she twisted and fired behind herself, taking advantage of the still activated technology. Good old gravity, that one thing that in

the past had always been so very inescapable turned out
to be their doom— in seconds they all hung there, limp
and lifeless at the end of their rappeling cords; in another
instant, Violet hit the grating at the top of the shaft with a
crash! and exploded through it without having a clue
about what was on the other side. She somersaulted up,
then came back down as her body's inner ear adjusted itself and intervened. When she landed, she was straddling
one of the skylights and already belting out hundreds of
rounds at the waiting security forces. They went down
easily, and before their superiors could think to regroup
and send more, Violet leaped off the skylight and ran for
the edge of the roof. Again without bothering to look, she
vaulted over the side.

She swung and, for the barest of seconds, went into
free fall. Did birds feel like this? It was wonderful—
weightless and giddy—and it was a damned shame she
didn't have the time to enjoy it. Then her trajectory, an-
gled ever so slightly, took her back against the side of the
building. She touched it and stuck, then instantly sprinted
down its slick metal side. When she came to a huge plate-
glass window, she jumped over its ten-foot expanse; there
would be security forces on the other side of the glass, so
she beat them to the draw and fired into it, showering
them with jagged pieces of glass and the remains of the
window frame, driving them solidly back into the interior. They returned fire even as they fell, until what was
left of the heavy plate glass seemed to be going in all directions at once.

She sprinted onto the earth-gravity surface of the alley
behind the building with the gyroscope still giving off a
reassuring pulse at her hip. She blinked once and started
to turn, then froze as she looked eye-to-barrel at the auto-

rifle pointed directly at her nose, a mere half a foot separating her skin from the cold metal.

For the first time since she'd come out of the air shaft, Violet realized it was raining. Not that hard, but enough to coat her skin and slick her hair down against her scalp at the same time it drifted against the face visors of the seven Command Marines surrounding her. Raindrops trickled slowly down the dark shields, making it impossible for her to see the eyes of the men she was about to kill.

No matter. She never did.

She whirled within the circle of rifle barrels, becoming a blur that was moving too fast for them to see, much less track. Then she stopped and simply stood there, and for a very long moment no one else moved—not a muscle twitch, a word, or even a gesture with the end of a weapon. Then, almost as one, all seven Marines just . . . toppled over backward and lay still, their abdomens now nothing more than wide, gaping wounds matched edge for edge with the next dead soldier.

Violet glanced at them indifferently, then held up the chisel-nosed sword she'd used to kill her would-be assassins, holding it out so the rain would wash the blood from the Hindi-Thai script that scrolled the length of the black blade. When the last of the scarlet drops had run off the end and disappeared, she slid it back into the flat-space sheath strapped under her wrist. The sound it made—a strange cross between a tinny clanging and a whine—was the only sound in the alley besides the gentle thrum of the rain.

With a sudden rush of adrenaline, Violet spun and gripped the white briefcase tighter. No one with a great cause works alone and she was no different; her comrades had made sure her method of escape, a metallic midnight-blue motorcycle, would be parked at this pre-arranged location. She jumped on the throttle hard and slammed it into first gear, hearing the hopped-up motor respond instantly. Then, as the last of the medication she so loathed finally diluted and cleared out of her system, her other eye finally slid away from the brown into full violet-blue. She blinked a couple of times and grinned wickedly, then Violet hammered the bike into a tight spin and screamed out of the alley in a cloud of hot, white smoke.

In another few seconds, the rain and the scant breeze had washed away the last trace of her existence.

EIGHT

Violet guessed she had maybe ten seconds to contact Nerva before the L.L.D.D.'s forces would figure out her escape method and come after her. The rain was a nice touch, but when it really counted, it wasn't going to help much. Ten seconds wasn't a whole lot of time, so she'd better make good use of it.

The bike thrummed beneath her like a huge cat hungering for freedom, wanting to stretch its body and run. She wasn't pushing the engine—not yet—but the time would certainly come. For the here and now she skimmed along rapidly but not at a breakneck pace; this way she could put some distance between her and the compound and avoid messing up her front wheel and getting blood—very traceable—on the motorcycle by running over any human security forces. Pedestrians were just as annoying.

Violet leaned smoothly into a right turn, then steadied the bike and jabbed a finger at the screen phone built into the console. A red digital readout flashed across the screen, but she couldn't read it and drive at the same time. It didn't matter, anyway—all this software cared about was her vocal cords. "It's me," she said breathlessly. Every time she did this, she worried that the computer wouldn't recognize her. How could her voice sound the same when sometimes she was running for her life, and at others her day was about as exciting as a farmer watching the chickens peck at the gravel.

But it *did* recognize her, and an instant later, after the computer had double-verified her voiceprint, Nerva's image appeared on the display. Even via the motorcycle's communication's package, his dark eyes burned with intensity and rebellion. Nerva was the epitome of darkness, a man who, when he contracted the disease, had immersed himself in the lifestyle of a Hemophage and reveled in it. In fact, Violet often wondered if he had been made for it all along . . . destined. His pitch black hair and matching clothes emphasized skin the color of fine ivory and lengthened the bruised-looking shadows beneath his eyes and under his cheekbones; when he talked, Violet could clearly see the elongated incisors in his red slash of a mouth. His passion and anger at the way Hemophages were treated and the way he had responded— waging his own war against those in charge of the uninfected masses—had earned him the unofficial sobriquet as the "Che Guevarra" of vampires. It was a reputation he thoroughly enjoyed and strived to maintain.

"Did you get it?" he demanded.

"Yes." Violet's gaze darted from left to right as she checked her side mirrors. Oh, yeah—there they were. The lights of a Command Security Tanker just appearing in the darkness far behind her. They were the only vehicles on the road allowed to have gold headlights. Even though her motorcycle was a lot lighter, the tanker would have more power. They would be relentless, and it wouldn't take long for them to catch up. "But they're serious about not letting me keep it."

"Fine," he retorted without hesitation. *"The objective is the destruction of the weapon. If you can't make delivery, destroy it."*

"Copy that." The tankers had cut the distance in half, and now she could clearly see them in the mirrors. She felt like a tidbit fleeing from a pack of hungry wolves. "Will determine nature and destroy."

"No!" The unexpected vehemence in his voice made her blink in surprise and glance at the tiny com screen. *"Categorically* not, *V! Under no circumstances are you to look inside that case! If you are compromised, you* must *destroy immediately. Do you read?"*

She frowned and swerved sharply around trash containers that had been left in the center of the alley. Strange that Nerva and his cronies wouldn't want to know what the weapon was . . . unless he already did. That wouldn't surprise her a bit. She risked a glance over her shoulder. Speaking of not being surprised, the tanker pursuing her was close enough so that now she could actually see the helmet and visor of the driver. A second or two after she glanced backward, the tanker ran over the trash cans, flattening the plastic and metal like an ant under the heel of a soldier's boot. As for the weapon, there was no time to argue about it and besides, she, too, was a soldier—obedience was second nature. "Read," she said, and hit the disconnect button. Obedience or not, she had a dozen questions, but they would have to wait until later. It was imperative that she and Nerva keep their conversations as short as possible to avoid a satellite trace.

The Command Security Tankers were nearly on top of her now—she could hear their engines screaming right behind her. The comfort zone she'd been maintaining was gone, so Violet went for the left turn coming up, sliding so long that she nearly put the bike on its side and the side of her tight leggings, made of a nifty combination of leather and armor, grew uncomfortably hot from the friction of the concrete. The two Tankers behind her weren't quite that agile and they had to slam on the brakes and skid to a stop, then jam the transmission in reverse before they could reposition and turn. Great stall, but it wouldn't take long before they were breathing down her neck all over again. She had maybe fifteen seconds, but that was all she needed to snap the line of red switches at the top of the motorcycle's console; where the gas tank would normally be installed—a slim, double-sided version that held just enough fuel to complete the mission ran up and under the uncomfortably modified version of the seat— was another gyroscope. This modified 'scope was big enough to handle a whole lot more than the weight of her slender frame.

The top of the gas tank slid open so the heavier-duty gyroscope could lift itself out of the cavity on miniature hydraulics. The machinery was a work of art, and it needed less than two inches to operate; when it spun to life with a whine that she could hear even above the roar of the motorcycle's engine, Violet grinned wickedly and aimed the motorcycle straight at the rounded front end of a clunky-looking street cleaning vehicle parked up ahead. A sharp jerk of her shoulders lifted the front wheel over the street brushes on the front of the machine and the bike climbed up the vehicle's front grillwork and kept going, up and up until it was airborne. The gyroscope reoriented the bike's gravity base and then she was skidding, right up the side of the nearest building. Violet got the motorcycle—and herself—righted and left a trail of heavy white smoke as she fired off in a diagonal direction while the Tankers raced along on the street below, following her weaving trail as best they could.

When the edge of the building suddenly appeared, Violet pulled the bike on its side and stopped, bringing it back upright at its corner just as she teetered on the very edge. A normal person would have had vertigo, but not Violet. Oh, no—suddenly she gunned it, hard, and the Ninja went over, launching her straight down and away on the opposite side of the building.

A sound, like a hot buzzing, worked into her hearing, loud enough to be heard over the scream of the motorcycle's straining engine. Violet jerked and looked over her shoulder, scowling at the two Whisperjet helicopters that had swung around the corner of the building and were headed after her. They looked like gigantic black wasps, with their fronts bubbled out and the rears extending back and tipped by dual stabilizers. In another situation she might have been annoyed by the myriad and multisized windows pocking the side of the building at random intervals, but today those same windows might be saving her life—it was having to hot-dog the cycle around them that kept the heated lead from the helicopters' 70mm machine guns from taking her down.

Another edge, and this time Violet gunned the motorcycle and felt it swing into open air, projecting her across the intersection far below and ramming the tires onto the face of the next building with enough force to make her teeth jitter inside her mouth. Bullets chewed up the metal and mortar behind her like blades whipping through soft butter, and the window glass blew inward with sounds like mini explosions. Leave it to the L.L.D.D. to care little—if at all—about the people behind those windows; the pilots were probably leaving a trail of blasted, blood-soaked bodies. She had a single second to orient herself and look forward—

And she skidded onto the surface of the huge bay window at the front of the new Harlem and Irving Mall.

There was no way Violet could avoid it. The cycle went on its side and slid like a downed skater across an ice rink, and all she could do was hold on and hope. The gunfire from the Whisperjets followed her, eating up the glass around her, the pilots still not giving a damn about anyone else getting hurt. This expanse of glass didn't so much shatter as disintegrate, and then there wasn't even time to think about what to do next. Violet kept everything together on instinct and autopilot, and when she fell, the only thing that saved her butt and got the motorcycle turned nose-downward into normal gravity was good old-fashioned training . . . with a heavy dose of extraordinary reflexes.

A couple hundred shoppers screamed and fled in all directions as Violet spun onto the mall's concourse and revved the engine. She took off before things could get worse, dodging the scrambling people as quickly as they tried to get out of her way. She'd seen a lot of things in her life, but even Violet couldn't believe it when four Whisperjets hummed into position in front of the great, jagged hole left by her untidy entrance . . . and then the front one opened fire on full auto. Men, women, children—the bullets didn't care who was in front of them as they chewed everything in their way to nothing but piles of red and bleeding mincemeat. It seemed to go on and on, but in reality it didn't take long at all to empty the rest of the oversized magazine—the gunner on the helicopter had already expended most of his ammo trying to take her down on the outside. Suddenly the screams stopped, the gunfire stopped, and the only sound in the mall, besides a few sad sobs and one faraway and pathetic store alarm, was Violet's motorcycle engine and the dry clicking of the minigun's magazine.

Violet came to the end of the concourse, then revved the engine into a skid that spun it around to face the remains of the plate-glass window and the helicopters hovering outside. There was a long, quiet moment . . .

Then she looked up and sent them all an evil grin.

The gunner gaped at her. Violet couldn't see his eyes behind his safety goggles, but she'd bet her life that they were as wide as golf balls right about now.

"Oh, shit!" he suddenly screamed in a voice loud enough for Violet to hear above the motorcycle *and* the helicopters. He twisted around in his seat, gesturing wildly to a munitions crewman she couldn't see in the tail of the helicopter. *"Load the next drum! Load the next drum!"*

Violet jumped on the throttle and went wide open.

Tires belching foul black smoke, she ate up the distance on the concourse and headed straight for the front helicopter, banking everything on the idea that the pilot would try to be a hero and stay in place rather than move aside so the next Whisperjet could take his place. The gunner was still screaming—

"Come on—COME ON!"

—as her speedometer hit a hundred fifty. She didn't hear it as the terrified crewman finally got the drum locked into place, but she knew it was coming by the tri-

umphant look on the gunner's face. She was well below
the bulletproof shield on the motorcycle before the first
burst of bullets hit, but even this top-notch custom shield
wouldn't hold for long against this kind of a barrage.

But that was okay. It didn't have to.

At sixth gear, Violet and the bike went airborne and
sailed out of what was left of the window. They flew
through bullet-riddled air and hammered right into the
open-sided helicopter, obliterating the pilot under the
front tire, and the gunner and the rest of the tiny crew
with the bike's machine pistol. As Violet came out the
other side of the copter, something in the cockpit—a
spark or maybe a short caused by one of her bullets—
suddenly turned the Whisperjet into a great blazing ball
of hovering flame. It sagged slightly in the air, then careened into the one next to it. That one exploded . . . and
then the next one, and the one after that, like a great game
of giant, fiery dominos in the sky.

Violet and the bike smashed through a window in the
building across the street. The motorcycle fell onto the
crash bar on its side as she slid down the entire length of
an office's central corridor, taking out furniture, chairs,
piles of paper, and anything else that was unfortunately in
the path of her vehicle. There was no easy out through a
window here, and when it was obvious that the end of
the road was a wall of Sheetrock—probably covering
reinforced metal studs—Violet made sure she had a
firm hold on the briefcase and thrust herself off the bike,
using her leg muscles to propel her as far away as she
could. She spun to her feet at the same time the motorcycle boomeranged into the wall, tangling itself into the
studs and a piece of some kind of heavy furniture—
maybe an executive desk—on the other side. Wiring

sparked dangerously amid the ruins, and she could see currents of raw electricity zinging along the now-exposed steel studs.

She twisted and spotted an exit door off to the side. Head held high, Violet strode smartly through the wreckage in that direction, moving as though she completely belonged there. She ignored the whining of the weak, uninfected humans as they peered from beneath their desks, makeshift hiding places that had she really wanted to do them harm wouldn't have helped them a bit. One guy looked like he wanted to say something, but she waved him away and he changed his mind; in another moment she'd left that office behind and ducked into a different corridor branching off it, winding her way through the maze of interior hallways and staircases toward the ground floor. There was only one nerve-wracking moment when she came out of a utility door and spotted a couple of security teams just entering that hallway only a few feet away; a quick backtrack and a few turns gave her a fresh perspective on which way to go. A few more turns and Violet was on the edge of the expansive lobby. Amid the expensive green marbling that was on the floors, walls, and ceiling, she watched the security teams stream into the building and tried to mingle with the throngs of bewildered office workers. That in itself was nearly impossible. The way she moved, her dark and vaguely exotic beauty and clothing, her bold self-confidence—all these things were working against her right now. While everyone around her was babbling about the "situation" in the upper levels of the building and when could they get up there to see, all she could think about was getting the hell out of the building and *not* being seen.

Violet discovered a small alcove off to the side and

ducked into it, pressing her back against the wall as her heart jackhammered and she tried to steady her breathing. She dug her mic-phone out of the tiny, flat-space pocket behind her ear, then activated the hand phone. It bleeped at her instantly. "It's me," she said. She inched forward and peered around the corner, keeping an eye on the people milling curiously about, making sure the security forces stayed well away from her as they rushed back and forth through the crowds, occasionally stopping to manhandle someone. This alcove was an easy trap so Violet couldn't risk getting caught in here.

Nerva's image shimmered into place on the tiny liquid crystal screen, but it was so small she could barely make out his expression. *"Three-D me,"* he ordered tersely.

That was probably not such a good idea given her situation, but Violet was used to obeying . . . at least for the most part. She pressed a nearly invisible button and his image fanned out from a pin-sized beam in her telephone. As he stood in front of her, Nerva was slickly dressed and life-sized; only the faintest of shimmers in his image identified it as anything but the real thing. *"Are you clear?"* he asked.

That, more than anything, was the telling aspect of the "man" standing in front of her—he had no idea what was going on around her. Sometimes he could be so utterly clueless. Or was it careless? "Negative," Violet shot back. "They're everywhere. I don't know if I can make it."

Nerva's eyes bored into hers, so close to lifelike it almost made Violet shiver. *"You're carrying the bomb?"*

"Of course," she answered.

"Then detonate it now," Nerva ordered without hesitation. *"It'll level the entire block."*

Violet's heart rate jumped a bit and she pressed her lips together before responding. "May I suggest an alternative?" She glanced at the white briefcase in her hand and her eyes narrowed. "Let's open the case and use the weapon."

"*Negative!*" Nerva's voice was sharp with anxiety. "*Do* not *open that case, V—Detonate! Right* now."

Her grip on the briefcase handle tightened until her knuckles were white and Violet licked her lips. Her fingers squeezed tight until she could feel the pulse of the blood inside her veins. "But my life loss and the collateral human loss may not be necessary. If the weapon's effective against us, it can be effective against them, too."

The face on Nerva's image twisted into something nearly resembling rage. "*And I'm telling you this is not subject to debate,*" he growled. "*The entire fate of our race is tied up in that case. Detonate the bomb. Destroy the case—destroy* everything. *Now!*"

Violet licked her lips and didn't say anything.

Nerva's image stared coldly at her, showing no emotion. "*Good-bye, V.*"

She opened her mouth to reply, but nothing came out. She closed it again.

"*V, I said* good-bye.*" He stared at her, hard and expecting. Unyielding. Here was a man used to having his underlings obey him, even if they weren't sure why or if his orders made sense. Even if it meant their death.

She managed to swallow again, but it was really more of a spasm in her dust-dry throat. "Yeah," she finally croaked. "Good . . . bye."

She snapped off the telephone and slipped it back into its place, then reached inside her coat. The detonator was in there, ready and waiting. Like all of her "toys," it was concealed inside a flat-space pocket where, until she removed it, it was as weightless and free of mass as air. All she had to do was pull it out and simply push the button. That little piece of plastic and machinery would then, supposedly, solve everything. The hotshot secret weapon would be history, the rebellion would be fueled, and the L.L.D.D. would be significantly hurt . . . although they would probably never be stopped. Was it worth it? Maybe. Her own waiting for the ultimate finality would also, finally, be over.

Just that one little *push.*

Push . . .

Nine

Violet was on the run again, bouncing through the crowds of people on the sidewalk outside like a pinball firing across the electronic surface in one of those late twentieth-century arcade games. She left a trail of muffled—and sometimes not—curses and sarcastic comments in her wake, but she didn't care; by the time she made it out of the lobby of the building, the L.L.D.D. security forces were only about a quarter block behind her. Now the only thing keeping her out of their grasp was the pedestrians on the sidewalk—everyone trying to get where they were going as quickly as possible in the busiest part of the day.

Violet knew she wasn't going to make it like this. There were too many soldiers and only one of her—she was outnumbered and while they didn't have the same level of technology she did, they did have more of it—more guns, more power, more variety. The only chance she had of escape was blending in and walking away, literally, right under their noses.

There was a woman coming toward her, dressed in a classy pin-striped suit and carrying a light-colored brief-case. Her hair was about Violet's length and strawberry-blond above dark, fashionable sunglasses, and she stepped confidently through the crowd, paying no mind to the other people—she was a woman with a purpose and a place to go, and she was exactly what Violet needed to be. Businesslike, brisk, and completely generic in her surroundings.

As she and the woman passed, Violet's fiber-optic-coated hair shimmered to match the woman's at the same time her mood coat did the same. Without saying a word, Violet did an about-face and fell into step at the woman's side, moving as though there was nothing in the world out of place that she should suddenly look like this stranger's twin sister.

Three seconds later, she and her new silent partner walked directly into the middle of the security forces.

The uniformed team streamed around her, not sparing a glance for the two women—they were far too focused on catching up with the dark-headed Violet. Not a single soldier registered the white briefcase that Violet swung loosely from her left hand as though it contained nothing more than a few office presentations. Maybe it was the light, maybe it was a trick of the mind, but when they saw what was in Violet's hand, they saw what was in her mirror image's. It was perfect.

When the last of the soldiers had stepped around them and moved on, the woman Violet was mimicking happened to glance to her right. She had only enough time to gasp, then Violet's coat and hair reverted to their normal colors and she dodged across the woman's path, then crossed the street and disappeared into yet another mass of daytime workers.

Down one block in the other direction, then one more, and Violet ducked into the doorway of a small DVD shop. As small as the shop was, it still managed to cram at least fifteen television screens inside its space, each one playing the latest and greatest of entertainment, all with the volume muffled to where together it combined to stay at a low, mind-numbing roar. Keeping her back to the street but making sure she could watch the reflection of the world outside of the alcove in the window, Violet pressed one shoulder to the glass and acted like she was browsing the most recently released of the selections, some flick about some little girl being transported to a fantasy land—a remake of *The Wizard of Oz*? Maybe. Violet's heart was tripping along inside her chest, adrenaline and fear adding to her already super high metabolism. When she tried to draw in air her breath was more of a strained pant than anything else.

It took a precious quarter minute for Violet to calm her breathing enough so she thought she could be understood over the telephone. Finally, she pulled out her mic-phone and hit the redial code. Without realizing it, she'd left it in 3-D mode, and now Nerva's darkly handsome form snapped into position in front of her without warning, his three-dimensional image so lifelike it was enough to make her heart stutter all over again. She had some explaining to do to her boss and it wasn't going to be easy.

"V, what the fuck is going on?" The image of Nerva's face was twisted with fury and frustration.

She swallowed. "I'm clear."

"I told you to detonate!"

Violet ground her teeth at the rage in his voice. "I said

I'm *clear.*" Her sense of propriety—she *had* disobeyed orders, after all—warred with a suddenly blossoming resentment. He was clearly furious that she was still alive. Had it really been so easy for him to order her to her death? Had he cared so little for her well-being?

Well, that figured. As long as it wasn't himself, why should he care what was lost in his great and grand struggle?

The image in front of her spun and took a step, then came back—he was so enraged that he was pacing. Before Nerva spoke again, his overly long incisors worked at the soft flesh of his bottom lip. *"You have the case?"*

"Affirmative." Her voice was crisp, back to that of a Hemophage soldier obeying orders. Inside, though . . . such indecision.

He paused and she tensed, waiting for his second round of orders for her to self-destruct. This time he surprised her when he finally nodded. *"Bring it in."*

Violet's breath hissed out between her teeth and she felt her shoulders relax a little. "What's your status?"

The image regarded her from beneath half-closed, sleepy-looking lids, a deceptive expression that she had learned not to underestimate. The man was a wolf in disguise, a true predator. She shouldn't have to be reminded again that he ultimately thought only of himself, no matter how grandiose and unselfish his words might seem. *"The Needle,"* he answered. *"In the Chinois Gau."*

She gave a curt nod. "Ten minutes."

≹

If the Caucasian part of the city had been hectic, the Chine-Buddikhan sector was nothing short of true chaos.

The people here were three times as numerous, most of them spoke at least two languages (and switched from one to another regularly within the same conversation), and children were as thick in the streets as the flies above the sidewalk vendors crammed along the outsides of the buildings. Saying it was noisy didn't really cover it—it was more like an out-of-control industrial metal band with undertones of eclectic Asian music. Every now and then someone going by would catch a glimpse of what things could be if only the pace would slow down a bit . . . but that glimpse was immediately devoured by the way reality had actually manifested itself.

It was hard for Violet to tell whether she was in the midst of some kind of celebration or the masses of people were just out to browse the daily sales and look at the advertisements. There were too many colors and banners and signs, too much yelling back and forth and hawking of street goods. It was a good thing Violet had left the motorcycle behind—she didn't think she'd have been able to get the bike through all the people. The pièce de résistance was in the center of the street, one of those huge, three-headed dragons made of papier-mâché and wire; its body was segmented into at least twenty pieces that gyrated and hopped, propelled by the people hiding inside it who manipulated the wires. The whole thing wiggled and twisted in time to a cacophony of sound pouring from digital speakers set high on poles set at regular intervals along the sidewalk, and while the sound quality was excellent, Violet sure couldn't find any kind of a rhythm to it.

Her goal, called the Needle by its builder, was the tallest skyscraper in this sector. Its appropriately named apex seemed to go up forever, or at least until it pierced

the cloud cover that was, thankfully, blanketing
Chicago—those clouds made things a whole lot easier on
her oversensitive eyes. But even here, in the heart of the
Asian community where the most independent—and
dangerous—of the nationalities lived and worked, the
L.L.D.D. had managed to make its presence widely
known. Security teams were everywhere, their helmets
and black visors swiveling from left to right as they pa-
trolled the crowds and ignored the street hawkers who
tried, outright sarcastically, to sell them a few useless
gadgets and snacks. The resentment felt by the neighborhood residents toward the security forces was more than
obvious—it permeated the air and carried on the belliger-
ent voice tones, scissored from person to person on narrow-
eyed glares. Still, the Asians, like Violet, suspected that
ultimately there was no winning the war . . . just the little
battles now and then.

Were the security teams looking for her? Violet didn't
know, but it was a good bet that if they hadn't already re-
ceived word of her theft via their microphones, it would
happen at any second. Like most of the people passing
the guards, she kept her gaze downward as though she
needed to concentrate on exactly where her feet would
land—it was easy to use the jagged curbs and the trash-
and people-lined sidewalks as an excuse. But behind the
ruse, her gaze constantly darted in every direction as she
tried to keep her distance from the black-suited L.L.D.D.
guards. The security people were even inside the Needle
itself, which made things doubly tricky—she didn't dare
do something to attract their attention and, God forbid,
invite them to follow her. This was the last place in the
world she wanted to lead them.

For a change Violet managed a little kiss from Lady

Luck and there was an elevator in the lobby waiting to begin its ascent. She shouldered her way through the office workers who were waiting for it and pushed inside ahead of several others, ignoring the barbed, angry glances. Her breath was shuddering as the doors finally closed—she'd become convinced that at any instant a couple members of the L.L.D.D. security force would charge onto the elevator and open fire. There was just no way to run—an elevator was way too much like a coffin built for a dozen people instead of one.

It was nerve-wracking to have to share the ride with several other people, but there was simply no avoiding it. Short of standing on her head on the counter in front of the security desk, Violet could think of no faster way to point to herself than to bodily remove her fellow passengers. Instead, she inched to the back wall as casually as she could, pressing her spine against a smooth, cold surface—fake marble—that matched the real stuff back in the lobby. Anxiety was making her flush and the chilly material against her back did nothing to help; she could feel nervous perspiration gather along her nose beneath the hard bridge of her sunglasses. To her own mind, she was glaringly noticeable—black hair, black coat, and sunglasses . . . how could she *not* be? Then again, maybe not. There were a lot of black-haired beauties in this Chinois community, and a lot of them favored the black outfits that made them look almost anorexic. To prove that her outfit gave her the desired measure of anonymity, her fellow passengers disembarked one by one, until only she remained, one lone woman headed to the upper floors.

Floor after floor ticked by on the digital display above the door, and now that she was alone in the elevator, Violet suddenly became aware—maybe too much so—of the white briefcase hanging from her left hand. Her fingers were still clenched around the handle so tightly that her knuckles were bloodless and stiff. Despite herself and the strict instructions from Nerva, she couldn't help but wonder what was in it. Just what was this strange and magical, *powerful* weapon that was supposedly going to wipe out all the Hemophages but not harm the humans? Common sense dictated that it had to be something biological, a devastating agent designed specifically to target the mutated DNA structure of the Hemophages while bypassing that of humans.

Or . . . no. Maybe the uninfected *would* catch it, but their immune systems, being slower and more primitive, might be able to fashion an antibody to the agent before their likewise sluggish metabolisms ran the disease—assuming that's what it was—throughout their system. It wasn't hard to imagine if one likened the possibility to that of the now eradicated Ebola virus of the former African continent, the last of which had finally burned itself out in the bat-filled caves of the Republic of Congo after the global eradication effort. During its heyday, Ebola would often manifest and disappear again almost immediately, simply because it would kill its host—some sad and unlucky human or primate—far too quickly for its own reproductive cycle. Something modeled after that and intended for the Hemophages could be deadly, indeed.

Was that something like what Violet carried in this mysterious white briefcase? Surely not—if so, it didn't make sense that Nerva would instruct her to detonate the bomb that had been affixed in her clothes since she'd left the meeting place this morning and started on her mission. An explosion was too risky, wasn't it? After all, detonation had to mean taking a big chance of spreading the virus, or whatever was contained in this case, on the air currents afterward. It would mean every piece of debris left in the explosion's wake might be contaminated, a potential avenue for mass dissemination of the virus.

Violet glanced down and saw that her forefinger had involuntarily moved to stroke the cool metal. She had risked her life for this briefcase, fought against and beaten down countless soldiers as she took the chance that she might be caught and tortured or killed at any second. She'd given so much and asked for so little in return . . . didn't she have the right to know what was inside?

She was two floors away from her stop when she reached out and pushed the emergency stop button. The elevator stopped with a jerk, but unless she intentionally pushed it, the alarm wasn't going to sound. It was just her, and the silence . . .

And the briefcase.

She looked down at it in indecision—

No, that simply wasn't true.

There wasn't any indecision about it.

With a senseless glance behind her, Violet knelt and swung the pizza-box-sized briefcase around until it was flat on the floor in front of her knees. Her heart was racing again, this time in anticipation and . . . oh, sure. That thrill, the one she sometimes got when she was about to do something she knew she wasn't supposed to, like a kid in a toy store getting ready to filch something small but which still had the potential to get him prosecuted. Her personality had always been that of a rebel, a woman who took chances for sometimes nothing more than the fun of doing so.

Another glance, this time at the floor indicator to reassure herself that the elevator hadn't moved, then Violet slid her thumbs down and broke both of the DNA lock-latches. It was strange that there was no secondary combination lock on the case, but there was no time to think about that now. She drew her breath in and instinctively held it, then quickly lifted the lid.

What she saw inside the case made her breath explode from her throat as she flung herself backward hard enough to slam against the back wall of the elevator.

She stood there for a long moment with her hands splayed at her sides, frozen in place, trying to process what she'd seen. No, it couldn't be . . . it simply wasn't possible. *This* was the great and grand weapon? *This* was the object of all destruction for her and her fellow vampires?

A *child?*

Violet wiped the back of her hand across her mouth and registered vaguely that her lips were dry enough to crack, then she cautiously approached the briefcase again. No, she hadn't been imagining it—there he was, a boy child no older than nine years, curled into a cramped, still fetal position in the flat space inside the case.

He was human (nowadays it wasn't unheard of to come across human-primate mixes, creatures bred to work in hard labor situations), with huge, clear blue eyes that stared up at her beneath a crown of fine, close-cropped light brown hair. While he blinked at the sudden light in the elevator, there was no indication that he had the Hemophage virus inside him—his pupils reacted normally to the light and while his skin was pale, he still had a nice, healthy blush to his cheeks, the kind that fled a Hemophage's body by the end of the third month of the disease. Violet's extrasensitive hearing could easily pick up the boy's heartbeat, and it was normal and steady— *thrum thrum thrum*—as though he had nothing in the world about which he need be concerned. When his gaze focused on her face, he opened his mouth to say something—

And Violet quickly slammed the briefcase shut again.

She wasn't sure how long she sat there, trying to comprehend what she'd seen, attempting to subconsciously run through the hows and whys of it. Eventually the self-preservation node in her brain kicked in and reminded her that she'd held up this elevator for quite some time, and there was a damned good chance that pretty soon some kind of auto-alarm would go off. Finally, she stood and picked up the briefcase, then squared her shoulders and pressed the button to get the elevator going again. It started again with barely a hitch, the miracle of modern machinery.

Sometimes a person just had to do whatever was necessary, including some things that he or she really didn't want to do.

Life was just like that.

TEN

By the time the elevator arrived at her floor and the doors slid soundlessly open, Violet had gotten her uncertainty under control and her appearance was once more completely composed. With the briefcase swinging at her side, she strode down the hall with all of her normal self-confidence, her boot heels clicking smartly along the polished tile floor, her head held high, and her face utterly expressionless. At the far end was an unmarked door with a DNA reader set into the wall and covered by a sliding panel that was indiscernible to those who didn't know it was there. There was no one else in the hallway, so Violet quickly pushed up the panel and pressed the tip of her ring finger against the reader; she didn't even feel the sting as the surface of her skin was punctured by an air needle and her blood instantly analyzed and identified. In the two seconds it took to process the results, she withdrew her hand so the panel could slide back into its hiding place; when it did, the plain, recessed door slid to the side to admit her.

Nerva turned to watch her enter, as did his several other deadly-looking companions, all Hemophages and probably top-ranking assassins like herself. None of that mattered to Violet. She ignored them and strode directly to the mahogany conference table in the center of the room. She swept aside a handful of file folders with no regard to the ones that scattered on the floor, then placed the case on the table and began removing the gravity leveler that had helped her keep hold of it during the fight to escape from the L.L.D.D.

"Bravo, V!" Nerva's voice was jovial, his smile wide and bright, but Violet didn't trust his appearance. He could be so devilishly handsome at times, debonair and impeccably mannered, but the dark good looks that so intrigued many of her female coworkers garnered a zero reaction in Violet. As a result, she also wasn't subject to the mind games he liked to run on people—she just wasn't so easily played or swayed by false compliments, a pretty face, and people who feigned support to get what they wanted when the truth was they cared little about what actually happened to anyone but themselves. There might have been times in the far-flung past when her body had made her act differently, but no more. Now she was just here to do a job. That was it. "Bravo!"

"It's not a weapon," Violet said flatly. Although the gravity levelers were now disabled, she still had a death grip on the handle.

Nerva's eyes momentarily widened, then his face lost the air of cheerfulness and he scowled. "What are you talking about?"

"It's not a weapon," she repeated. Violet gestured down at the briefcase with her free hand and met his dark, angry gaze without flinching. "It's a child—a *human* child. I risked my life for *nothing*."

For a long moment, all Nerva could do was look at her in disbelief. He took a step toward her and actually seemed to stumble, then he used one long, almost delicate finger to steady himself against the side of the conference table. Finally he managed to choke out, "You opened the case?"

Violet's mouth twisted and her voice dripped with venom. "What's the difference? It's not a fucking *weapon*." She squeezed her eyes briefly shut as she recalled the Chief of Research's self-satisfied story about what they were using as a decoy. "We were played," she said derisively. "They probably took the *real* weapon out in the armored convoy!"

At his sides, Nerva's fists were opening and closing. His companions were wisely remaining silent, unwilling to become involved in what they could sense might be an upcoming war. "I told you *not* to open the case!"

He reached for it, but Violet pulled it out of range and turned away. "I think I had a right to know what I was willing to die for," she said sarcastically.

Nerva glared at her, then yanked the briefcase out of Violet's hand before she could react. Sometimes his speed, borne of age and experience, could be nothing short of incredible. He swung it back onto the table's shiny surface, where the white case stood out in dark relief against the wood so brightly that it could have been backlit by neon. Without hesitating, he clicked open the top. As he stared down, the other Hemophages in the room dredged up their courage and crowded around so they, too, could gaze upon the so-called weapon. Violet could see the out of control curiosity and fascination on each one's face crumble away as each got within viewing distance. Fascination was soon replaced with bewilderment, then with a much wider repertoire of emotions: anger, uncertainty, disappointment.

Violet stood back a few feet and watched them tensely. From the flat space in the case, the boy's huge eyes blinked at them. "See?" she finally asked. She shrugged as if to give weight to her declaration. "It's *nothing*."

Nerva glanced back at her contemptuously. "Nothing?"

"It's not a weapon," Violet said, automatically going on the defensive. "It's a child."

But Nerva only shook his head and gave her a thin smile. "It's both." Violet and the others regarded him without understanding and he jerked his shaggy head back toward the boy. "It's a weapon *and* a child. Its blood is swarming with cultured antigens that would kill any one of us on contact." Nerva's gaze was flat and deadly, full of self-importance. "If they atomized its tissues into the atmosphere, it would be like . . . insecticide to people like you and me." He nodded to add emphasis to his words. "It would find us, and it would kill us. *All* of us." His mouth turned up in hate. "He's a living petri dish."

Violet's gaze snapped to the boy folded into the flat-space interior, trying to reconcile Nerva's statement with the frightened little boy she'd first encountered in the elevator. Could this be true? No . . . yes. God, she didn't know. But still, something wasn't right. The pieces weren't adding up . . . such as Nerva telling her to blow up the boy, and herself. Would that not have done exactly what he'd just warned them about? It didn't matter; Nerva would never bother to explain himself to her. "So then . . . what are we going to do with him?" she finally asked.

Nerva lifted one eyebrow, and that simple gesture made it clear he expected her to already know. "Destroy him, of course." He held out his hand and one of the other Hemophages was already stepping forward to place a laser gun in his palm. A shot to the head would emit a beam that would kill the boy but instantaneously seal the wound—there would be no particle aftereffect, no spreading of the so-called antigen that Nerva believed the boy carried. At least if Nerva really *was* going to kill him, this way would be a lot cleaner and safer.

But he was just a child.

Violet opened her mouth and involuntarily took a step forward. "Nerva, wait." She swallowed and tried to formulate her words so that they made sense, so he would understand. "You know how antigens work. If an accelerator for H.P.V. is in this child's blood, then so is the counteranalog for *decelerating* it."

Nerva held up the gun, then set the strength of the laser. It was all too clear that while he was paying attention to her words, he'd already made up his mind not to give them any credence. "What are you saying, V? A cure?"

She hesitated, then plunged ahead. "Wouldn't it be better than infecting innocent people?" She gestured at herself and the others. "It's better than living like this."

Nerva's hard expression relaxed a little and he almost smiled at her. "Living like this? *Living* like this?" He closed his eyes for a long second, then reopened them and fixed his glowing gaze on Violet. "Wake up, Violet— the disease and the having of it is what *defines* us. And as far as a cure goes . . ." Now he actually did smile,

although it certainly wasn't a happy one. "Yeah, sure—
Garth might fix your body, but do you think he'll ever be
able to cure you of the things you've done?"

Violet stared at him and realized she was trembling.
How could she make him understand that her past wasn't
the issue here. There was something bigger, more pro-
found at risk. It went beyond her and Nerva and the other
Hemophages in this room. It had to do with omnipotent
things like destiny, and whether a good chunk of the
human race would actually be able to continue existing.
How could he be so narrow-minded? "All I'm saying is
that this child could provide the choice."

Nerva ignored her and thumbed the safety lever on the
side of the laser gun to OFF. The gun responded by hum-
ming to life, emitting a high-pitched, almost indiscernible
whine that literally made her ears *itch*. "If there's a
choice, V," he said coldly, "I've already made it."

He raised the gun and aimed, but Violet reached out
and snagged the cuff of his shirt, jerking his arm off to the
side. The electric red dot of the laser aim wobbled around
and snaked across a couple of the other vampires. They
shifted nervously. "Oh, for fuck's sake," she said in exasperation. "It's a *child!*"

Nerva turned and fixed her in his cold gaze, then with
his free hand he grabbed her by the wrist and yanked her
face to his. His mouth covered hers in a hard kiss, one
completely devoid of any warmth or feeling.

Violet pulled free and stared at him in surprise. What
the hell? She could feel the way her lipstick had smeared
across her face, taste his saliva on her lips. It was utterly
revolting.

"This is the end of us," he said carelessly, then shook

himself free of the grip she still had on his gun hand. "Your work's done. You can go."

She took a small step backward, then hesitated. Freedom? From what? Nerva and his little pod of power, but to what end? A few more weeks or days, maybe less, of her severely troubled life, and then . . .

A quick glance around the room confirmed that she was way outnumbered here—these weren't weak little humans dressed up in armored clothes and helmets with misconceptions about her abilities. These were 'Phage assassins, fully mature and well transfused just like her, as strong and fast as she was and just as highly trained. The humans were annoying, but in reality they were mostly just . . . entertainment. These Hemophages had the potential to be *deadly*. As if to confirm this, their eyes tracked her like dueling hawks zeroing in on a lone rabbit with no place to hide. She was that rabbit.

Violet swallowed. "For the record," she said, "I don't agree with this."

Nerva and the others simply stared back at her, unmoving. Uncaring.

As much as everything inside her wanted to fight it, Violet was smart enough to know that there was no way she could win here. She waited one more moment, then inhaled deeply and glanced at the boy in the briefcase a final time. Ultimately, without saying anything else, she turned and strode out of the conference room.

She didn't turn and look back as the door slid shut behind her. Everything she was leaving behind seemed to be in slow motion, but Violet didn't dare increase her pace or look over her shoulder—she couldn't see any surveillance cameras, but that didn't mean they weren't there. Nerva and the other Hemophages could be watching her right now—in fact, they were probably doing just that—making sure she was well out of range before Nerva decided to do his dirty little deed. Speaking of dirty, she reached up and used the back of her hand to scrub at the lipstick smeared across her mouth, wishing she had soap and water so she could wash away the traces—the *smell*—of Nerva on her face. His scent lingered on her flesh like the last traces of disease, something insidious and worse than the HemoPhagic Virus itself. Very shortly, there were things that she would have to do, consequences for her actions, so many what-ifs that were all about to happen that Violet felt like her mind was racing at light speed. Even that wasn't fast enough for her to find all the answers, and what was coming down at any second, everything about to happen back in that room, would only generate more questions, not reasons.

She wasn't in the conference room, but the events that were taking place there weren't a mystery. Right about now, Nerva would be stepping up to the table with his laser gun charged and ready. The cold-blooded bastard was probably enjoying it; in his former life, Nerva had been an egotistical graphics design guru, a man on the fast track to being a dot com millionaire and loving every bit of it. He'd had a high-rise condo with a city-wide view, fast cars and faster women, and all of that, as well as his passion for high-stakes, public gambling, had crashed around his ankles when he'd caught the virus. The clubs he frequented refused his business, and no amount of money could convince them to look the other way when he came calling. His oh-so-loyal employer had kicked him out on his ass—clearly the equal opportunity and nondiscrimination laws didn't apply to Hemophages, especially once the uninfected stopped considering them human. No job, so no income, and eventually even his careful investments were bled out by the decadently high payments on his mortgage; he lost it to the bank when none of the real estate agents would sell it for him, and no potential buyers would look at it when they found out he was a 'Phage, anyway. The bank was less than overjoyed, although after sending in a hard-line decontamination team, then ripping out everything and redoing it, they were finally able to put it on the market as "sanitized."

Becoming a Hemophage had twisted Nerva's mind and made him worse than human, worse than 'Phage. Filled with bitterness and the desire for revenge, he convinced himself that he *enjoyed* blood and the sight of it, the smell, even watching it ooze from an open wound; Violet wouldn't have been surprised to discover he drank it like the ridiculous legends of the old centuries, just because it *was* legend.

If they had any common sense at all, the others in the room would back away from Nerva, make sure they were out of firing range just in case something went wrong and the heat scal component on the gun failed or, worse, he got caught up in his killing. As it was, Violet thought Nerva was a fool—if the child's blood could kill them, why was he so eager to destroy the boy and take the chance of exposing everyone? Because he was bloodthirsty, that was why.

At the end of the hall she turned the corner. There wasn't any reason to even think about it—she knew he would never reconsider. Right about now the tall, dark-eyed Hemophage would be pointing the barrel of the laser gun at the child's head. He would smile that pleased-with-the-world smile, and then he would squeeze the trigger.

Halfway between where the hallway turned and the elevators was an AutoVend machine, its plasticized front cheerfully advertising soft drinks, snacks, and a few health-conscious mini-lunches for the few and far between who actually tried to keep their bodies healthy rather than just get a pill for it from the doctor when they were older. Seated on the floor next to it, with his back against the wall and his knees drawn up to his chest, was the boy who had been inside the white briefcase. He was an obedient young boy, and he'd stayed in precisely the position Violet had ordered, clutching her activated cell phone so that it would train on his own unmoving body as the three-dimensional object continued to project.

Back in the conference room, the air would be full of the smell of hot fabric—the case's softer, inside upholstery—and metal, but not burned flesh. Nerva's expression would have initially been shock, but now it would be twisting into full rage. After he waved aside the sparks and smoke, he would reach inside the briefcase and yank out the charred and twisted remains of Violet's micphone, that handy little piece of advanced technology that had allowed her to project the three-dimensional image of the boy inside the case's flat space.

And then Nerva would start bellowing for her.

The young boy looked up at her with placid brown eyes that made it clear he had no idea how much danger he and Violet were now facing. What would it matter if he did? It wasn't like there was anything he could do to save them, or even buy them time. Violet snatched the cell phone from his hand, then pulled him to his feet and hauled him roughly toward the elevator. Before he could ask—if he even wanted to—she shook her head. "Don't overthink it," she told him tightly. "It just turns out I was right and we're getting the hell out of here."

The elevator door was already opening as they ran up to it. Violet could see Hemophages crowded up to the inside of the door as it was opening—Nerva must have already sounded an alarm. They hadn't expected her to be right there so she had the element of surprise. She used it to her advantage, too, yanking one of her machine pistols out of its flat-space holster and firing into the control panel, not caring if any of the Hemophages got hit. Their life spans were limited anyway, and if they were Nerva's flunkies . . . well, they were probably close to being just like him.

But it wouldn't be long before the vampires inside the elevator pried the doors fully open and came after them. The fire stairwell was their only option, and Violet made short work of the locked metal door, kicking it so hard that she nearly took it off its hinges. She wanted to go down, but it was a good thing she leaned over to double-check the way. Already she could see a couple Hemophages clambering upward, their hands skimming along the surface of the banisters. Pushing the boy behind her, she took a precious three seconds to aim carefully and track the team as it climbed. When she was ready to fire, her bullets literally vaporized the two hands that were showing.

With all that screaming, Violet and the boy didn't even have to try to be quiet as they ran up and toward the roof.

ELEVEN

He had never been more angry in his life.

Nerva skidded to a stop in front of the closed elevator and his furious glance took it all in at once, the mangled door, the shredded control panel. He didn't even need to hear the words of his waiting lieutenant, Luthor, to know what Violet's next move had been. He could hear the screams in the stairwell, so she'd already made mincemeat out of the two soldiers who had been dispatched to stop her from fleeing toward the ground floor. God, had they even slowed her down? Doubtful.

"She went up," Luthor said uselessly.

Nerva almost couldn't say anything. Why had Violet done this? Her behavior made no sense at all, and she was endangering everything she'd worked for, including the survival of her own species. Did she think the humans were going to help her? Forgive her? *Accept* her? How ludicrous.

"So go after her!" Nerva snarled.

Luthor swallowed visibly and wouldn't meet his gaze.

"The Blood Chinois control the top ten floors of this building," he finally mumbled.

Oh . . . not good. It was a nasty but necessary reminder for Nerva. The Chinois were a testy, ugly-tempered bunch to deal with—they had a tendency to fight first and ask questions later. Ironically, that was exactly how the vampire population had been forced to act thanks to the ArchMinistry of Medical Policy. It had taken a very long time—years—and a lot of bloodshed on both sides to convince the Chinois that a peaceable existence between the two factions of society was a good thing; a major basis for that settlement was the ironclad promise from the Hemophages not to trespass on their turf. To violate that treaty today would be to reopen a never-quite-healed wound. "Call them," Nerva finally said. It was the only thing he could think of that might help them handle this; if Violet wasn't stopped before she managed to leave this building, they might never find her.

Luthor activated his phone and looked at Nerva knowingly from below half-closed lids. "Kar Wai's no fool," he told his boss. "He knows he'll lose resources if he stacks against Violet." He raised one eyebrow. "He'll want his pound of flesh."

Nerva's lips pressed together grimly and he thought about it again. That was true, and the price would likely be heavy. But the boy was too important to let Violet escape. "Whatever he wants," he finally said with reluctance. "Give it to him." He turned away and headed back to the conference room, while off to the side his two injured soldiers slumped against the wall. Their wrists were bound with tourniquets and their faces were pale with pain and blood loss; beneath the bandages, their fingers were mangled and more than significant chunks were missing. Too bad they couldn't regenerate their appendages—had the vampires in the old legends been able to do that? He didn't know, but these two were scarred for whatever remained of their life span. He wondered how many more of his kind would end up sacrificed just so that he could get that "weapon" back and destroy it. He glanced back at Luthor and saw the other man talking animatedly into his phone, then grimaced and thought of Violet going up against Kar Wai. He thought the Chinois and his men could take her down, but they were going to pay hell doing it.

And then it would be his turn.

"I'll probably never have to pay it anyway."

※

Violet pulled the slender boy up to the final landing at the top of the stairwell, then slammed open the door and hauled him onto the rooftop with her. She got three feet, then skidded to a halt. There were more than twenty Chinois already waiting there, spaced at carefully calculated intervals that would never allow the two of them to escape . . . at least, not easily. How the hell had they gotten here before her? Via other entrances, of course—this was their territory. They probably had all kinds of tricks at the ready.

She pushed the boy behind her and he stumbled backward a few steps, then stayed there—so far so good. Walking slowly, keeping her hands visible at all times, she moved closer to the center of the roof. Then, with excruciating slowness, she drew out her machine pistols and held them up so each one of them could see her as she let them fall at her feet. She wasn't sure if they knew about her flat space weapons, but she sure wasn't going to reveal that secret card unless there was no other option.

When none of them moved aside, her eyes narrowed and she turned to face the leader, Kar Wai. She'd never met him face-to-face before, but she, like everyone in the upper third of this building, knew who he was. The Asian man was slickly dressed in an expensive black suit with a bright white oriental shirt collar showing above it— maybe even real silk rather than synthetic, a real rarity since the silk worm had gone extinct—but the fashion didn't fool Violet. These people could fight wearing anything—in fact, that was one of their pride points. Kar Wai smiled with exaggerated patience, like a middle manager assigned to do a job no one else wanted. "You're not ArchMinistry," Violet finally said. "You're not even vampire—you're Blood Chinois. Let me pass."

Kar Wai shook his head as though he were talking to a slow-learning child. "Sorry, Violet. Can't do."

Violet regarded him dispassionately, not particularly surprised that he knew her name. Nerva would have told him that much when he'd offered Kar Wai the job. But with the Blood Chinois, life was all about the numbers— they valued quantity above almost everything else. Money, property, inventory, lives. Maybe it would help to remind him of the consequences he would face if he crossed her. "You're going to lose resources, Kar Wai."

But he only stared back at her with dead, black eyes, still with that slightly smug smile playing across his mouth. "Can't be helped." His small smile stretched to a full-out grin and he glanced around at his men. "But I don't think you're going to make it off this roof."

Violet inhaled deeply, feeling the chilly air up here seep into her lungs. After the stale, overprocessed air inside the building, it was refreshingly cool, revitalizing as it sank into her dry lungs. "Watch me," she said simply.

The real world wasn't like in the classic old Chinese martial arts movies that people still enjoyed, where the hero faces a hundred opponents and defeats them one by one. No, the battles fought in real life, the *street* battles, were much more brutal and tiring, devoid of all the showy movements and graceful choreography. There was nothing beautiful about the way they all came at her at once, where it was only a matter of who could reach her first to get in a good shot—competition was the goal here. But, of course, in the end it was useless—they were just humans with nothing but martial arts training. All the years of training and skill in the world just wasn't going to help them against a fully mature Hemophage with Violet's deadly expertise.

Kar Wai, however, was something else altogether.

He let his men go down first, one by one, watching and, Violet was sure, learning from their deadly mistakes. Most were simply too slow, and the ones who were fast, just couldn't cut it in the strength department. Violet could take a blow three times harder than a normal human man could deal before it hurt to any degree, so the little punches and kicks Kar Wai's men delivered did almost nothing to slow her. When they were all finished, Kar Wai hung back rather than approach her, and Violet wasn't stupid enough to think it was because he lacked courage. No, he was evaluating her, processing the moves and errors he'd seen from his defeated team and calculating just how he could best use those same things to his own advantage. They had been soldiers.

Kar Wai was a warrior.

He came at her long and low, like a tiger. Indeed, his

fighting style resembled that ancient mode: fearless and unpredictable, unbelievably quick.

Kar Wai's attack on Violet was sudden and brutal. He sprang through the air, and even though he missed—she was way too fast for him—Violet had to admire his attitude of fierceness, the way he seemed to believe that he alone of his men was completely indestructible. Violet couldn't help but gain a measure of respect for this small, lithe human—his courage was incredible and he seemed not to notice the blows she dealt him. For a little while, it almost seemed as though Kar Wai really *was* indestructible.

But in the end, he was only human.

She held back, the sense of growing esteem for her opponent making her want to see him live, even though she knew she must still defeat him to have any hope of escaping. Time, however, was a precious commodity, and each fifteen-second increment that passed while she toyed with this Chinois martial artist was a deduction on the scale that might slide to freedom for her and the boy. Her patience was slipping as Kar Wai finally slid under her outstretched arm and tried to catch her in a Pencak Silat trap; she turned her body out of range and, with lightning speed, brought her elbow down on the back of his unprotected neck.

Just a little too hard.

Oops.

Even a tiger has to die sometime.

In the end, Violet left them all, Kar Wai included, lying in crumpled little piles on the roof's dirty black surface.

The final victory over Kar Wai and the exertion left her a little breathless, but when she could stop at last and look around for the boy—

For a moment what she saw took away the rest of Violet's ability to breathe.

The child had abandoned the area by the stairwell door in favor of the roof proper. She would have felt all right about that—after all, every child likes to explore a rooftop—had he been on the roof's actual edge—that, at least, was a good eight-inch wide strip of concrete. Instead, the crazy kid was on the quarter-inch-thick wire *above* it, perfectly balanced on the cheap contractor's answer to a safety railing. Beneath the feet that he was nimbly moving around like a child ballet dancer was a sheer drop to the city sidewalk more than a hundred stories below. The trip down might be like flying, but the landing was going to be one hell of a jolt.

"Holy *fuck*," Violet whispered to herself. As if just to taunt her, the wind suddenly picked up. Moist air swept over the back of her head and her cheeks; the boy's hair was cropped too closely to make the breeze visible, but his clothes fluttered briskly. Her heart jumped as she saw the wire sway back and forth; his body moved with it almost instinctively, like a motorcycle rider leaning his machine into a hard curve.

Violet took a cautious step forward. "Hey there," she said. Was her voice shaking? She was trying to sound soft and calm, no surprises here. What if she scared him enough to make him jerk? She could never reach him in time to stop him from tumbling off that damned guard wire. "Hey—" Before she could think of what to say next, he turned on the wire, moving effortlessly on his toes as if the surface on which he was balanced was flat earth rather than a quarter-inch steel cable. She had to admire that. She also had to resist the urge to scream at him like an angry mother.

"Whatcha doing up there?" she asked, forcing her voice to stay within normal conversation range. She gave him an easy smile, hoping it didn't look as sick as her stomach felt right now. She'd managed to get directly in front of him, but he didn't seem concerned . . . about her, about the battle that had taken place only a dozen feet away, about *anything*. The thousand-plus feet between him and the ground and the wind making the wire swing and dance . . . those things might as well not even have existed in his universe. The boy's face was calm, almost beatific—if Violet could believe the expression on the child's face, this moment was the penultimate one in his thus-far short life.

The wire swung a little more strongly and Violet swallowed back the protest that wanted to come bursting out of her mouth. "Good view up there, huh?" She smiled up at him as best she could, then cautiously moved to stand directly below where he was balanced. "Help me up. I'd like to see, too." She looked up at him expectantly, then stretched out her hand toward him, as though there were no reason in the world why she wouldn't climb out there and join him on that skinny little line fluttering across the abyss of space beneath him.

The boy looked at her hand, then at her, and for a long moment Violet wasn't sure he actually understood what she'd asked. He had to at least understand *something*—after all, he'd stayed put in the hallway outside Nerva's meeting room, clutched the cell phone in just the right position as she'd told him. Would he take her up on her request?

He hesitated just a moment more, then offered her his hand.

As quick as a rattlesnake, Violet grabbed his wrist and

yanked him off the wire, pulling him toward her and onto the safety of the roof. Now she could let her anger at him show without being afraid the vehemence in her voice would somehow make him fall, the weight of her fury drive him out and into deadly space. Now she could say what she thought of this ridiculous stunt.

"What the hell is wrong with you?" she demanded. She fought against the urge to shake him. "Are you *trying* to get fucking killed?"

Before the boy could formulate an answer—*if* he could do so—the doorway to the roof suddenly banged open, belching more of Nerva's soldiers. The bastards scuttled across the tarred surface like cockroaches coming after a good meal.

"Damn it," Violet hissed. Snagging the boy's arm, she hauled him toward the exit on the opposite side of the roof, moving as fast as she could before they were spotted, although it wasn't like they wouldn't find the obvious leavings of her miniwar with Kar Wai.

Later, Violet still wouldn't be able to retrace the route she took in getting the boy child down to street level. She wasn't even sure why they'd made it, how they'd negotiated stairwell after stairwell, catching the occasional short elevator ride just to throw off the soldiers pouring down the staircases. Maybe they were successful only because all the Hemophage soldiers chasing them had expected her to go over the edge, bounce from building edge to building edge as she had when she'd first escaped the L.L.D.D. That only showed their ignorance about her equipment and how stupid Nerva was for not sharing the details of their highest technology; none of his poorly briefed soldiers would know that her gyroscope was calibrated only for her weight plus a few pounds for the briefcase—it would not support her weight and the boy's.

It wasn't until Violet and the child reached the lobby that it all caught up with her . . . or at least the Laboratories for Latter Day Defense troops. Even if they *had* followed her, Nerva's troops wouldn't face off against the ArchMinistry's, not in broad daylight and in the very building where they had, at least up until now, held countless secret meetings. Violet wasn't sure how the ArchMinistry's troops had traced her here, but things weren't looking on the good side right now.

Before she could lead the boy out of the lobby, more human Command Security Teams than she could count skidded to a stop outside the building. She couldn't go back, not unless she wanted to face both the Blood Chinois—and boy, they were going to be pissed at her for killing their leader—and Nerva's ugly-tempered little blood warriors. That left only forward, so Violet yanked out a machine pistol and made chopped glass of the biggest plate-glass window that stood between her and freedom.

The glass shattered and spilled onto the sidewalk, and she and the boy fell with it, easily slipping past a half-dozen Security Commandos who instinctively ducked to avoid the glass rain shower. One of the security vehicles was parked crookedly at the curb and Violet shoved the boy in front of her and they dived into it. As escape cars went, this one wasn't much—it had no speed and hardly any maneuverability; on the other hand, it was heavily armored and therefore definitely better than physically running the soon-to-come gauntlet of lead and laser. Twisting the wheel and thinking ahead to her escape route, Violet started to ram her foot onto the accelerator—

Then a Deployment Tanker screeched to a halt directly in her path.

Practically screaming in frustration, she twisted around and looked behind her, but that way was blocked, too—at least three more cars had pulled up and parked behind this one in the preparation for the initial on-slaught.

They were trapped.

Violet knew there would be no courtesy warning, none of the familiar Hollywood "Drop your weapons and come out with your hands held high!" She pushed the boy down on the front seat and dropped on top of him; an instant later, the windshield of the car was blasted apart by full auto-fire. The bullets chewed up the dashboard and the vinyl upholstery over their heads as Violet tried desperately to figure out how she was going to get out of this one.

"No no no! Stop—STOP!"

She barely heard the shouting above the gunfire, but someone else must have because all of a sudden the gunfire stopped. It was a shocking difference, one that made Violet realize just how much her ears and head were throbbing from all the horrendous noise. And that voice—where had she heard it before? If her ears would just stop ringing and get back to normal, maybe she could identify it. In the meantime, moving as fast as she could while still trying to remain a nonviable target, Violet risked a glance out of the blown-out hole where the windshield had been. Oh, yeah—she should have known. It was Daxus, of course, the darling Vice-Cardinal of the ArchMinistry of Medical Policy. If the Catholic

Church had still been in existence, the man would have been the next best thing to the Pope . . . except, at least in her opinion, that would have meant that Satan was running the show.

As Violet peered out at him, Daxus gestured sharply at the dozens of Command Marines standing at the ready, most of whom had their fully automatic weapons pointed at the vehicle in which she and the boy were sequestered. "Seal the building," he ordered briskly. "Any others inside—I want them hunted down." As they spun and moved off, Daxus turned back to the nearly destroyed car and approached it cautiously. There was no hiding—Violet knew he'd already seen her. Where was she going to go, anyway? When she bared her teeth and started to bring up her machine pistol, the man pulled off his breathing mask and held up his hands. Both were gestures of goodwill that she didn't believe.

"Easy now, Violet," he said in a soothing and clearly practiced voice. "Do you know who I am?"

Violet's mouth twisted. "How could I not?" she spat. "Tyrant, phobic, egomaniac, narcissist." Her grip on her weapon tightened reflexively; of its own accord, her finger stroked the trigger. "Horse veterinarian stumbles into a power vacuum in a revolution he didn't create." Violet's lips pulled into an even uglier sneer. "That about sums it up, doesn't it?"

Daxus pressed his lips together in irritation, then his features smoothed out. She could imagine him thinking that it wouldn't do to have his men see that this female Hemophage could get to him simply with verbal insults. Sticks and stones and all that. "Yes, Violet, it's true," he said calmly. "I may have 'humble' origins and my justified sense of pride may sometimes be . . ." He paused and smiled slightly, struggling to think of the appropriate word. "*Misunderstood*. And I may even have quirks." He shook his head, and again Violet had the impression it was a clearly rehearsed move. He'd clearly passed *How to Deal with Underlings 101*. "But that doesn't mean I'm stupid," he continued in an oily voice. "And it certainly doesn't mean you can make a single move without me knowing about it first."

Violet almost snorted. "Bullshit. You would have killed me long ago."

Now it was Daxus's turn to give her a calculating stare. "Are you quite sure about that, Violet?" he asked.

The ever-so-slight lift of one of his eyebrows portrayed enough smugness for Violet to realize he was, at least about this part, telling the truth. Her eyes narrowed dangerously and Daxus raised his hands to placate her when he caught her expression. When he spoke, his tone had gone matter-of-fact, as if he were doing nothing more than reading a set of statistics and rules. "Listen," he said, "the child is of no use to you. He's laboratory bred, vegetative." Daxus tapped his head for emphasis and his dark eyes held hers. "He's practically brain-dead. Just give him to me and you're on your way."

Violet gave a bitter chuckle. Did this stupid man really think she would ever believe him? Did he think *anyone* would? "Sure I will," she said sarcastically. Her gaze flicked to the left, then the right, and she didn't have to check the shards of glass that used to be the side mirrors to see she was surrounded. "Because you're going to use him to kill me and everyone like me anyway."

"It's not like that," Daxus said flatly. This time Violet thought he sounded impatient, as if he felt he was wasting his time. Of course he did—all the uninfected felt the

Hemophages were a waste of time. "The boy's not what you think."

Violet raised an eyebrow. "No? Then what *is* he?"

Daxus opened his mouth, then hesitated. Finally he said, "He's . . . my son."

Her eyes widened, then her gaze cut to the boy's face. If Daxus's words had any meaning at all for him, the child certainly wasn't showing it. But it wasn't so far-fetched. In fact, Daxus probably *was* the boy's biological father, but only in the most clinical sense. Anyone could see that it was inarguable that the second part of Daxus's claims were also true—the child was laboratory bred, devoid of emotion, deprived of all the simple things that a child should have, like toys, fun, sunshine . . . *love.* To Violet, fathering a child but neglecting these other things negated any connection, biological or otherwise. He was no better than a normal human who'd abandoned his offspring and pretended the boy—or girl—never existed. After a certain length of time passed, he simply had no rights.

She caught movement out of her peripheral vision, and when Violet glanced at the rearview mirror—how amazing that it hadn't been blown to hell—her suspicions were confirmed. This mouthy bastard was just killing time, while behind her more Deployment Commandos crept ever closer. Any possibility of escape was going to disappear way too fast, but it hadn't yet—not too far behind the men was the luckiest break she could think of for her and the boy: a subway entrance.

She cleared her throat, then stared the older man straight in the eye. "Hey, Daxus," she said in a falsely conversational voice. She put a perky, curious tone in her words, but in the meantime she never lost sight of what was going on around the car.

If he could have rubbed his hands together in anticipation, Violet thought he would have. His grin was toothy and sharp. It looked a lot like the mouth on a shark. "What?"

"You're full of shit." Miraculously, the car's engine was still running, and she rammed her foot down on the accelerator at the same time she threw the transmission into reverse. The vehicle's engine choked and almost died; for an overly long moment, her heart was in her throat, beating and beating and beating, and drowning out every other sound in the world. Then the engine caught, revved, and they shot backward; when the rear bumper plowed through the Commandos heading toward it, they scattered like pins in an old-fashioned game of bowling.

Without slowing the vehicle, Violet yanked a machine pistol out of a flat-space pocket, then screamed "Cover your ears!" at the boy. But he only looked at her, his wide, dull gaze obviously uncomprehending. Did he have a clue at all? About anything? With a growl of frustration, Violet slapped a hand over the side of his head that was closest to her, then pushed his head down and against the upholstery. A moment later, the back of the vehicle crashed hard into the dual stone banisters that marked the opening of the subway entrance she'd spotted a moment ago. They bounced off one and stopped, then Violet slammed open the door on her side and she and the boy were spilling out and dashing down the stairs into the crowded station.

They might as well have stumbled into another world, one full of people oblivious to all the danger and excitement of what had been happening above their heads. Office workers, maintenance people, blue collars—literally *thousands* of people going in every direction, and not one of them at anything less than breakneck speed. Down here it was damp and cool and *noisy,* so much so that none of the subway riders or vendors had even heard the shots or the shouting or the scream of the vehicle engines on the upper street level. These people had one purpose, and one only—to get where they were going. Whether it was work or home or somewhere in between, they hadn't a clue about the problems at ground level. They weren't concerned about it, and they certainly weren't going to let anything as petty as the police or a criminal chase get in their way.

Yanking the boy along behind her, Violet ignored the startled look of the cashier and went over the turnstile rather than through it. She half expected some kind of an alarm to sound, but nothing happened—apparently the girl had gone back to inspecting her fingernails and being utterly bored. Violet kept heading down, practically dragging the child as she pushed to the side of the line of non-moving people on the descending escalators—if these idiots were in such a hurry, why didn't they *move* on the escalators and get where they were going twice as fast?

They passed the billboard ads along the walls so quickly that they were little more than colorful blurs spotlighted by different neon colors and blinking LED displays. Papers and discarded fast food containers not yet swept up by the auto-cleaners crunched beneath their feet. Now, as the areas closest to the trains became more crowded, people *were* starting to stare and grumble at Violet as she forced a path through.

The final set of escalators, and she and the boy had finally made it to the train platform proper, where an express train was readying itself to pull out of the station. Before its doors could close all the way, Violet raised her machine pistol and put one shot into the door mechanism, leaving it jammed open despite a good two-foot gap and the fact that it was already moving. Ignoring the startled screams of several passengers, the two of them leaped onto the car at the last second. Then the train was on its way, leaving the overly bright platform behind for the dark anonymity of the train tunnel.

Gasping for air, Violet turned around and grabbed the boy by the shoulders, examining his face and neck and ignoring the rest of the train riders. He *seemed* okay—no signs of blood or bruising—but that didn't mean he hadn't been injured somewhere that she couldn't see. "Damaged," she managed to get out. "Are you damaged?" But the child only gazed back at her and with sudden dismay, Violet suspected that not only could he not understand her, everyone else on the packed subway car was staring at them suspiciously, filing away their images in their memory banks for later identification whether they realized it or not. Swallowing past her uneasiness, Violet grasped the boy's small hand and tugged him after her as she threaded her way through the people in the narrow center aisle until she could cross into another car.

This one was better, almost empty—like dumb cattle, the people had crowded through the door and stayed where they were rather than find more comfortable surroundings. With the boy at her side, Violet slumped onto one of the double seats, then her shoulders sagged and she put her head into her hands. Her heart was still pounding in her chest and adrenaline still washed the nerves in her body. She could feel her hands trembling against the skin of her face. "What the hell have I done?"

she whispered out loud. For that question, she had no answer, only a thousand repercussions.

Something made her look up again, and Violet realized the boy was no longer next to her. For a second, she panicked, almost unable to fathom that the object—living or not—that she'd thrown everything in her oh-so-limited life away for was gone. Then she saw him a little farther down in the car. He was wandering, looking left and right over his head and studying the bright paper and LED advertisements as if he'd never seen such things. There was one for a family counseling center, another for a medical center that "specialized in H.P.V. prevention"—as if such a thing were possible. Another, done in a child's primary colors, touted the latest and greatest in robotic toys while the one directly across the aisle was an online university's gloating missive about the famous people who had taken its courses. Yeah, he'd probably been missing this stuff all his limited life.

"Hey!" Violet snapped. Even though she'd spoken loud enough to be heard, the child ignored her. *"Hey!"* This time he turned and looked back at her. She caught his gaze and gestured sharply at the seat across the aisle from her. "Park it," she ordered. "Right there." But although he looked where her finger pointed, he made no move to obey. She scowled at him. "Don't make me tell you twice," she said ominously. *"Sit!"*

Still he paused, and Violet felt her irritation rising as she thought he wasn't going to obey. Then he surprised her by moving slowly back and settling himself on the seat, looking at her without saying anything. "And don't get any cute ideas, either," she told him testily. "The only reason I saved your life is because what's in your blood can save mine." She grimaced and ran her tongue across her dry lips. "If they corner us, suffer no delusions—I'll kill you."

The boy didn't move, just sat there with his hands folded in front of him like a good little robot in neutral gear.

Violet grimaced under his implacable scrutiny, realizing that what she said made no sense. If they were cornered, she wouldn't kill the child—if she broke the surface of his skin, whatever was in his system would be instantly released. An airborne disease, especially if released outside, would be unstoppable. Her species would cease to exist in . . . what? A week? A month? They were nearly there now.

She looked at him again, but he still wasn't speaking. Her hand waved in the air impatiently. "What am I doing?" She scrubbed at her face, wishing she could wipe away some of her tiredness. "It's like talking to a bag of rocks."

The hiss of the train's hydraulic brakes made her jerk and look up as the train slowed and rolled into the next stop. Tired or not, it was time to go. Moving quickly, she stood and grabbed the boy's arm, then pulled him out the door while it was still opening. Violet could see Command Security Teams streaming down the stairs at the far left of the platform, so she and the kid headed in the other direction until she found a different set of steps. Keeping her head down so no one could see her face, Violet pulled the kid up and out of the tunnel.

The street outside was packed with more people, hundreds, maybe thousands of worker bees. Didn't these men and women have jobs to go back to after lunch? It never ceased to amaze Violet just how *many* people there were in the world. On the surface it seemed like a coldhearted thought, but why the heck was the ArchMinistry so concerned about the Hemophage virus anyway? Maybe it was God's way—if she believed in God, that is—of controlling the population, thinning the herd before mankind completely overran this planet and sucked up all its fragile natural resources. Of course, when you became infected with the virus the point of view about that changed drastically. Now that she was on the receiving end and watching her life dwindle away to nothing way too soon, Violet could understand why they wanted the spread of the virus to stop.

But that didn't make it all right to exterminate the poor bastards like herself who were already its victims.

Concentrating, she made the bright colors of her overcoat tone down so she could blend in more easily with the distinctively office-type crowds in this neighborhood, then headed toward the building directly in their path. Called Pearl Tower, it was massive and tall and beautiful, its outer surface covered in a simulated pearl-coated granite that reflected the light and made her Hemophage eyes ache nastily even behind her black sunglasses. Hauling the kid around was like tugging on a confused and unruly dog—he gawked at everything, twisting and turning, trying to step backward so he could see people and things that he'd clearly never thought existed. Finally Violet found the staircase she'd been looking for and hurried down it, by now practically dragging him. She could tell in an instant that it wasn't safe to go right through the lobby. "We're going to have to go around instead of straight through the middle, so stick close," she told the boy in a low voice. "I know someone who might be able to help us." She glanced over her shoulder, then jerked to a stop when her eyes focused on nothing but an empty space. Where the hell was he now?

Three long steps took her back up to street level. There—right smack in the middle of the sidewalk, staring up in awe at Pearl Tower while everyone who passed him on the sidewalk stared at *him*. Great. "Unbelievable," she muttered. Then louder, she said, "Excuse me!" For the amount of attention he paid her, she might as well have been mute. "Hello?"

Nothing. She might as well have not even been there.

"Damn it," she growled under her breath. She was going to have to go get him. Glancing nervously around, she marched over and tapped him on the shoulder. "Hi," she said. "Remember me?"

He turned his head just quickly enough to see her, then went back to staring at Pearl Tower. "Look, she said. "Do you have *any* clue how serious this is?" Still no response, and she'd had enough. This time she pulled him roughly around to face her. "These people will *kill* you— do you understand that? Without even thinking. In fact, they *have* thought about it, and that's exactly what they intend to do."

God, why was she even trying to talk to him like this? Because for some incomprehensible reason, she just couldn't accept that this boy didn't have enough brain cells to register what she was saying. She *had* to keep trying. "So I suggest you stop acting like a newborn fawn and straighten up before your actions start to affect my ability to survive."

Okay, maybe that diatribe had been a little over his head, but what did it matter? He *still* only looked at her blankly, and suddenly all the wind went out of her. How the hell was she going to reach him? Even if he did understand her, she wasn't even sure that they spoke the same language—it was entirely possible that he could hear her but not know how to talk. For all she knew, that monster Daxus had ordered the boy's vocal cords surgically removed as a way of ensuring his silence, and it was highly doubtful he knew how to write. She knelt, then realized the boy still had biometers attached to his clothing; angrily, she started tearing them off. "Look," she said, "all I'm trying to say is . . . you know, it's for your own good. Do you . . . do you understand me?" She sighed and shook her head as she yanked off the last meter she could find. She felt like a dog too hungry—or dumb—not to keep braving the fire to get at the last possible morsel of food. "Just stick by me," she finally told him in a tired voice. "Close, like glue. Nothing more complicated than that. Just stick by me. Okay?"

The kid still didn't say anything, but he did surprise her by reaching out to curiously touch her face with his fingertips. She pulled back instinctively and she saw a slight frown cross his forehead, then he settled for brushing his hand across the surface of her LCD coat instead. Before she could think of what to say about this, over his shoulder she spotted a double security team pushing its way through the people on the sidewalk.

"Not good," she said through gritted teeth. Without bothering to explain, she grabbed the boy by the hand and yanked him into the crowd in a different direction.

TWELVE

They were on the move again—when was she *not?*—
and working their way quickly through another maze of
people at yet another crowded mall. What a crowded
planet it had become, twenty-four hours a day, three hundred sixty-five days a year—never an end to it. Part of Violet hated the hustle and bustle, the overpopulation, and
the normalcy of life all around her; on the other hand, if
it wasn't for that very same environment, she and the boy
would both be dead by now.

Without stopping, she pulled a new mic-phone out of
one pocket and slipped it behind her ear, bringing the mic
attachment around to her mouth. Her gaze darted in every
direction, on high alert mode for the first signs of a Command Security Team as she pushed a code into her memory keypad.

"Garth, it's me," she said urgently. "I screwed up—I
screwed up *bad*. The case had a freaking kid in it, and
I . . . I crossed Nerva."

Garth's voice came back immediately, but it was

scratchy, a bad connection getting worse with each passing second because of the reinforced bars crisscrossing the mall's roof. *"I know—he called. Don't even think about bringing it here, V."*

She felt the hairs on the back of her neck rise in instant anger, almost like a wild dog's. Was he really that easily swayed by Nerva? Or was he just scared? "Damn it, Garth—this kid might have the answer in him, but he's got all the collaborative ability of a *cow.* I'll be lucky just to get him out of here alive. I *need* your help!"

Nothing.

"Hello? Hello?" She tapped the mic frantically. "Garth? Hello?" Hissing with frustration, Violet snapped the phone closed. *"Damn* it! I can ride a motorcycle on the frickin' ceiling, but I *still* can't get a decent cell signal!"

Violet turned to the boy, and wouldn't you know it— he was gone again. She spun but her panic was short-lived . . . at least as long as he hadn't been noticed. He was only a few yards away, backed against the plate glass window of one of the stores and staring in openmouthed wonder at all the different people hurrying past. Right now, at least, no one seemed to be paying any attention to him. Violet was at his side in three seconds, her fingers digging firmly into his forearm. "Are you crazy?" she demanded. "What part of those bullets whizzing past your head didn't you *get?"*

As usual, he only blinked back at her, although this time he seemed a little taken aback by her forcefulness. Again, she squashed the urge to shake him and instead waved a hand back and forth in front of his face. "Hello? Are you functional? Do you understand *anything* I'm saying to you?"

Not a word . . . not a single, damned word. Just that same lightly wary expression she'd almost come to expect and which was growing increasingly infuriating. Violet exhaled, and her air came out through gritted teeth. Some kind of techno-classical crap was blaring through the mall's speakers, and the burbling, pseudo-happy notes coming from every direction made her feel like screaming. Who the hell chose that stuff? "Look, let's start simple. They had to call you something, right?" She pointed to herself, then tapped her chest with a forefinger. "I'm Violet. Pleased to meet you." On a whim, she grabbed his limp hand and gave it a perfunctory shake, then dropped it. "Your turn," she said. "Go."

But the boy only stared from her to his hand, as if he couldn't believe she'd done what she had, that she had given him a touch that was friendly and not meant to just hold on to him and run, or maybe drag him back to her. The smile that slipped across her face was one of grim resignation. "I could just as easily be a barking dog, couldn't I?" Still no response. "Hey," she said as an idea occurred to her. She motioned him to come closer and he obeyed, regarding her cautiously as she leaned down and put her lips close to his ear. "Woof."

When the child only stared at her with wide, amazed eyes, Violet sighed and straightened, scanning the crowd automatically for signs of trouble. Just as automatically, she glanced back at the boy—

And jerked when she realized he was holding up both his hands, one with all five digits splayed and the other with only his forefinger raised. Now it was her turn to be confused, but at the same time she felt more than a little desperate—she *needed* to be able to communicate with him, to understand. "Six?" she asked. "What's 'six'?"

He didn't answer, but that no longer annoyed her. They were making progress here—maybe he couldn't speak, maybe he wasn't physically capable of doing so. She wasn't a doctor and she hadn't a clue how to check, so his sign language would have to do. As if to confirm this, the boy raised his hands higher, trying to reinforce whatever he wanted to tell her. Violet chewed her lip for a moment, then experimentally put her hands over his, intentionally folding his smaller fingers into fists. When she let him go, he brought up the same six fingers. At least now she knew it wasn't an accident. "So . . ." She tried to think, to turn it over and work it in her mind like it was a Rubik's Cube. One plus one, two plus two. "So 'six' is . . . is . . ."

The child looked at his own raised index finger, and when he was certain she was also looking at it, slowly turned the end of it around and pointed at himself.

Violet stared at him, her mouth dropping open. Of course! "It's *you!*" she blurted. "It's your *name?* Your name is *Six?* Like a number?"

This time he actually nodded. She watched the up and down movement like it was in slow motion, then abruptly the moment ended as she caught a glimpse of another damned security team headed in their direction. God, they multiplied like lab rats. "Damn it!" She started to pull the boy in the other direction, but a wild glance over there showed a second team already on its way. Would this never stop? They hadn't been spotted yet, but it was only a matter of time . . . of seconds. She had a moment of crazy indecision, then she knelt jerkily in front of the child and pulled a syringe out of a flat-space pocket in her coat. "Give me your arm," she said and reached for it. But no one was more surprised than she when he pulled away from her. "Give me your arm!" she repeated sharply.

But something about Six had changed at the sight of the syringe—his eyes had narrowed while his brow had twisted in terror. His eyes were so wide that the whites completely surrounded his blue irises. Any trust she'd managed to establish in the previous few minutes had been swallowed up by the accusation that was suddenly in the boy's eyes. "Damn it," Violet growled. She glanced over her shoulder—so far, so good. "I may not be able to get you where I need you to go, but I sure as hell will get your blood there. Now give me your fucking arm before I take the whole thing!"

Perhaps she had misjudged his level of comprehension, or—and this made her feel very, very small—maybe the things the ArchMinistry had done to Six in their lab were so heinous that the memories overrode every other rational thought in his head. It was a horrible thing to consider, but right now none of that mattered. "Trust me," she said in a low and dangerous tone. "As bad as these people are, the real monster you don't want knocking down your door is *me*."

She grabbed for the boy's arm again, and once more he back-stepped out of her reach. Before she could leap for him, he shocked her more than he had since she'd first opened the white briefcase and found him curled up inside it. "If I scream," he said in a quiet and trembling voice, "we'll both be dead."

Violet gaped at him. "So," she said after a second, "it speaks." She jerked her head left and right, then slapped the syringe back into one of her flat-space pockets. There would be time for a get-to-know-each-other conversation later; right now, they had to get the hell out of this mall.

≹

Three hallways, two escalators, and an EMPLOYEES ONLY exit later, Violet pulled Six to a stop in the dubious safety of the shipping and loading alley behind the mall. She pushed him bodily against the wall before kneeling to where she could look him straight in the eye. "Daxus has no idea that you can talk, does he?" When Six finally shook his head, Violet didn't know whether to be amazed at the boy's ability to keep a secret or at Daxus's stupidity in not realizing the learning potential of his lethal little lab experiment. Either notion made a slow smile dust her lips—good for Six. And this little guy? Well, he had a surprising amount of moxie.

"But you *do* talk," she said thoughtfully. When he nodded, the next step Violet had was trying to work out in her head just how big his vocabulary was, how much she would have to dumb down her conversational skills. She wasn't skilled in talking to children, had hardly been around them at all since becoming a Hemophage. She also wasn't pleased that he had put her through what he had—why hadn't he just spoken up right from the start? Fear, maybe—he had probably been afraid that her getting all the information she needed right from the start would make her abandon him.

"English," he said suddenly.

Violet started, then stared at him in amazement. "English? English-*English?*" When he nodded again, she had no choice but to accept it. "*That's* what they spoke at the L.L.D.D. labs?" She couldn't help being astounded when he just kept nodding. "Ad Rasul," she said, more to herself than to him. "Probably for secrecy—no one speaks that anymore. But you understand Thaihindi . . ." Another nod, so she continued. "And you *speak* Thaihindi." This time when he nodded, she didn't bother to hide her look of relief. She took a deep breath and studied the child. "What do you know about what's going on?"

He didn't say anything, but that was all right—she was no longer worried that he didn't understand. Growing up in a lab, he had no social skills and he certainly wasn't going to be a conversation whiz. She would have to carry the weight here and trust in her understanding of basic body language. By the expression on his face, it was a good bet that the kid knew next to nothing and he was mightily frustrated because of it.

"Okay," Violet continued. "Look at me, Six. You at least understand that there's a war going on, don't you? Between vampires and humans?" For her trouble, Violet got that same look of bewilderment. Strike one—why would they bother giving him that information? "Okay, it's not important." She made a quick, instinctive check of the alley, but for a change they were doing all right. "Just trust me—there's a war to the death between humans and vampires and . . . and . . ." Her voice faded, then she tried again. "And, well, Six . . . you're human, and . . . you're human and . . ." She swallowed and finally just looked him straight in the eye. There was no way around the simple, stark truth. "I'm a vampire."

Clearly he understood the concept, because Six's eyes widened, then his breath hitched a little and his gaze darted toward the questionable safety of the well-populated sidewalk at the other end of the alley. She placed a hand on his arm, careful not to grab—this time, she just wanted to be reassuring. "Look," she said gently. "It's not like I suck blood or anything. I'm just a little . . . sick."

When he looked at her, it was with that same overly wary expression, but at least he didn't seem like he was getting ready to bolt at any second. Violet gestured at herself. "Just listen, okay? Do you remember that I said what's in your blood might be able to save my life?" When he nodded, she gave him her best gentle smile . . . although it'd been so long since she had had a reason to look that way, she couldn't help wondering if it was convincing. "Six, your father, Daxus—if he really is your father—he put something in your blood." She hesitated, then shook her head. No, that wasn't right. She didn't know why it seemed so important that she make him understand, but it was. "He *grew* something there," she corrected. "And whatever it is, the antigens, they may hold the key to saving my life. But they were first and foremost built to kill me—and everyone like me."

Six's eyes narrowed again, but this time with understanding. "Then . . . those men," he said slowly, "they're all—"

She nodded, and the look she gave him was more serious than anything he'd seen from her before. "Yes. They're after *you*. Right now, you're the most valuable object on the planet."

≥

At the Needle, the battle was far from over.

Thanks to Violet's incredible lapse in obedience and what Nerva could only believe was her sentimental stupidity—what else would you call her having feelings for some experimental human lab rat, anyway?—he and his only remaining two soldiers were facing the most disastrous situation they'd had in years. The human security forces were nipping at their heels like skinny little wolves hot on the trail of their next meal, and the insulated safety of their once-secret conference room was now forever out of reach. He and the other two Hemophages had gone into the stairwell after Violet when they'd gotten the report that she'd destroyed the Blood Chinois team, then they'd gotten trapped by the humans before they could get all the way down. Now they were in even worse shape—the humans had sent forces not only from below but dropped backup soldiers onto the roof from helicopters. They were headed back up and so far they'd managed to stay one floor ahead of their hunters, but now, on the twenty-fifth, they could go no farther. Each landing was segregated from the one previous and the next by locked entry doors, but they wouldn't be alone long. Even through the metal fire doors, Nerva could hear the men's boots tramping along the stairs from both directions.

To drive that fact home, Nerva and his men whirled and brought up their weapons as someone burst into the stairwell. So far, so good—it was only another 'Phage, a man they hadn't realized had managed to survive the outside attacks. His black and violet eyes were wild with fear and fury. "They're right behind us!"

Nerva gnashed his teeth, feeling the razor-sharp edges of his elongated canines sting against the sensitive skin inside his bottom lip. "They're not going to stop until they've hunted us down and killed every one of us," he growled. "We have to stand here." He jerked his head toward the ceiling. "The lights," he ordered. All three of his men immediately raised the barrels of their guns toward the ceiling; an instant later, at the same time as the hallway door burst open and the human soldiers spilled onto the landing, the roar of their gunfire was washed over by sparks and the hissing of electricity as they shot out the lights.

In the wink of time between the harsh glare of the fluorescents and the sudden darkness, Nerva's gaze crossed the small expanse of space and locked with the lighter but just as fierce gaze of Daxus himself as he followed his team into the tight confines of the stairwell.

Blackness.

"Night vision!" Daxus shouted. "Go night vision!"

"Sir, we are not equipped!"

The semi-panicked whisper from one of Daxus's men generated one overlong frozen moment of silence, then one of the humans' form was silhouetted by a blast of gunfire. Nerva actually laughed as the Hemophages moved around the human like wraiths, enjoying his dark moments of victory as they happened again, and again. In the space of mere seconds there was no gunfire, and no sound.

Clunk! Clunk! Clunk!

Red emergency lights suddenly clanked on around the landing, casting a dark glow on the bloody human bodies crumpled on the floor. Of the humans, only Daxus was still standing, and as Nerva looked over at him, the Hemophage let a wide and ugly grin spread across his mouth. He knew Daxus and what the man had done, and it was high time he paid for his sins of genocide against Nerva's brothers and sisters.

Incredibly, Daxus only smiled back at him.

Then sidestepped out the door.

Nerva snarled and moved after him. With Nerva leading, the Hemophages went after Daxus, following in an unhurried, ominous line as the Vice-Cardinal of the Arch-Ministry walked down the hallway and turned into a doorway labeled SNACK ROOM. Just because they could, the Hemophages watched Daxus as he pulled out a sterile packaged sanitary wipe and ripped it open. He chose a clean coffee cup from a cluster on the counter, then peered into it and grimaced; finally, he cleaned it thoroughly, inside and out, with the sanitary wipe.

"So," Daxus said without bothering to look up. "Are you going to kill me?"

Before Nerva or any of the others had a chance to answer, Daxus stuck his hand beneath his jacket; his fingers came back out wrapped around a small pistol wrapped in a medical-grade sterile covering. A small smile played at the corner of Daxus's wide mouth as he methodically unsheathed it and fussily dropped the leftover packaging into the trash. "Do you think you *can?*"

The Hemophages' eyes widened at Daxus's nerve, especially when the human set the gun down on the counter, then lifted a coffeepot from one of the burners and filled his cup, all the way to its rim. He returned the pot to the coffeemaker, then carefully picked up the overfilled cup.

While Nerva stood back and watched warily, his soldiers saw their chance and went for it, yanking their guns up as they counted on the fact that the human was more concerned with his precious coffee than his own safety.

And Daxus killed all three of them before any one of them could so much as squeeze a trigger. One shot each, no fanfare. Just a triple blaze of incredible, almost superhuman speed, and that was it.

Daxus lifted his gaze to Nerva's astounded one, then

raised the coffee cup he still held in one hand, toasting the Hemophage with it. Not a single drop had spilled over its edge. "Now," said Daxus as he brought the cup to his lips and took a sip, "I think you and I have matters of mutual self-interest to discuss."

THIRTEEN

You're unbelievable, Violet. You jeopardize *everything* by coming here!"

Violet faced Garth with her shoulders and back ramrod-straight, although she really wanted to wilt beneath Garth's accusing stare. He was right, of course—the traveling eighteen-wheelers that the vampires used as bases of operations, medical labs and facilities, and weapons storage were safe only because no one but the Hemophages knew about them. The boy was human, and everywhere he went the human security forces eventually showed up. The semitrailer in which she and Garth were standing right now could be closed up and out of here inside of five seconds, but God forbid the humans should actually find out just *how* the vampires had been avoiding them all this time.

She swallowed hard and made herself meet his intense, intelligent eyes. "The humans want me," she finally said in a voice that sounded very, very small. "Nerva wants me. I . . . didn't have anywhere else to go."

A muscle in Garth's jaw ticked in anger as he stared at her without answering. His normally calm face was hard along the edges beneath his light brown hair. She didn't think he'd ever looked at her so sternly, and it wasn't like she hadn't pulled enough stunts to justify it. But this one . . . oh, boy.

"Besides," she gave him a smile that came out weak, "You have all my guns."

He opened his mouth to snap at her, then shut it as a reluctant smile softened his tough, worried features. Finally, he looked back into the trailer, where the boy—Six—was nosing through the laboratory equipment. Clearly he was familiar with this kind of machinery; he kept his hands safely in his pockets and while he examined everything, he touched absolutely nothing. "So what's his story?" he finally asked.

Violet tilted her head, feeling a little of the anxiety bleed out of her muscles. Paranoia had worked hard at her, and she'd had the horrible notion that Garth was going to stand strong and turn her away. That would have been a death sentence for her and the boy. "You tell me," she ventured. Instead of answering, Garth inhaled deeply. Then, his face troubled, he climbed inside the truck and motioned at Violet to follow.

Thanks to flat-space technology, the interior of the trailer was much more spacious and well equipped than the outside implied. Rows of lights gleamed overhead, illuminating space that stretched out to at least four times more than the outer walls implied. The floor, like all the countertops and the walls, shone with medicinal cleanliness—Garth was a stickler for that, and just as anal retentive about having things put away where they belonged. His habits couldn't be faulted; on more than one occasion he'd saved her life by knowing just where the right surgical instrument was to close up a badly bleeding wound, just what to combine to bring her back from the edge of eternity. In times past, Violet had wanted that, though now she was feeling her age and exhaustion.

Still not daring to speak, Violet watched Garth pull on a pair of sterile surgical gloves, then kneel in front of the boy. Maybe it was the laboratory environment, or just that Garth looked much more like a medically oriented person than Violet, but this time the child didn't protest. In fact, he didn't even move—just stayed utterly still as Garth pushed up his lips to check out his gums, then first one of Six's eyelids, then the other, checking the child's color and pupil dilation response. Seeing the child used as a lab rat made Violet's muscles tense involuntarily, but it was also something she had to get past if there was any chance at all of finding out what was so special about this boy. When she spoke, her voice was even and unemotional, completely masking the turmoil she felt inside. "Can you make an assessment?"

Garth stood and yanked off his gloves. They made an unpleasant echoing sound inside the trailer, something that must've brought back unpleasant memories for Six. He winced instinctively, then was still again; Garth noted the reaction and looked down at the child thoughtfully. Steady once more, Six looked back at him, his face as emotionless as Violet's. She had an idea that, like her, Six was hiding his feelings. "I'll need to take some blood," Garth finally said. His eyes searched hers. "It'll take a few hours."

Take blood? Violet couldn't help but remember her struggle to do just that less than an hour ago, the way Six had resisted her efforts and threatened to scream. But when she and Garth glanced back at the boy, he was already obediently rolling up his sleeve. Was it the laboratory environment here in the trailer and the sense that he had nowhere to run, or did the child have some empathy for Violet's kind after hearing her recount the circumstances of their war? She had no way of knowing. What Violet *did* see was that Six's arm was a clinically organized mass of scars, a road map of physical evidence detailing how often his body had been tested and cruelly used in the past.

She could stand almost anything, but sometimes the sheer senselessness of the world and how it treated the most innocent of those who lived in it just made her want to cry.

⚡

The night sky was an ink-soaked blanket of stars and brilliantly colored explosions. She didn't know what they were celebrating in the city's interior tonight, but they had fireworks—the display went on and on and on, coating the interior of the truck's roomy cab with flashes of scarlet, green, yellow, and blue, more colors than Violet could name. It was inexplicable, really, the way she couldn't stop herself from watching, the way her gaze was drawn to the fire in the sky in much the same way as her ancestors, the ancient ones shared by her kind and humans alike, had probably been mesmerized by the red and orange flames of their first cooking fires. They—

Something inched into Violet's consciousness before she could complete the thought, a sound that was out of place. She'd left the passenger door open to catch the breeze, and when she turned her head she saw Six look up at her from the open side. For a second, she wasn't sure what to say, then she patted the seat. "Come on and sit." When he obeyed, she told him, "Just don't move. Or . . . talk." A silly thing to say, really—most children were chatterboxes, but this kid hardly ever spoke a word.

Right now it was no different. He sat next to her and stared out the windshield, leaning forward slightly and placing his hands delicately on the dashboard so he could have a better view of the overhead show. Violet could see the colorful little explosions mirrored on the surface of his eyes, watch as his gaze flicked from side to side across the windshield as he tried to keep up with each new fireworks display. He was, she realized, seeing this for the first time; while somewhere in her consciousness she had known that, the epiphany was that she herself was doing the same . . . through him.

Finally, even though he hadn't asked, she felt compelled to explain. "Humans," she said. "Celebrating something." When she realized what she'd said, Violet couldn't stop the bittersweet feelings that spiked inside her, little memories that brought nothing but sharp, spiked pain. She had been human once, but the war had taken that away. The ArchMinistry wanted the world to think it was the virus's fault, but that wasn't true. Humans were prone to plenty of viruses, and hardly any of the other illnesses segregated its victims the way this one did. The ones that had? Eradicated. The key part was that the *diseases* had been eradicated, not their victims. The truth now was that the sickness part didn't matter. Even the death part was only a piece of the whole pie. Sickness and death—those things could be easily tolerated, carefully treated, even contained. What couldn't be allowed to continue was the strength, the speed, all the things inherent to H.P.V. that made its victims *better* than humans. It was all about *power*, not preservation. There was nothing blatant about the ArchMinistry's extermination of vampires. It was all subjective, much like killing in the name of religion.

But then, there had been entire eras over the course of mankind's existence that had been devoted to just such battles, hadn't there?

Six shifted on the seat, bringing Violet's thoughts back to the present. He seemed to be carefully pondering what she'd said about the humans celebrating, then he looked like he'd finally made a decision. Digging into his pocket, the boy came up with a worn piece of paper, looking at her sideways at he pulled it out. He unfolded it carefully, trying his best to smooth out the sharply creased edges; after another moment's hesitation, at last he offered it to her. "So you know where this is?" he asked with his customary seriousness.

Curious despite herself, Violet took the paper from him and studied it. The image burned into her eyes, and once again she fought the lump that rose sluggishly in her throat. Behind the stoic facade she kept up, she could feel her eyes burn. Thanks to the fireworks and the moonlight, she could just make out that she was holding a timeworn drawing of a playground. A dozen kids played on the swings and the teeter-totters, more ran happily alongside a merry-go-round. Everyone in the drawing was having a great time, and it looked like an antique advertisement for schoolyard equipment. Six, of course, had never known anything like the scene on the crumpled piece of paper. His question made it clear that he wasn't even sure such a place existed, and Violet thought he would probably never see one for himself. Sometimes destiny could truly screw over those who deserved it the least.

"When I was a kid," Violet told him quietly, "a little girl, I used to dream about this . . . old dusty road. There were beautiful daisies growing tall on both sides—bright yellow and for as far as I could see—and they would sway in the wind. I'd walk down it for a long time, and at the end would be a schoolhouse, a red one like in the old movies, with a yard in the back where they'd have stuff like this." Violet pointed to the picture, then her gaze cut to the window and the beautiful faraway fireworks. "In that dream, I had a family and best friends, and we'd play house and everyone lived happily ever after. It was a happy dream. But then you realize, as life settles in around you, that those places don't really exist." She refolded the picture and pushed it back into Six's hands with a sigh. "Not in this world, anyway. Now I just dream about losing things." She felt him staring at her and shrugged, suddenly feeling stupid. There wasn't any explaining what she'd just said, and he wouldn't understand her anyway. He was too young and naive—

"You're dying," Six said suddenly. She jerked and turned to stare at him. The child's eyes were clear and without guile as he reached up and brushed his fingers over her eyelids inquisitively. "I can see it."

Violet swallowed and returned her gaze to the windshield, tilting her head to get out of range of his questing fingers. Outside it was just beginning to rain; the weather report said the precipitation would get heavier as the night wore on, and soon the fireworks would be chased away by the moisture. "Yeah," she said hoarsely. "Yeah. I'm . . . winding down. I can feel it." She shrugged again, trying desperately to appear nonchalant, like this was the last thing in the world that bothered her . . . or at least that she had accepted it. She had, right? After all, it wasn't like she could *do* anything to stop or stall the inevitable, even with Six at her side. Whatever secrets were in his blood probably wouldn't be revealed in time to do her any good. Stuff like that took years to figure out. She didn't even have days. "By this time tomorrow." Violet nodded thoughtfully, then pressed her fingers against her temple. She could hear her heart beating rapidly, that accelerated Hemophage metabolism. It was killing her. "I don't imagine there'll be much left."

The boy was silent for a moment. "I'm sorry," he finally said, and he sounded like he meant it.

They looked at each other for a long moment, then Violet raised her left hand and spread her fingers. There was still enough light from the lessening fireworks display to illuminate the beautiful Indo-Narai script tattoos that twined around three of the fingers. "Do you read Thai-hindi script?"

Six shook his head and peered quizzically at the writing. Obligingly Violet ticked off each one and folded it back into a fist as she recited its meaning. "Comrade," she told him. "Lover. Wife." She stopped with only her blank forefinger extended. "This one was going to say Mother," she said quietly. Was her voice shaking? She hoped not. "But I never got that far. I got infected and all that became . . . impossible."

The boy's gaze was frank and liquid, blatantly melancholy for her. It was heartbreaking to realize that the only person in the world who truly sympathized with her was a child who had never experienced—and never would—all the things she had lost in her life. "So when you're gone," he said softly, "there really will be nothing left of you."

That went beyond even what she expected, and Violet didn't know what to say to that. How could this boy, raised in the emotionally cold and sterile prison of a laboratory, even understand the concept of death? Of nonexistence? Or maybe it was *because* of his upbringing that he understood it better than most adults. Eventually Violet couldn't stop the dark smile that stretched across her mouth. "My last act was going to be to walk into the ArchMinistry of Medical Policy," she told him, "the very *soul* of all this rot, and blow it to pieces with a bomb strapped to my chest."

Six tilted his head and Violet could see his eyes. They were sparkling, full of questions and the reflection of the rain and the last of the fireworks. "But now you won't."

A chill rippled across her skin, raising the fine hairs on her arms and neck. She let a minute pass, then two, then squared her shoulders. "Oh, yes—I will." She sucked in a breath. "Nerva may have given up, but I haven't. Before I leave it, I'm going to take this world back to what it was. At dawn I'm going to leave you here with Garth, and I'm going to walk into that building—guards or not—and before they can gun me down, I'm going to *destroy* it." Violet glanced at the boy and nodded slightly. "That's what's going to be left of *me*."

Me, she thought, and her gaze wandered back to the blackness of the night sky overhead.

And, just for a moment, Violet closed her eyes . . . and remembered.

She is maybe twenty pounds heavier, and her hair is different—cut differently, a different shade, a whole other her. Her white nurse's uniform is starched and bright white, smart-looking even if it has gotten a bit on the snug side across the breasts and hips because of certain recent circumstances. It is those exact same circumstances that she's going to discuss with the doctor just before she goes on her rounds and passes out the doses of medicine carefully measured out in the syringes arranged on her tray. She has a smile on her lips and a bounce in her step, all those things now lost over the course of time's passage and the way her life has changed.

She turns the corner and ducks into the hospital laboratory. The man she's come to see is carefully going over a stack of X-ray films spread out on one of the light tables. His dark brow furrows in concentration as he compares one to another, then quickly scribbles notes on a clipboard to his right. Despite her best efforts at sneaking up on him, he looks up and catches her.

"Doctor," she says as seriously as she can manage. "It's been decided." He stands as she approaches him. His head tilts curiously and a small smile, hardly noticeable to the unaccustomed eye, starts at one corner of his mouth. She has never seen him look so handsome. "I'm getting a new tattoo." Standing in front of him, she holds up her hand and her splayed fingers reveal the Indo-Narai script with which he's already so familiar. The fluorescent lights overhead make the small diamond ring on her third finger sparkle cheerfully above the words—

    Comrade

       Lover

          Wife.

"Here," she says softly and holds up her forefinger.

His eyes widen as the realization sinks in that she's talking about the word "Mother," and that means she's going to have a baby. His smile is so filled with happiness it's dazzling. "Oh, my God, Violet—" He can't finish, so instead of talking, he entwines his own tattooed fingers around hers and pulls her to him for a sweet, sweet kiss—

—that breaks abruptly apart when the wild-eyed man barges into the lab and skids to a stop just a few feet away.

The intruder is tall and anemic-looking—dark eyes squinting at the lights from a bone-white face fed by ramped-up adrenaline. Violet's instinctive impression is that he's on drugs, an almost overdose of cocaine, PCP, or crack—no matter what the police do, they can't seem to clean that stuff off the streets. Even so, there's something odd about him that she can't put her finger on, a sense of strength, energy, and danger, of clarity, that she's never seen in the hundreds of addicts she's seen come through the emergency room.

"One suggestion," he snarls at her and her husband. "Stay the fuck out of my way!"

She steps back automatically as he round-shoulders his way farther into the room. His watery gaze scans the lab, then stops on the oversized stainless-steel refrigerator against the wall. A red-on-white sign warns CAUTION: BLOOD PRODUCTS, *but this seems to be exactly what the guy is looking for. Without hesitating, he strides toward it.*

And just as unhesitatingly, Violet's husband bodily steps into the man's path. "Hey," he snaps. "What the hell do you think you're doing?"

It happens so fast—one second her husband is speaking, the next he's slammed against the refrigerator and the intruder's fingers—only one-handed—are pressed so deeply into his windpipe that Violet can't even see the attacker's fingernails. Her husband chokes and fights, clawing at the grip on his throat. "Violet!" he manages and gestures wildly at the tray of syringes she's set aside on the counter. "Tranq—tranquilizer!" The word seems to infuriate his attacker, who brings up his other hand and folds it around her husband's neck, cutting off the rest of his air. Violet is paralyzed with fear, her feet leaden on the floor—never has she faced something like this, she doesn't know what to do, what if she drops the syringe, or misses, or doesn't even pick up the right one—

"What the hell!"

She spins helplessly and sees one of the hospital security guards standing in the doorway, a coffee cup held in one hand below his incredulous face. The attacker releases her husband and whirls to face the guard, dark, sweaty hair circling around his head like a flock of bats; as her gasping husband slides down the wall, the crazed man leaps forward. But the guard is too quick—he lets go of the coffee cup and has his gun drawn and aimed even before the cup hits the floor and shatters.

BAM! BAM! BAM!

Three shots to the chest and the man goes down . . . but not before he actually lingers upright for a moment, somehow managing to turn his head enough to make eye contact with each of the three people who will watch him die, practically at Violet's feet.

Shocked, all Violet can do is stand there and stare downward. Oddly, something on her hand tickles, and when she looks down—

—then feels her face—

—both are splattered with the dead man's blood.

She turns her head and wordlessly locks gazes with the horrified eyes of her husband . . .

FOURTEEN

Something—some*one*—was close enough to make her eyelids open with a snap. Violet started to jerk upright behind the truck's steering wheel when a gentle hand— Garth's—held her in place. Jesus—she must have fallen asleep. Forcing herself to relax, she glanced to the side and saw Six, also asleep, curled into a protective ball on the passenger seat. A pressure at her wrist made her look back at Garth; he'd slid his fingers into position so he could take her pulse and now he was frowning. When he met her eyes, he looked slightly embarrassed at being caught playing mother hen. Even so, he pressed his lips together. "You're not looking so good," he told her. "I need to transfuse you."

Violet started to protest, but as she tried to sit up, she realized how utterly *rotten* she felt, weak and drained of what little she had going in the reserves department. She looked up at him and nodded, then found enough energy to reach over and touch Six on the wrist to wake him up. He came out of whatever dream he was having with a jerk, and for a moment he looked around wildly, like he was ready for the worst; when the boy's eyes focused on her and Garth, the change was instant. His eyes cleared and Violet could literally see his muscles release. More evidence, it was clear, of bad lab memories.

In the laboratory portion of the trailer, Violet settled herself as comfortably as she could on the stainless steel chair in the center. It only took Garth a few minutes to get an IV hooked up and start pumping fresh blood into her; a transfusion usually made her feel better almost immediately, but not this time. Now it was just new liquid going into her while the bad liquid went out, like the old-time dialysis sessions for kidney failure patients. Her sickness had changed over the last couple of days; now it was a strange sensation—her joints felt swollen with a sort of flulike ache, her head was achy and heavy, and she was so *tired,* despite the nap she'd just had and the fresh blood being pushed into her body.

Garth fluttered around her like a moth in front of a porch light at twilight, checking her vitals, jiggling the sterile plastic bag, consulting his portable computer, and holding up the continuing printout of her blood gases. She didn't have to ask about the results—the darkening expression on his face said it all. "It's not days anymore, V," he told her in a low voice. She could hear the pain in it, the regret. "Now it's more like . . . hours."

She didn't move or say anything, just stayed where she was on the cold, uncomfortable chair. She was nearly numb anyway, and it wasn't as though the news was a big surprise.

"Maybe if you stayed," Garth suggested hesitantly, "I could do something. Prolong you—"

"To what end?" Violet interrupted. She looked at him

out of the corner of her eye, waiting. If he had a good reason, something that could actually justify maintaining her miserable, sickly existence, she certainly wanted to hear it.

Instead of replying, Garth bit his lip and looked away. After a moment, he brightened and held a piece of paper up so she could see it. "Did you do this?"

Violet peered at it and it took her a few seconds to comprehend that what was on it was a mass of mathematical equations . . . at least, that's what it looked like. She shook her head wearily. "What is it?"

Garth pulled it back and studied it again, but his expression remained bewildered. "I'm not sure," he finally admitted. "It looks chemical, but it seems like it's done in the old Pre-Collapse form of Western notation."

Her eyes narrowed thoughtfully, then her gaze cut toward the boy. He was off to the side, standing in front of one of the computers and gazing at it like he expected it to do something at any second. His stance—waiting— was enough to raise chill bumps on her arms. "Must have been him," she said.

Garth shot the child an unreadable look, then gave a small nod and shoved the paper into his pocket. His face was morose.

"What is he?" Violet asked under her breath.

Unaccountably, Garth stiffened. "I know what he's *not.*" When Violet waited for him to continue, he seemed to struggle to find the appropriate words. "He's not someone who has a single molecule of vampiral antigen in his blood," he said at last. Violet could easily picture Garth agonizing over how to tell her this while she and Six had been sleeping in the truck, oblivious to the rest of the world. "He's not someone who's any good to us. Daxus was telling the truth."

Violet sat up on the chair, making the IV line stretch out and Garth frown at it. She felt like someone had just punched her in the gut. *"What?"*

Garth folded his arms protectively, but he didn't back down. "And if that's not bad enough," he continued, "the kid's *hot,* V. Practically radioactive. He's got a tracking device in him accurate to about a hundred yards." Violet gasped and reached to pull the IV out of her arm, but Garth's hand stopped her. "We're shielded in here."

She sank down again, feeling the cold from the metal chair back seep through the flimsy fabric of her shirt. She should have known—hell, hadn't she already suspected it when every time she dragged Six off to a new and safe spot, a human security force showed up within minutes? Of course she had, but she'd ignored it, reluctant to face the truth. And how dangerous was that? With her free hand, she pushed her hair off her forehead, then rubbed at her eyes. They were burning with an exhaustion that the transfusion simply wasn't chasing away. "I don't understand," she said at last. "Then why did Nerva want me to get him so badly? Why were the humans guarding him so closely if he's not a vessel for a vampiral antigen?"

Garth shook his head. "I don't know, but . . ." He hesitated just long enough for Violet to look sharply at him. In response, he wouldn't meet her eyes. "Whatever they did put in the kid . . . it's killing him, V." Her eyes widened. Garth shrugged, but the motion was anything but careless. "It's some kind of aggressive antagonistic protein, with a very predictable decay." He stared unhappily at the floor. "He's got a shelf life of no more than another eight hours." Finally, Garth lifted his saddened gaze to hers. "The kid's toast, V."

She sat there, frozen with disbelief, then abruptly pushed out of the chair. The IV tore free of her arm and leaked blood onto the floor, but she didn't feel it—the transfusion was complete anyway. Her hand closed around the first thing she saw—a rack of empty test tubes—and she hurled them against the side wall with a curse. The boy spun in surprise and stared at her, but she couldn't look at him, not right now. Not yet.

Garth sighed and spread his hands, but he made no move to clean up the mess. "What can I tell you?"

"That I should expect this?" she demanded bitterly. "After all, they're humans."

Now Garth frowned. "Violet, you sound more and more like Nerva. We're *all* humans—we're just sick." His expression deepened into a scowl. "And what's so wrong with being human, anyway?"

For a moment, Violet couldn't answer as she fought to keep her jaw from trembling. Besides being a species that automatically wanted to exterminate anything more powerful, more beautiful, or better than it in any way, what, indeed? Finally, she gave Garth the only answer she could think of that seemed to cover it all.

"It's *weak*."

⚡

It had taken a while to calm things down—including herself—after Violet had thrown the test tubes, but finally she and Garth had calmed Six down enough to where they actually got him to sleep. In the way of room and board, what Garth had to offer wasn't much: a cup of instant chicken noodle soup and a small, fairly uncomfortable cot with an old synthetic military blanket, but it seemed to more than satisfy the child. Six had lingered over the soup, seeming to enjoy the scent of it as much as the taste as he rolled each spoonful several times around in his mouth before swallowing it. Afterward, he'd tugged the scratchy blanket up and under his chin and settled on the lumpy cot mattress with obvious pleasure and smiled slightly as his eyes fluttered and closed. Violet could feel her internal anger building again as she watched him. Had he ever had anything but capsulated food and water? Had he slept on anything besides a sterile metal shelf?

Right now Six looked like a sleeping angel, some kind of otherworldly creature that didn't have a single care about what did or didn't happen in the world of mankind or Hemophages. He was innocent and helpless, vulnerable to everything, and Violet couldn't stop herself from reaching down to touch his cheek.

But no—she pulled her hand back before her fingertips actually made contact with his skin. She mustn't wake him up or disturb his sleep. He needed his strength to—

Who was she kidding?

All the strength in the world wasn't going to help him, and she knew it. That wasn't why she couldn't touch him. No, it was the *contact,* the actual act of *touching* him as she would a human being about whom she actually cared. She couldn't do that—she couldn't touch him because she mustn't *connect* with him. He needed to be just as much an inanimate object to her as she needed to be to him. After all, in another eight or twelve hours, neither one of them was going to be alive.

But in that case . . . why not?

Because it would hurt them both just too damned much.

Garth stood off to the side, and by the expression on his face, Violet knew he wished he could figure out something comforting to say. He couldn't, of course, and so the best he could finally do was hold up something for her to see. "I . . . made you this," he ventured. An object dangled from his fingers, a sturdy necklace with a white metal disc hanging at its apex. "It's meta-crystal," Garth explained. "It tracks biorhythms. It's white now. When it's black . . ." He didn't bother to finish but Violet already knew the rest of the sentence.

When it's black, you'll be dead.

A hell of a gift, that.

Even so, Violet managed to find a smile as she reached for it. "Been a while since a man gave me jewelry." She stopped, then suddenly offered it back to him. Her smile had faded. "I don't think I'll be needing it."

But Garth only gave her a tight-lipped glare. Instead of accepting it, he folded his arms stubbornly. "V, come on—this isn't the way."

Her eyes flashed. "Haven't you heard, Garth? Violence is just another word for change. Now if you don't mind—"

Instead of moving aside, he caught her by the arm when she tried to step past him. "Still playing the good little revolutionary?" he asked bitterly. "If you're going to go out like this, don't you think you ought to at least own up to why you're *really* doing it?"

Her lips stretched into a grimace, but before she could retort, both she and Garth jumped as someone blurted a string of unintelligible words at them. When they jerked around, they saw Six standing right behind them. His gaze was fixed on Violet, his eyes blurry with sleepiness and fear. Before she could think of what to do or say, he repeated the words, his hands fluttering urgently in the air between them as he tried to make them understand.

"Six," Violet began. A third repeat of his words, even louder and more frantic than the rest, cut off the rest of what she was going to say. She had to remind herself not to get impatient, to realize that no matter how dire her circumstances or anyone else's were, she was still dealing with a child . . . one who was apparently prone to sleepwalking on top of everything else. He had limited intelligence and zero life experience. "Six, calm down—it's okay—"

Obviously, *he* didn't think so. Now he was so worked up, he was nearly hyperventilating. Violet knelt in front of him and gripped his thin shoulders, forcing him to focus on her face and mouth. Easy, now. "Remember," she said with false calmness, "I don't speak English."

It was almost as if a light went off in the child's head, chasing away the sleep fog and making him realize where he was and what he was doing. "I said—" Six had to pause to catch his breath, then he struggled to find the right words. "Please . . . don't leave me."

Before Violet could stand or pull away, Six pushed forward and wrapped his arms around her in a tight, fierce hug.

⚡

Dawn.
The sweet, quiet night had passed much too quickly, especially considering it was the last one of her life. As

usual, Six wasn't far away, this time just inside the shielding structure of the trailer—no sense in having his tracking device fire up any sooner than necessary—and admiring the meta-crystal that Garth had given him. Right now it was a strange shade of pearlized gray, a tiny but terrifying step down from the bright white it had been at the onset.

"Look," Garth said under his breath. His voice was filled with urgency. "Just leave him with me. I'll figure something out."

Violet and Garth were standing at the very end of the truck, intentionally out of earshot of the child. Now that he was fully awake and bored with the meta-crystal, Six had gone back to wandering around the flat-space interior and inspecting the equipment and computers, looking quizzically at the firearms and other weapons neatly stacked in strategic areas. Sometimes he looked completely baffled, but now and then it was like something would clear in his head and he would understand completely whatever it was he happened to be staring at. To the casual observer—or, as was the case with Violet and Garth—the child's behavior was downright eerie.

Violet waited long enough to make Garth think she was actually considering his suggestion, then finally shook her head and sighed. "No. He'll try to follow me . . . and he's smart. Maybe smarter than you or me." Her knowing gaze cut to Garth's. "There's no guarantee you'll be able to contain him. He'll lead them right back to you."

Garth's eyes softened and a ghost of a smile played across his lips. "Well, then. Maybe you'll have to stay here after all. With him." There was something else in his tone, something unspoken. No, she didn't want to go there, not now. She *couldn't.*

Violet forced herself to meet his gaze and swallowed, but she couldn't hold it. Before she turned her head, she knew he'd read the answer in her eyes—that wasn't going to happen. "No," she said. The word came out as a croak and she cleared her throat harshly, impatient with the ways in which her body was revealing its growing failure. "What you're doing is too valuable to jeopardize. Listen, I'll get him to Kristensen. He's got the equipment—he can get the tracker out of him."

Garth's expression went back to being matter-of-fact, unyielding. The face of a man who looks soft from the outside, but inside just won't buy the bullshit. "You know they're likely to lock on to it and intercept you long before you make it that far."

She refused to look back at him. "That's a chance I guess I'll have to take."

"And the ArchMinistry?"

Violet shrugged. "What about it? I guess it'll just have to wait for another lifetime."

Garth looked at her warily, then shook his head. "V, I wish I could, but I don't *trust* this. As much as I care about her, the Violet I know would be too stubborn and too blind to do an about-face for a child she doesn't even *know.*" He didn't say it, but the rest of his statement was there, hanging in the air between them.

And too smart.

This time when she gazed at him, Violet managed to keep her face utterly bland—no emotion, no fear, *nothing.* All she did was nod, like an agreeable little robot soldier. "Good-bye, Garth," she said simply. Six had wandered close enough to where he heard her words and he looked over at her in alarm; without turning to face him, she held out her hand. A moment later his smaller one slipped into hers and he jumped down out of the trailer. As they left, walking quickly to put as much distance between the boy's tracking device and the oh-so-precious trailer, Violet didn't look back at Garth.

"Where are we going?"

Sometimes, there was just nothing as good in the world as the truth. "You've got a tracking device inside you," Violet said bluntly. "We're going to get you someplace safe."

Maybe.

FIFTEEN

It was almost like déjà vu, a rewinding and restarting of any one of several of yesterday's adventures.

Except that it was early morning, and this time the crowds of people were going *to* work instead of having lunch or leaving the office to add to the evening's rush hour.

And, of course, except that this was one of her last few hours alive.

Violet and Six moved briskly through the crowd. While Violet felt oddly like she was a walking clock with a dying battery, this time Six seemed to be a little more attuned to the world around him. Apparently he'd embraced the idea that he needed to keep up rather than gawk at all the things he'd never seen before. Violet thought that was too bad; in a part of her mind that she didn't want to acknowledge, she wished she could slow down and take the child shopping, buy him bags full of the toys he'd never had and never would, then take him for pizza and ice cream. There was one of those children's pizza parlors down at the other end, next to the video outlet store. Had he ever tasted things like pizza and ice cream? She didn't know for sure, but Violet doubted it—the only image her mind would provide when she tried to imagine his life at the lab was a tiny white room with a sterile metal cot, a toilet, and a slot through which someone shoved bowls of nutritionally complete mush, perhaps coupled with the nutritious capsules that Violet was convinced had been the bulk of his diet. Probably an overreaction, but the way he'd been so overwhelmed by the everyday made her wonder.

So far, so good—they hadn't seen any security forces, but Violet was too smart to think that would last for long. They might already be within striking distance, this time holding back and quietly surrounding them, waiting for whatever strategic purposes might suit Daxus best. By now there had to have been fallout from the humans who'd been hurt in yesterday's manhunt, and it remained to be seen whether Daxus was willing to risk a repeat of that. Then again, this was the ArchMinistry she was dealing with, and that entity thought it could do anything.

"Why aren't you photokemic, too? Like him?" Six asked suddenly.

Violet blinked, then frowned down at him. "Photo say what?"

"Kemic," Six repeated. His expression was curious. "Negatively phototrophic. Like Garth—sensitive to light."

She smiled self-consciously, secretly impressed. How strange that he knew nothing about some things, but more than her about others. "You mean, why am I a freak among freaks?"

He returned the smile, but he looked a little doubtful,

as if he wasn't sure if what she was saying was truly funny. "Yeah . . . I guess so."

Violet shrugged and glanced around again, letting her mind automatically process the crowd and gauge their safety ratio. "I converted with only mild"—she made quote marks in the air with her fingers—"Photokemia— sort of a reverse albinism. Everything else can be suppressed chemically." She stretched her mouth into a mock grimace that showed all of her teeth. "Teeth ground down. See?"

He peered at her mouth and she could feel with her tongue that her incisors were already starting to elongate again. That was an interesting phenomenon, something that continued to happen no matter how close a Hemophage got to the end of his or her life span. Six nodded his approval. "Neat," he said.

She couldn't help chuckling—only a child would find vampire fangs appealing. "They come in handy if you can't find a can opener," she joked.

He grinned, then his face went back to being serious. "What's it like, Violet?"

She started and looked at him for a moment. How much should she tell him? How much of a *child* was he really, anyway? Like her, he was doomed, and in some way that neither of them could quite grasp, it was for the same reasons. He deserved to know the truth, or at least as much of it as she could convey. "You contract," she finally said, "then you convert. There's a deathlike paralysis for several hours. Then you just . . . wake up." She didn't try to hide her sad smile. "The fucked-up irony is that you've never felt so *good.*"

They kept going, with Violet pushing a little harder, a little faster. They streamed along with the morning workers, just two more fish in a vast ocean school. Their luck had held so far, but the laws of fate were never on the side of the fugitive. It wouldn't—it *couldn't*—be long now until Daxus's forces made their appearance.

"V?" Violet looked down at the boy, but didn't stop moving. When he spoke, his words were punctuated by his footsteps as he struggled to keep up with her ever-increasing gait. "Back on that rooftop?"

She raised an eyebrow. "Where you were doing your high-wire act?"

"Why are you so good?" He paused, trying to find the right words. "Why are you so much *better* than everyone else?"

Violet grinned. "Aside from All-Pan-Asia Women's Gymnastics?" She glanced at him, but he didn't get the joke, so she finally just squared her shoulders and stopped trying to make it funny. "I'm not," she said simply. "I'm just a whole lot angrier." Before she could elaborate, the ringer went off on her cell phone, making her jump. She pulled it out and frowned at it before flipping it open. A name flashed across the finger-sized screen and her frown deepened into a full scowl. Panic made her snap the phone shut hard enough to stress the hinges.

Six picked up on the anxiety in her features immediately. "Who was it?"

"Daxus." Violet felt her heartbeat increase and she struggled to at least keep her voice calm. "My number changes every sixty seconds." She didn't elaborate; she thought the boy was smart enough to figure out that meant the ArchMinistry had probably been able to lock on to their location.

Violet quickly led Six deeper into the stream of people headed for their offices, hoping the crowd would at least let them blend in. After a few minutes, just before heading down a staircase to a lower level, she tore off the glove phone and dropped it into a trash can; at the bottom of the stairs she spied a vending machine and they made a detour to it. A few dollar bills later and the machine obligingly spit out a cellophane-wrapped temp phone. She unwrapped it quickly and keyed in Garth's number. All the while her gaze skipped suspiciously over the faces of the crowd, trying to spot anyone out of place. She wouldn't be surprised to learn that Daxus had an entire squad of undercover people, just like the drug teams. If he did, they were doomed; she'd have no way to recognize them and they could be surrounded in a heartbeat.

"Garth," she said when she heard him answer, "it's me. They may have been tracking my phone. I'd get moving if I were you." She closed the phone and scanned the crowd again, then her gaze stopped on Six. He looked small and quiet, like nothing so much as an out-of-place child on an overcrowded city street. And yet, he had so much of that . . . dangerous potential. "Or maybe . . . it's me," Violet murmured. A final glance around gave her the entrance to the subway, thankfully only about a quarter block away. She grabbed the boy's hand and headed toward it. "We've got to get under some concrete."

Once they were past the entrance and headed down again, Violet felt a small sense of relief spread over her. "We'll be shielded in here," she told Six. Was it the relief bringing a flush to her cheeks, or her sickness?

But before she could decide which way to go next, Six grabbed her arm and pulled her to a stop. "Violet, wait."

She stopped and blinked back at him. "What?"

"What are we doing?" he asked. His eyes were clear and guileless, searching.

Violet frowned. "Well, what do you mean? I told you—we have to get you someplace shielded—"

But the boy shook his head and folded his arms protectively across his thin chest. "V, why didn't Garth believe you when you said you'd take care of me?"

She opened her mouth to reply, but nothing came out. Then, on the edge of her peripheral vision, she saw a security team. They were moving slowly and without purpose, like sharks trolling the waters . . . so far. The quiet was about to erupt into a storm.

Violet knelt so that she could look the boy in the eye and drop out of the guards' field of vision. "Because Garth is a jaded and cynical being with no faith in human nature," she said. The instant she said it, she felt like some kind of super hypocrite—how many times had she made it clear that she considered humans inferior? Hadn't she told Garth only an hour or so earlier that to be human was weak? Well, yes . . . but this was a different thing and one she couldn't explain right now.

To keep the boy—often he was too smart not only for his own good, but for hers—from catching her inconsistency, Violet managed a smile. "Speaking of which, I'd be neglecting my duties if I didn't get a growing boy fed, now, wouldn't I?" She reached down and snapped off the bracelet on her wrist, then pressed it into Six's hand. When he looked at it quizzically, she told him, "Untraceable single use credit card. Good for the purchase of any and all goods and services." There was a bank of vending machines only a few yards away and she turned the boy so that he was facing them and gave him a little push in their direction. "Why don't you go and see if you can rustle us up something worth eating? We've got a big day ahead of us."

Six looked from her to the machines, then back again.

Violet smiled as encouragingly as she could. "Go on," she prodded. "It's about time you learned how this world works."

The child hesitated again, then startled her by handing her the blue jacket that Garth had given him before turning back toward the machines. It wrenched her heart to see the resignation on his face, but she told herself there was nothing she could do about it. She had so little time left—she couldn't save him anyway . . . and there were other things she needed to do before she left this world.

He'd taken only a few steps when Violet found her voice. "Six."

He stopped and turned to face her, but didn't come back. She swallowed. "You should . . . really put up your mask."

He stared at her without saying anything for a long moment, then reached beneath his collar and pulled up the breathing mask, that useless piece of portable protection that was supposed to keep the uninfected from becoming just that. Before he tugged it into place, he said quietly, "Good-bye, Violet."

Violet swallowed again. "What . . . what're you talking about?" she managed, but they both knew the question was a farce. He gave her a final look, then found a smile for her, sad and serene—like the face of a child martyr ready to go on to the final step to canonization. Turning his back, he threaded his way through the crowd and over to the machines.

Steeling herself, Violet turned her back on the boy, then draped the blue jacket over the edge of a waste receptacle where Six, if he turned back to the crowd to look for her, surely wouldn't miss it. She wasn't going to need it, and she certainly wasn't going to be taking it back to Garth. Before she could change her mind—she mustn't be weak!—she melted into the crowd, striding purposely as fast and far away from the child as she could without drawing attention to herself.

But even so . . . she couldn't resist one final glance over her shoulder, right before she began climbing the stairs that would take her out of the subway and put him completely out of her sight. Six was still there, right in front of the vending machines where she'd sent him. He wasn't looking at her—thank God—but he had defiantly pulled down his breathing mask. Now he simply stood there, his face utterly expressionless and his eyes closed. It was almost like he was feeling the press of people around him, their nearness, their passage, while he . . . *waited* for something.

His destiny, perhaps.

SIXTEEN

Violet had made good time, and she was almost at the top when the first security team passed her on the descent side. She averted her eyes automatically, then realized they weren't looking for her—oh, no, they were focused on something much more important, something that kept their shielded gazes straight ahead. They had purpose in their step, purpose and ... *direction*. They knew what they were tasked to find, and let's face it, so did she. It wouldn't be long before they had the boy in their sights, literally, and soon after that he'd be dead.

She told herself, again, that there was nothing she could do about it—hell, she couldn't even help herself, much less save a doomed child. If she tried, all she'd get for her trouble was dead, and that, before her already shortened life span. To make it even worse, trying to keep the child alive would be a futile effort that would break her heart with the final result, and if she was going to die and she couldn't take out that fucking ArchMinistry like she'd originally planned, shouldn't she go quietly? Not for the benefit of anyone else, but for her *own* peace of mind, her own sense of go down gracefully and fade away with time. After all, people always said you should grow old gracefully, and she took that to mean she ought to die that way, too.

Another half-dozen strong security team streamed past, again too focused on their mission to notice her. This time, however, she did catch something from them—

"Signal locked on child and are in rapid response!"

—and she shut her eyes as tightly as she could.

A useless gesture, of course. There was no way to erase from her mind the grainy sound of the man's radio transmission, no way to wipe out the sight of the cruel stone-slash of a mouth beneath the black visor.

No way to forget the face of death.

"Damn it," Violet whispered. She made herself keep going, up and up, until she came to the last riser of the staircase and realized she was standing in front of the trash can where she'd dumped her cell phone. For the moment there were no more security teams, so after a quick double glance around, Violet leaned over and scanned the trash. There, just under a half-empty cellophane bag of health chips and the crushed remains of a disposable cup—thankfully empty—she saw her glove phone. With a quick snap, Violet retrieved it from the pile of litter and slipped it back on her hand. She'd been foolish to think Daxus had found her via the phone; now it was obvious that he'd gotten a satellite lock on the boy and his computers had simply jumped the signal over to her phone. He might have a lock on the kid, but with the phone turned off, there was no way the Vice-Cardinal could keep tabs on her. Besides, she'd already seen plenty of proof that his soldiers were on their way to the boy and not her. They didn't even know she was there.

But she could change that.

She could.

"Damn it." She jumped at the sound of her own voice before she realized she said it again. She was up and on the sidewalk now, pushing through the heavy crowd and trying to make headway, then suddenly jerking her face to the side as yet another security team barreled past her.

"Damn it."

No—she couldn't save him, she *couldn't*. He was too far gone, she was too far gone—

"Damn it!"

—and she wasn't some kind of fucking messiah! She strode on, trying desperately to ignore the objects beneath her coat, but suddenly they all seemed too big, with an overabundance of sharp edges that raked her skin and excessive weight that banged painfully into her muscles and made her flesh ache.

"Damn IT—"

Barely registering her own frenzied movements, Violet kept surging forward, but this time she was yanking things out from under her coat, those objects that had weighed so heavily on her, freeing herself of them as she tossed them from left to right along the curb and never even registered that they rolled into the dirty street and were instantly lost in the crush of feet and forgotten—

The fuse.

The detonator.

The dozen packets of C-10 explosives that had been strung together around her waist, the chemical composition at least a hundred times more powerful than its early plastic explosives predecessor.

And, finally, all that was left of the small bundle of quick-connect wiring.

Abruptly Violet went down on one knee, but the pain of her kneecap striking the sidewalk did nothing to ground her as her hands came up and cradled her head.

There would be no bomb, no final, beautiful, deadly end to the ArchMinistry.

"DAMN IT!"

Her head was splitting, throbbing with indecision and rage and regret. She couldn't think straight, couldn't see, couldn't make a damned decent *decision.*

Someone touched her lightly on the shoulder. "Are you okay?"

"Damn it," she whispered, ignoring the voice. "Damn it damn it damn it . . ."

The person touched her again, this time more insistently. "Hey," he said. "Are you okay?" Suddenly the touch of his skin ate into hers, feeling like a hot poke instead of concern.

Violet's eyelids snapped open and her face jerked up toward his. He gasped and back-stepped as her eyes blazed at him. "Touch me again and you'll lose your arm and half your torso with it," she snarled. The man's face twisted, first in fright, then in anger and revulsion when he realized she was a Hemophage; without a word, he spun and disappeared into the crowd.

Violet pulled herself to her feet, pushing away the twinge of guilt—the man had only been trying to help her. Was the last of her . . . *humanness* truly gone? Was she like Nerva now, not much more than a cold, hateful vampire, a bitter, bloodthirsty creature without the capacity to care and who existed only for the pleasure of revenge?

Yes.

Maybe.

No—she would *not* be like that, she wouldn't *let* herself.

"Damn it," she whispered a final time.

And turned around to go back to the boy.

Violet started walking, first quickly, then trotting, then finally outright running, leaping down the stairs and back into the subway. She was painfully aware that she'd taken too long to come to her decision, surely the security teams were practically on top of Six already. But things were still quiet, notably free of screaming or gunfire— maybe their orders from Daxus had changed, maybe they were only going to retrieve the child and return him to the ArchMinistry or the Laboratories for Latter Day Defense, back to the science lab where he'd been born and bred, a reintroduction to life as a lab rat. It wasn't much of an existence, but it was better than nothing, and if they were intent on bringing him back, surely they knew how to stop whatever was in his blood—

Someone she couldn't see shouted a string of words over the heads of the knot of people in front of her. Violet managed one more step forward, then the unmistakable sound of machine-gun fire shattered the dankness of the afternoon subway, immediately punctuated by the startled screams of people on the sidewalk. Violet froze, then hurtled forward, shoving people aside as she tried to see beyond the growing crowd of people gathered around a couple of security team men and something crumpled on the sidewalk. She elbowed past the last line of gawkers and sucked in a burning lungful of air as the thing on the sidewalk filled her vision, momentarily blotting out everything else in her life—

The small, bleeding body of a boy wearing a blue jacket.

The world went on around her, but all Violet could do was stand there, paralyzed. Had she really failed, after coming this far? Had she really let this happen because she could think only of herself and her so-called mission, that useless, personal pilgrimage of revenge that she had cultivated for so long? And had it cost this sad and lonely little boy the only thing in the world he had, that he had *ever* had—

His *life?*

She stood there with a hundred other passersby and watched as the security team soldiers clustered around the pathetic little body. The entire time, all Violet could think was, *It should have been* me. *It should have been* me. *It should have been ME!*

"It's not him."

One of the team members' gruff voice cut through the fog bubbling through her brain and for the first time Violet registered that the man was holding a scanner over the dead child's face. Her eyes widened, then she instinctively looked down at the sidewalk, as though one of her shoes—even though she was wearing boots—was untied, turning her face in any direction but where one of the guards might look over and see it. Before the soldiers dispersed, she saw that it wasn't Six at all, just some poor, hungry street beggar who'd thought finding the blue jacket on the edge of the trash receptacle had made it his lucky day. Now he was nothing but a corpse, and even the security team that had mistakenly killed him couldn't be bothered with gathering up his remains and seeing to a decent burial. The bastards looked down at him, then turned and started scanning the crowd as they sought their real target. God, but this world was getting to be a colder and more savage place with every passing minute.

Careful to stay unobtrusive, Violet took a couple of steps to the rear and blended back into the onlookers, barely hearing their grumbled comments about the street child's death and the uniformed men who had murdered him. Nothing much would ever come of it, anyway—humans were big on talk but small on action. That much had been obvious from the way the civil rights groups had failed miserably to defend the Hemophages. Violet wasn't going to be like that—she'd made the decision to give up bombing the ArchMinistry in favor of saving Six, and that was exactly what she was going to do. She just had to find him, and logistics demanded that he couldn't be that far; she'd start with the row of vending machines where she'd last seen him. All little boys loved ice cream, and while it was a long shot that he'd still be there—she really figured he was too smart for that—it was as good a place as any to start her search.

But the vending machine area was empty, at least of anyone resembling the little boy for whom Violet searched. There were no security teams converging on the area so far, so something must have managed to break their signal lock—too much concrete, one of the two-hundred-miles-an-hour trains, an electrical burst from the tracking satellite. Whatever it was had left them with only the last known description of the fateful blue jacket. Violet cared only that it had done the trick; now she just needed to find the boy and get him out of here.

But which way would he have gone? For a few seconds she turned back and forth, mired in uncertainty. Then something on the ground caught her eye, a thin, gold object shoved against the wall over by the entrance to the lower subway tunnels.

Her bracelet.

Violet didn't bother to pick it up as she dashed into the tunnel—she probably wouldn't live long enough to go shopping again, anyway. It wasn't that long of a distance, but it seemed like miles, pushing through more and more people, dodging around shopping bags and briefcases that were probably full of business papers relevant to a world in which she no longer belonged. But the boy wouldn't be here, not in the midst of this crush of people—although his life span had been short so far, he had learned too much for that and he was smart enough to know that out in the open like this he was nothing but machine-gun fodder, a target easily locked on and eliminated. No—he would go for something more clever, something hidden and not so easily accessed. Something small—

The catwalk.

With a quick glance around to make sure no one was watching or following her, Violet slipped onto one of the concrete catwalks that ran on either side along the track and headed deeper into the dirt-encrusted darkness of the train tunnel. Stretching ahead of her for as far as she could see were evenly spaced lights, but they did little to break the long, gloomy expanse of the train tracks. Each light, nothing more than a dull, bug-filled dome over an energy-saving bulb, was positioned over an alcove large enough for a worker to slip into as the train passed; inside each alcove were iron handrails set into the concrete walls, and the workers needed these to hang on to since the train's momentum could easily suck a man right off his feet. Violet figured that some of the alcoves would have doors leading to maintenance tunnels or storage areas, but she had no idea which ones actually did. That didn't matter; if she had to, she would check every single one in case Six was hiding inside. The distance between alcoves wasn't far because there was damned little time from when a person first heard the train coming and its actual arrival, and safety—*survival*—depended heavily on how fast you could get to those precious handrails.

But Violet needn't have worried. There was no sign of an impending train by the time she'd sprinted her way around several curves and finally spotted the boy several blocks ahead. Yes, he was definitely smart—there was no way the security teams' trackers could lock on him this deeply beneath the earth and the thick layers of concrete and metal overhead.

Of course, there were always the manholes.

As Violet moved faster to try to close the distance between them, she saw Six suddenly pause beneath one of the metal coverings. She frowned and tried to step up her pace, but it was difficult—the catwalk was narrow and slick with dampness and layers of old mold. She felt like she was slipping backward with each step, or at least going in slow motion, and when the child came to a full stop and craned his neck to see upward, she knew something was dreadfully wrong. He was standing in a shaft of hard, white light, almost like a spotlight. But there shouldn't be any light coming down from the manhole cover, those were supposed to be *closed,* and as Violet desperately tried to stretch an extra inch or two into her stride and slipped precariously on the thin ledge, she found her voice and called out to him—

"Six, *please!*"

And, as so often happens when the nightmare that's

called life is at its most difficult, something so much worse manages to take place.

Nerva.

Although Violet had used her own Gravity Shifter any number of times, she'd never been in a situation where one had essentially been used against *her*—she hadn't even known Nerva had developed one that could process so much weight. Now, stunned and still too far away to be able to do anything about it, all she could do was keep lurching forward as she watched Nerva calmly crawl through the open manhole, walk down the rounded side of the subway tunnel, and yank Six off his feet. It was a horrifying thing to see, like Nerva was some kind of giant, predatory spider in the darkness, but Violet wasn't sure who was more frightened—Six or her. The child must have been paralyzed with fear, because he made no sound at all as he hung from Nerva's grasp for a split second, legs and arms dangling limply over the tracks; then he was dragged up and through the manhole, and he disappeared into the circle of brutal, overhead light.

"Six!" Violet screamed.

She closed the final yards just in time to look upward and see Nerva's dark and not at all remorseful grin centered in the light of the street, silhouetted by the daylight behind it. "Sorry, V."

Self-preservation instinct kicked in and she dived for safety, narrowly escaping the sudden spray of machine-gun fire he sent through the hole. She flattened herself against the curve of the filthy wall, then jerked around the edge and into the nearest alcove as the bullets chewed up the concrete surface and sang off the metal train tracks. She'd pocketed her dark sunglasses back on the platform so she wouldn't seem odd to the other passersby, and now bits of concrete mingled with the bullets' spark showers and sent little star blossoms of light against her painfully sensitive eyes. By the time Violet rubbed them away, Nerva and the boy were gone.

And the hunt was on.

SEVENTEEN

Violet didn't give it much time—less than sixty seconds—before she decided she was clear, then she found and activated her own gyroscope. Sixty seconds . . . only a minute, but as she was scuttling up the side of the tunnel, then pulling herself out of the manhole, she was acutely aware that every second counted. Was Nerva going to kill the boy outright, or take him somewhere else? Nerva was already a wanted man and would be shot on sight if the security forces ever caught up with him, so why not just go on and do it? The notion of secreting Six away didn't seem logical—back in the conference room, Nerva had proved his intent when he'd pulled out his laser pistol and, he thought, killed the boy right there. If he truly wanted to murder the child, why hadn't he simply leaned through the manhole and gunned the boy down where he stood? No, something had changed—there was something else going on here, something she didn't know about.

Nor did she care.

Right now, all she wanted was that child. What happened after that . . . well, it could be negotiated.

Standing sideways on the subway wall, Violet jammed her sunglasses into place, then catapulted out and onto the street. A careless thing to do, and for her trouble she nearly got run over by a motorbike; the driver swerved and cussed her soundly, shaking his fist as he sped away. Violet ignored him and frantically scanned the street, but Nerva and Six were nowhere in sight.

She spun helplessly, feeling her anxiety spiral to the point where she wanted to simply fold in on herself. She wasn't sure how far they'd gone underground, or even in what direction. At least she'd been out here long enough for her eyes to adjust a bit; the sky over the intermittent buildings was a merciful shade of gray, layered in clouds that made the whole light-sensitive thing a bit easier to take. One side of the street was virtually empty—industrial, in fact. Somewhere along the seemingly directionless turns of the catwalk in the subway the world overhead had gone from bustling downtown to dirty manufacturing, a change that wasn't at all uncommon in the larger cities where rich neighborhoods could border on noisy airports and the seedier areas, such as this one, could be the backyard to cemeteries.

Such as the one across the street.

Nerva was headed into it now, dragging the boy along with him. Six wasn't fighting . . . but he wasn't cooperating, either. He was letting Nerva drag him along like some kind of life-sized, tangled-up marionette. The two figures twisted through the poorly maintained tombstones, all marked with the yellow and black biohazard symbol that identified them as victims of the Hemophage virus.

Violet started to dash across the street, then gasped as the boy surprised Nerva by suddenly twisting out of the vampire's grasp. He spun and ran for it, but he didn't get far. A pair of Nerva's soldiers—Violet had thought she'd taken care of all of them, but like flies, they seemed to come from nowhere—slipped in front of Six and blocked his way. With vicious speed, one of them reached out and slapped the boy, hard; he reeled backward into Nerva's outstretched hand and Nerva buried his fingers in Six's collar and hauled him along like a misbehaving dog.

For a moment, Violet's fury at the way the child was being treated blotted out everything—reason, sight, the *world.* When the red cleared from her vision she was already on the move, pounding across the pavement straight for the three Hemophages and Six. She didn't get very close, though—when they spotted her, one of the 'Phages yanked out a machine pistol and sent a deadly spray of bullets toward her, forcing her to duck and roll along the chilly, rock-strewn ground. The gunfire sounded like high-speed, pounding drums, the sound bouncing from building to building in the deserted industrial area. When Violet dared to raise her head again, the vampires and the child had once again disappeared into the sea of headstones.

She scurried into the cemetery, moving low and fast and working her way through the tall, desolate grave markers. It was such a depressing, soul-depleting place, a small but powerful testament to the millions who had fallen victim to the Hemophage virus, and the overcast sky just added to the morose atmosphere in the cemetery. Everything around Violet was a bitter reminder of the fate of her brethren and of her own impending death, and had any of the uninfected—those with the power and the

money and the resources like Daxus and the ArchMinistry—
worked to combat it? To find a *cure?* No . . . they had
only exterminated. In another ten or twenty years, unless
a miracle happened, the Hemophage virus would be
eradicated like so many other diseases. That, in itself,
was not a bad thing, but did they have to murder all of its
victims, too?

Violet swung around the corner of a double tombstone
and abruptly stopped, melting back into the concrete
camouflage provided by the wide stone wings of the
double-angel display on the top of the grave markers.
There, at either side of an overgrown, narrow rock pathway, were Nerva's two Hemophage soldiers. She had
never seen these two before, and they were grinning
widely, showing their confidence that she was nothing to
be bothered with when faced by the two of them. One
was tall and thin with long, lank dark hair, the poster
child for a nearly anorexic cocaine addict. The other was
like his negative image—platinum-blond hair cut short
and spiky; washed-out blue eyes peered at her above his
black sunglasses and his skin was so white it seemed
transparent in the gray light of day. Both of the men had
let their incisors grow long enough to hang out below
their upper lip. They curled their lips at her now and
showed their teeth, bright white and sharp like young,
ignorant puppies. In Violet's eyes, they were next to
useless—immature and foolish men more in love with
the vampire lifestyle than with survival, more concerned
with their carefully stylish hair and designer clothing
than reality. They wouldn't care about either for much
longer.

"Where are they?" she demanded. It would be stupid
to beat around the bush.

The taller of the two lifted his lip even more, creating an exaggerated sneer. "As if we'd tell *you.*" When she stepped toward him, he lifted his chin arrogantly. "Think what you're doing, V." He spoke like he knew her, but she wasn't lulled by the false camaraderie. Soon this baby vampire would be nothing more than the next statistic in the long line of today's deadly tally. "It's not Blood Chinois you're dealing with anymore."

The second one nodded and lifted a finely shaped dark eyebrow. "We're as fast and as strong as you." His voice was full of smugness.

Violet's mouth stretched into a dangerous, mocking smile. "Yeah . . . but are you even one-tenth as pissed *off?*"

But he had other things in mind than trading words. The roundhouse kick he sent toward her head was like lightning . . . but it still wasn't fast enough.

Fueled by rage and her inexplicable desire to protect Six, even as much as she didn't understand it herself, her retaliation was vicious, even for a vampire. She didn't care if she got hurt—there was little anyone in this world could do to her physically that would equal what had been done to her emotionally, anyway. That utterly callous attitude came with certain advantages: if she took a blow, it didn't matter; if she hit someone so hard she hurt herself, she didn't feel it. A flurry of strikes, a series of rapid-fire kicks, and it took her all of thirty seconds to wipe out both of them. When the fighting was done, Violet stood over their broken, bloody bodies, victorious but breathing hard and knowing that each time she did this, she lost a little more of herself and what small amount of time she had left in this world. But that didn't matter either—it was fitting even if it didn't make sense to spend that time and body energy trying to gain a few more hours of existence for a doomed human child. A person had to fight for something in his or her life, and it had been too long since she'd been fighting for a doomed cause. She had thought she'd lost everyone worth loving a long time ago; finally she again had someone for whom she could be a champion.

Where to go now? She scanned the grim-looking tombstones, then her gaze stopped. About forty feet farther down the path, exactly in the center of the cemetery, was a small and picturesque stone chapel. Despite the neglect this gathering place for the dead had undergone, this tiny building was still a haven for anyone—doubtful—who might come here to mourn or visit those who had passed on. The outside surface was made of smooth, rounded river stones, the kind you didn't see much in the more modern metropolitan cemeteries. The roof was made of heavy, iron-colored slate tiles, and it ran to a peak in the center, then up to a short steeple like an old-fashioned country church. At the very top of the steeple was a crucifix that in a burial place for Hemophages mocked the stupid old legends. Snowball bushes, their greenery ratty-looking but their flowers blooming magnificently, flanked the closed, unassuming wooden doors in the center of its front wall. She could smell their heavy, rich scent all the way out here, and it was to this little chapel, Violet realized, that the path she was on had led all along. Maybe her *life* had been designed to do just that—cycle around and bring her right here. Destiny wasn't something that was always clear to the common person.

Despite her recent victory, Violet approached the chapel cautiously. She'd already once wrongly assumed all of Nerva's henchmen were dead, and while she'd won the last battle, the war was far from over. The chapel itself wasn't a big building, but looks meant nothing in the world of the dead—maybe it had an underground area, or passageways that led to catacombs much like those from the Ancient Ages, the ones that had been lined with the skulls and bony remains of thousands who had died centuries before. From where she was, Violet could only see the front—there might be a long, narrow extension in the back, an add-on built specifically to house coffins and which disappeared into the trees that backed up to it. As her hand closed over the tarnished, old-fashioned handle and her thumb pressed down on the latch, she knew she'd have to be very, very careful.

She pushed and the right door opened smoothly and silently, as if it had been recently oiled. An interesting concept, since it wasn't safe for Hemophages to be seen in public anymore and no uninfected human would risk venturing into such a dirty place as a Hemophage cemetery. Once she was fully inside, it only took a few steps for Violet's eyes to adjust to the darkness, maybe two more for her to realize that the statues lining the walls weren't statues at all, but Hemophages, standing absolutely still, seeking refuge from her and the humans in the outside world. Really, it was the perfect place and the perfect type of camouflage.

She watched them with narrowed eyes, but when no one came toward her she went farther inside. There was something in the center of the chapel, something large and dark and round—a well, some kind of historical marker that had long since had the plaque denoting its original human history ripped away. The building had originally been constructed around it, but now it was going to serve a different purpose. There had once been a bucket hanging beneath the opening's roof, probably a replica restrung on a new rope. The bucket had been ripped away and Violet glimpsed it off to the side, where it had been tossed against one wall after Nerva had sheared it from the rope. In its place was Six, the remaining rough hemp tied tightly around his waist; he hung there like a sack of rice, swaying slightly. The scene was disconcertingly close to a hanging, where the body sways gently back and forth, pushed by some unrealized breeze. The other end of the rope was wrapped around Nerva's hand and he grinned and jiggled it playfully when he saw Violet. He'd pulled off his sunglasses in the dark room and a sort of manic glee shone in his ink-colored eyes. He jiggled the rope again and it slipped a couple of inches; Six gasped as he dropped slightly and Violet growled and automatically took a step forward.

"Huh-uh!" Nerva said sharply. This time he let the rope slide down a good half foot, stopping it with a jerk that made the rope dig into the boy's stomach. A small, involuntary cry escaped Six's lips, then Violet saw the muscles in his jaw grind together. Incredibly, the boy was trying not to show his fear as he shot Nerva a dark look.

Violet froze. If she rushed Nerva, he would let go of the rope and Six would likely plummet to his death—she had no way of knowing how deep the well was, but it was a good bet it went down at least sixty feet and perhaps as much as two hundred. There might be water somewhere at the bottom, and there might not. Even if there was, who could say the child knew how to swim? The odds were highly against it.

On the other hand, if she didn't try for it . . . well, what good would it do to just stand here? Time—and life—was ticking away and Nerva was just evil enough to drop the child anyway. After all, hadn't he wanted the boy dead all along?

Keeping her face carefully expressionless, Violet reached under her coat and drew a pistol out of a flat-space holster.

Nerva only grinned more widely at her. "Gunfire will attract the human security teams," he reminded her. He jiggled the rope again and although Six didn't make a sound, Violet's heartbeat jumped for him in sympathy. "You might win the battle, but you'd lose the war, V."

He was right, of course—and she'd thought the very same thing less than two minutes earlier. Besides, if she got pissed and shot the bastard just for the fun of it, he'd let go of the rope and Six would be killed anyway. Without taking her gaze from Nerva's, Violet grimaced and tossed the gun aside in exasperation. For a long moment, she just stood there and stared at him. Her mind worked furiously, turning over option after option like a computer working out the moves in a chess match. She had never been so trapped before, never so caught in a battle she couldn't find a way to win.

Well, except for when she'd been told she was infected with the Hemophage virus.

Damn it, if Six was going to die anyway, if there really was *nothing* she could do to save him, then why not die trying? And she would take Nerva and as many of the others with her as she could, her way, without intervention or misguided assistance from the humans who so despised her and those like her. The way of blood and steel rather than firepower.

This time, when she reached inside her coat, Violet's hand came back out with a long, carved steel katana in it.

The response from the Hemophages stationed around

the chapel was instantaneous—swords sang out all around her, the blades glittering in the muted light from the high, stained-glass windows along the chapel's side walls. Ignoring them, Violet focused on Nerva, but before she could leap for him, he held up his free hand. "V, wait." He sounded almost pleading. "Don't you realize what this child has *in* him?"

Her fingers gripped the sword's handle, trembling with anticipation, with the urge to kill. The metal warmed in her grip, thrumming with the energy bleeding off her body. "I don't *care* what he has 'in' him," she growled.

"It's not a vampire antigen," Nerva said quickly. His gaze flicked from left to right, making sure his soldiers stayed put. Violet knew he could call them down upon her with the merest blink of his eye. It was inevitable. "It's a *human* antigen," he continued. "Lethal enough to kill every human on the planet!"

Violet's eyes narrowed until they were nothing more than slits. What kind of talk was this? Trash, that's all, just more bullshit to stall the eventual bloodshed. *His* bloodshed. "I don't believe it," she said. "Why would humans create a human antigen?"

Nerva smiled but it was edgy, trembling nervousnessly. Even so, his fingers playing idly along the rope that controlled Six's life . . . or death. Whether he convinced her or not, he knew he held Six's life in his hands . . . literally. "Sweetheart, humans have been busily devising more and more effective ways to kill each other since the beginning of time." He licked his lips, his tongue momentarily probing the ends of his incisors in an oddly erotic gesture. "Why do I or even you care *why?* I just intend to help them finish the job."

Violet stared at him, unsure. Even now, after all this

time, it was so . . . *strange* to think of life as her against *them*, against the "humans." What Nerva was saying now just fortified that—he talked as if humans and vampires had been warring for millennia, but she had been human less than ten years ago. He had, too. Did he truly want to kill all the humans? If he did, that would effectively end humans, uninfected or otherwise, as a life form on this planet. It was unthinkable. Because really, wasn't she still just that—a human, but one with a disease? To kill off *all* the humans couldn't be right, it *couldn't* be. If he did that, their existence—*everyone's* existence—would suddenly shorten to a mere ten years, and that was assuming the vampires were unaffected by this ultimate weapon. And didn't people have a right to live longer than that?

"Why . . . didn't you tell me then?" she asked. It wasn't much of a question, but she was desperately trying to stall for time. God, she needed time to *think,* to work this out in her head and try to figure out the right thing to do. What was right and what was wrong, who should live and who should die—how had the responsibility to decide this on such a grand scale fallen on *her* shoulders?

"Because, darling, I didn't know." Nerva lifted his chin haughtily and gave her an oily smile, then shook his head. His long, curly hair flew around his head, making him look like an unruly wolf. "In the form of Daxus, the humans have offered us a most tempting proposal," he continued. "One that would finally even the odds for us." His gaze was piercing and the hint of a sneer tugged at one corner of his mouth. His expression said she should have known better. Violet's stomach twisted; she just hated to be in a position where this bastard could lord it over her. "So just walk away, V. *Walk away.*"

Suddenly, something high on the wall behind Nerva lit

up. Violet's gaze shot to the source of the light, then stopped. It was a clock that she hadn't noticed before, its mechanism built across a window of stained glass that matched the ones on the side walls. The clouds outside had finally parted and the sun was now bathing the clock window at just the right angle to throw Violet into a bright, multicolored spotlight. She turned her attention from the clock back to where Six dangled over the well and he caught her eye, then looked down at his feet. To the other people in the room, it looked like nothing more than her giving the boy a visual farewell before making her exit; only Violet saw him quietly push off his left shoe. It dropped unnoticed into the dark hole of the well and Violet's gaze cut back to the clock. Time seemed to slow and she counted in her mind—

One one-thousand

Two one-thousand

Three one-thousand

Four one-thousand

Five one-thousand

There was a faint *smack* as the boy's shoe finally hit water somewhere out of sight. It took her three more seconds to estimate twenty-seven armed Hemophages between her and where Nerva was holding Six's rope over the well.

Without a word, Violet brought her sword up and spun it expertly in the air in an outright challenge.

Nerva's mouth dropped open and his eyes widened. "Are you *insane?*" he asked incredulously.

As he had done only a few moments earlier, Violet lifted her chin with more confidence than she actually felt. "You need him more than I do," she said flatly. "You won't drop him."

The dark Hemophage's lip curled and his fingers went white around the rope in his hand. *"End her,"* he hissed.

A dozen of the Hemophages in the chapel charged her, springing from the long shadows against the wall like greased streaks of black. As they closed around her, Violet spun in the midst of them almost lazily, letting her mind and body go on instinct, parrying blows and striking in return with an almost ethereal precision. The kernel of doubt she had felt a few seconds ago bled away like water escaping a sponge. Such foolish, foolish brethren she had; by now she would have thought they'd known they could never win. Or maybe, like her—until she had found Six—they fought because they had nothing else left to live for. What a shame that your existence was so cheap that you could find no reason not to die.

The fight was over quickly, almost *too* quickly—she hadn't even worked up a sweat this time. Violet raised her head, then looked at Nerva from beneath half-lowered lids, and she knew, she *knew*, what he was going to do. He didn't disappoint her.

The vampire's teeth drew back in a grimace that was nothing short of vengeful and his face contorted with hatred. He knew she would be too fast for him, so he wasn't stupid enough to think about it or give her time to get ahead of his actions. He just . . .

Let go.

Six cried out as he disappeared below the lip of the stone wall surrounding the well. The rest of the Hemophages in the chapel lunged at Violet, swords slicing through the air all around her. Now that she knew it was there, now that it consumed her whole *world,* Violet could hear the damnable clock ticking over her head as each second went by. It sounded more like cymbals in her brain than anything muted or soft, like huge waves crashing against rocks—

Tick—

Crash!

Tick—

Crash!

TICK!

CRASH!

—with each one getting louder than the one before it.

She ran through the remainder of Nerva's Hemophage soldiers like a shark churning in a sea of bloody chum, taking down one group, then another, then another, each more viciously than the last, never forgetting the clock and the timing of it all, how absolutely *crucial* it was for her to be at the precise spot at the precise moment—

And finally, at the very last instant, only Nerva stood defiantly before her.

His blade whipped forward to meet hers and Violet easily swept his steel away with a strike that twisted her wrist and yanked the sword from his hand. It clattered off and was lost amid the bodies; Nerva spun and stared at her, his face twisted with more hatred than she had ever seen even as he realized he was looking death in the eye. In a final act of rebellion he spit at her face, but even that was denied him as Violet yanked her hand up and caught the saliva. His eyes bulged, then she slapped him, smashing his own spit against his cheek—

Right before Violet turned her sword and nearly decapitated him with its edge.

She stepped calmly through the spray of Nerva's blood and just barely caught the rope as it jerked wildly in the air. For a heart-stopping moment it ran through her fingers like a snake made of fire, then her hand closed around it, her skin smoking as she fought to ignore the pain and stop Six's descent. It was agony against her palm, the flesh blackening and filling the air with the sickly scent of cooking meat. Violet's teeth clenched and she squeezed her eyes shut; she would not give in, she would not let go no matter how bad the pain, she would not—

Until, mercifully, the rope finally yanked to a stop within her grip.

Without opening her eyes, Violet began hauling the child back up, hand over hand, ignoring the agony across her palm every time she switched hands. She could tell from the way the rope felt against her uninjured hand that there he finally was, rising above the edge of the well and swaying from side to side. When she opened her eyes, her gaze met his; his eyes were wide with fear and relief, and when Violet pulled him over the side and set him on solid ground, he threw himself forward and wrapped his arms around her, holding on as tightly as he could. She jerked and started to pull away, then just surrendered and held on with everything she had. Thirty-six hours ago she would have never imagined she would hold a child like this. "I'll get you fixed," she promised as he buried his face against her shoulder. Violet bent her head until her cheek pressed against his close-cropped hair, and she could feel his tears smearing against the skin of her neck. "I'm going to get you fixed . . ."

And, kneeling in the middle of the blood-soaked floor of the tiny chapel, Violet held him until his tears and sobbing finally stopped.

EIGHTEEN

Garth and the tractor-trailer were gone.

With Six at her side, Violet stood in the middle of the field where her comrade had been only a few hours earlier. "Gone," she whispered to herself. Her fingers tightened around Six until the boy's smaller ones squirmed in discomfort. "He's *gone*." On the one side, she couldn't believe it, but on the other . . . of course he was gone. Hadn't she called him herself and warned that there might have been a trace, telling him to move as quickly as possible? Garth was no fool. There was too much at risk. He would have taken her words to heart and moved out quickly, had probably had the tractor and trailer on the road literally within minutes. The fool here was her, for even thinking that he would still be here and . . . what? Waiting for her? Going to somehow fix everything at the risk of his own life and one of the extremely precious mobile lab and weapons storage units? Highly unlikely.

What now? Well, they would just have to move on themselves, keep going until . . .

Until . . .

Violet turned to look back at Six. The boy had pulled out of her grasp when it had become too painful and now she realized he'd dropped back a couple of yards, wandering off to the left. Her gaze locked on his face just in time to see him stagger slightly; his eyes met hers, then fluttered and rolled back into his head. She hurried toward him and got to the child's side just as he sagged to the ground and started to dry heave. It was a heartbreaking thing to watch as he bent over and retched, but there was nothing Violet could do to help, nothing she could offer that would bring him any kind of relief, no medicine to stop the nausea. Her sad and sorry best was to drape her arm across his shoulder and feel his small body shudder as he tried uselessly to vomit up the nothing that was inside his stomach.

Finally, Six found the strength to raise his head and look at her. His red-rimmed eyes were watery and all the rest of the color had washed out of his face, leaving his skin as pallid and gray as the bottom half of the meta-crystal still hanging around his neck. The top half of the stone was a troubling shade of black that was rapidly moving downward. "What's wrong with me?" Speaking was such an effort that his words came out in a gasp.

All Violet could do was shake her head and not respond. She didn't have the heart to look the child in the face and tell him he was dying. Ages ago, when she had been a nurse, having a cold and detached bedside manner had never been her strong point. "Can you walk?" she asked after a while. His answering nod was weak but determined. "Come with me," she said, and helped him to his feet. He stood on his own, eventually, but he was shaking at best and Violet wasn't sure how long it would be before she'd have to carry him. She would answer his question—she *had* to—but not out here, not in the open where they were vulnerable to an attack from the human security forces at any time.

Garth's location, now forever history, had been on the north edge of the city, where the lakefront curved around to the north and looked back at the downtown area. That northern location had given them that spectacular night-time view of the fireworks celebration, but it also hindered, too—now it took Violet and Six almost a half hour to get back to a more populated area so she could find a place for them to hide out. It was funny how the world had evolved—the urban sprawl had evolved out. Now there were overpopulated cities or desolate fields, and not much along the lines of a middle ground. It would have been nice to leave the people and the anxiety-ridden crowds behind but still be able to find a good place to hole up while they waited for the end, but that was nothing but a wild fantasy—in the real world, the best Violet could offer the boy was an abandoned tenement about six blocks into the city zone proper, just to the west of the old line of elevated tracks that hadn't been used in decades. It wasn't much but Violet couldn't hold out for better; Six's condition had gotten noticeably worse, and if she hadn't been holding on to him, the boy would have been staggering at her side down the pitted sidewalk like an adolescent drug addict.

With a quick glance behind them, Violet kicked in one of the side doors and dragged the boy inside, hopefully, too quickly for anyone passing by to notice or care. There wasn't much traffic around here, at least not of the desirable kind, but people were naturally curious . . . no, naturally *nosy*. Violet slammed the door shut again, then pushed Six in front of her and into the disused lobby area, where she could make him turn and look at her. It was a good-sized room that was filled with smashed-up furniture, old trash, and construction debris, but it was also blissfully quiet and empty of anyone else. Dust motes spun in the air where their footsteps had stirred up the layer on the floor, and off to one side was what was left of an old reception desk. It was curved and wide, with a cracked and pitted dark green granite counter, and in a previous lifetime it had probably been something special to see. Now Violet blew at the heavy mantle of dust on the surface, then picked Six up and sat him on the counter so she could look him in the eye. Gray light washed over them, diluted by the heavy layer of grime over the bank of high but unbroken windows along the ceiling line above the entry door. Violet wished it were dark instead of daylight; she'd done so many difficult things in her life, but this had to rank up there with the worst of them. She almost couldn't bear to meet his trusting gaze.

Six sat there in front of her, his shoulders slumped with illness and fatigue while his feet dangled limply over the counter's edge. He looked so afraid and confused, yet at the same time she could see the hope in his eyes, the heartbreaking glimmer of light that told her he believed that somehow she might be able to fix everything. How could she tell him the truth? Where to begin to explain the unexplainable.

Finally, she said, "Don't you see?" A foolish, incomprehensible start—of course he didn't. She was dying now, not just her physical self, but her emotions. All on behalf of this small, strange boy, and she was so very, very angry. "Don't you fucking *see?*"

But no, he didn't. He only looked at her expectantly, silent and waiting. And as before . . . *trusting.*

"That . . . *mechanism* inside you," she croaked. "The thing your father put in you. It's an antagonistic protein, very precise . . ." The word "father" was bad enough, but the rest . . . Her words faded. He was so very young. Was she being too technical? Did he understand any of it? Violet wasn't sure—her doubts about whether he was able to comprehend what she was saying went all the way back to when he'd finally started talking. But back then didn't matter right now; but she had to keep going, had to *try.* He had a right to know, damn it, to know it *all.* "It's . . . it's going to shut you down, Six."

Violet stared at him and he stared back, but still, he refused to say anything. He looked like an oddly blue-eyed rabbit frozen in the headlight of an oncoming motorcycle—paralyzed and terrified but physically incapable of doing anything other than staring at its impending death with huge, liquid eyes.

God . . . he was going to make her *say* it.

She took a deep breath, and the air rushing down her throat felt like it wanted to strangle her. "It's going to . . . *kill* you, Six. Just like that boy in the station." Did he remember who she was talking about? "It's going to kill you, unless I . . ." Her voice cracked and Violet struggled to steady it again. She was the adult here; she was supposed to be the stronger of the two of them, no matter what happened. "Unless I can figure some way—" She spun away. The hurt was too great—she simply couldn't meet his huge eyes any longer. "I just need a little *time,* damn it!" Her gaze flicked wildly around the abandoned lobby. "If I could have some time, just a little more *time*—" Abruptly she stood up straighter. "Wait here," she ordered the boy, then strode away.

A few yards down was a doorway to another room, just as trash-filled and empty of life as the lobby, but at least here she could have a little privacy. What she was about to do would take acting skills she wasn't sure she possessed, and Violet didn't need the boy staring at her and wondering what the hell she was up to, didn't need him afraid that she had decided to violate his trust.

She yanked out her phone, then jammed her mouth-mic into place and reverse dialed the last call that had come in; an instant later, Daxus's image flashed on the screen. She didn't find it at all surprising that he might have been expecting her call.

"Hello, Violet." His voice was smooth and disgustingly oily, the tone of the ultimate life insurance salesman.

"Come in on Three-D," she ordered.

Violet saw Daxus smirk at her for a moment, as if she'd said something he found mildly amusing and was deciding whether or not to laugh, then he shrugged and did what she'd asked. Instantly it was like he was there with her in the dirty room of the tenement house . . . well, maybe not. It ruined the effect to see the man's impeccably-attired figure sitting in front of her without the requisite chair beneath him—inanimate objects in the room with the call transmitter never came through on the transmission. As a result, Daxus's image looked like it was semifloating in midair, doing an impossible balancing act with his rear end extended and one leg folded over the other. This was why most people made sure they were standing up when they made a 3-D call; otherwise, they just looked ridiculous. Apparently Daxus simply didn't care, and somehow that didn't surprise Violet either.

"Well," he said. The amazed expression on his face was so fake that Violet would have laughed if it hadn't been a matter of Six's life or death. "This is a surprise."

Violet raised one eyebrow. "I doubt it," she said sarcastically. She paused for a moment, trying to figure out how to put this, how to negotiate. Who was she kidding? Daxus wasn't interested in negotiating, so why waste words? "I want you to turn off what was put in the kid."

Daxus leaned back on the chair that Violet couldn't see and folded his arms. Even floating awkwardly in the air like that, he looked absurdly comfortable. How she wished she could reach out and knock his ass onto the floor. "I wish that were possible, Violet," Daxus said. Like everything else, the sympathy in his voice was exaggerated. "But there is no cure for the antigen."

Violet swallowed. "I don't believe you." She couldn't. She *wouldn't*.

Daxus stared at her implacably. Didn't anything ever bring up a reaction in this bastard? "Just bring him to me, Violet. If you don't, the antigen will die with him and neither will be any good to anybody."

Violet's hands curled into helpless fists, the fingernails digging brutally into her own flesh. "You said you were his *father*, for God's sake!"

Before Daxus could answer—and she doubted she would have liked what he had to say, anyway—another voice cut across the room. "No, Violet." When she whirled, Violet saw Six standing shakily in the doorway. All the color had washed out of his face and one hand gripped the woodwork as he tried to steady himself. "I don't have a father," he said. She could tell from his voice that he was trying to be tough, and strong, and all the things that a boy of his age *should* be. All the things with which he had absolutely no experience. He sure was a fighter.

"No?" Daxus's 3-D gaze cut to the boy and now he sounded even more amused, like he might break out in a chuckle at any moment. As Six wobbled forward to stand by Violet, without giving any hint about what he was going to do, Daxus reached two fingers under his chin and pulled a piece of white material up from his shirt collar. As she and Six watched, Violet realized it was a sterile surgical mask, the kind typically worn by everyone nowadays. In another moment, the man had it covering the lower half of his face so that only his dark, glittering eyes showed.

Standing beside her now, Violet saw the child shrink back from the anonymous-looking image a few feet in front of him. The boy's eyes widened in fear and his hand came up and covered his mouth before he could cry out. The gesture made Daxus grin—Violet could tell what his expression was by the way the mask pulled tightly across the sides of his broad, square jaw. When Daxus pulled the mask back down, she saw that she hadn't been wrong. "More precisely," Daxus said smugly, "he's my *clone*. Number six in a series of eight."

Oh, if only Daxus were in the room with her so she could wipe that smirk off his face. Instead, she could only snarl helplessly. "What the fuck *difference* does it make? He's a child, you monster!"

Now Daxus laughed outright. "Monster?" he repeated mockingly. "And what are *you?* More to the point—what is *he* to you? Some sort of bizarre surrogate?"

Violet's mouth worked but she couldn't reply, and Daxus's mouth stretched into a scornful smile—he knew he'd hit a nerve. "A vampire and a dying human child— what a pathetic picture." His expression relaxed, the leer melting once more into his polished businessman facade. That was instantly replaced by an expression much more sly. "I'll make you another just like him, Violet," he offered. "One that's not . . . *broken*. You won't even be able to tell the difference, I promise." Amazingly, his voice softened to a tone that might have held a tinge of sympathy. "I might even be able to help you with that problem you have in your own blood."

She was so furious that her pulse was pounding in her temple—

thud

    thud

        thud

—nearly loud enough to block out the words coming through the phone's microphone. Quick as a snake, her fingers reached up and snapped on a button on her mouth-mic, then she snatched up the telephone and snapped its connection into place. "Trace!"

Again, Daxus's image laughed at her, this time with undisguised entertainment. "Why track the call, Violet? I'll *tell* you where I am. I *want* you to bring me the boy."

But Violet only looked at him from beneath half-closed eyelids. Her voice was low and very, very dangerous. "I'm going to bring you a lot more than that, you *fuck*."

His lips tightened—finally some reaction. Perhaps there was a bit of human left in him after all, some little part of him that rightfully still knew how to feel fear. "I have seven hundred soldiers here with me," he told her rigidly. "What do you really think you can do against that many men?"

Violet's lips stretched over her teeth as she stood perfectly still in front of the Daxus 3-D, but her expression wasn't even close to a smile. "I can kill them," she said flatly.

The complete confidence in her voice must have registered somewhere in Daxus's brain, because she could see his cheeks go pale, the loss of coloring even more apparent beneath the crown of his nearly black hair. He leaned forward quickly on his invisible chair, obviously reaching for his phone, but it was too late—a schematic of the city flashed on the screen of Violet's cell, a small, blinking red blip indicating the origin of the call. Violet tilted her head and glared at Daxus. "The ArchMinistry," she said. She didn't need to say anything else, so she just killed the call and watched Daxus's suddenly terrified image wink into nothingness.

NINETEEN

Violet stared hatefully at the spot where Daxus's image had been, then inhaled sharply and turned back toward Six. "Let's go meet your maker—"

The boy was lying on the floor in the doorway.

Unmoving.

Crossing the few yards to get to him was like moving through ancient, chilled amber—it took hours, days, *years*. All the muscles in her body tensed and Violet felt the uneven tile beneath the soles of her boots as she moved toward Six, but at the same time, she *didn't*—every nerve ending in her body had gone suddenly, shockingly numb. She could walk and balance but she had to do it on autopilot, had to allow her body to lead the way and hope she didn't fall, because if she did, the notion of putting out an arm to stop herself was unfathomable—her thoughts were far too focused on the boy for anything else to interfere.

Her knees bent, then thunked hard against the cold floor. She didn't feel the pain of the impact. "Six?"

No response. She could see his chest still rising with each inhalation, but each movement was jerky and un-evenly timed with barely an exhalation to push the used air from his body. If he heard her at all, it was clear he didn't have enough strength to answer.

Violet didn't have time to waste on being afraid or try-ing to help him when she had no medicine or tools—if she wanted to make any kind of a difference, she had to move and she had to move *now*. There was nothing she could do for him anyway short of CPR, and he wasn't at that point yet. Violet bent and gathered Six in her arms, then stood and strode out of the abandoned building, try-ing to stretch each step out and gain as much distance as she could without actually running—bouncing his body up and down was the last kind of trauma he needed right now. To the outside world it was bad enough that she was carrying a child in her arms who was as limp as a dead body and clearly sick; running would *really* call attention to the two of them. All it would take was one call—some-one on the street who wanted to be anonymous and was using a disposable cell phone—and she'd have the Arch-Ministry's security forces chasing down the two of them with nothing but extermination orders. At least if she could get him to the ArchMinistry there might be hope. Damned little of it, but still . . .

It was still overcast outside, cooler and a little dimmer now as the afternoon wore on and the sun went lower in the sky. She wished it were full dark—the night could be so forgiving of those in the world who were forced to hide from the rest of humanity. The neighborhood here was still empty and quiet, but a short couple of blocks would take the two of them back into the city proper, and then she could bet her little "package" would be noticed right away. No . . . she had to find another method of transport.

But that would be easy. After all, she was what she was, and the people walking around here?

They were only humans.

≽

"Hi there."

The guy looked up in surprise and his sale, a prostitute with a scarlet-colored wig and a strapless red velvet minidress, backed away and took off—but not before snatching a packet of something unidentifiable out of the guy's hand. He glanced at Violet, then at the fleeing street girl, and gave a sign of disgust.

"What?" he said. "You a cop?"

He was a nice-looking guy and Violet could see how he made his way—once he drove that car of his, a black Viper Series XII, out of this 'hood and back to the New Gold Coast area, he'd look like just another one of the up-scale young lawyers who lived, worked, and played up there. Apparently the legal field wasn't quite cutting it, though—places like this held a little more bang for the buck as far as paying the law school loans.

Violet grinned at him, but it was anything but genuine. She'd left Six sitting propped up against a trash can around the corner, carefully concealed beneath an over-sized piece of cardboard, a piece of an old appliance box. It was a degrading thing to do to him, but it was the best she could offer on short notice. Stumbling across this idiot and his extremely nice ride was a piece of luck that she wasn't stupid enough to let pass them by. "Do I look like a cop?"

He eyed her warily and stepped back a little, moving to the inside of his still open driver's side door. Not good—he probably had a gun in there, something small and easily concealed that he could slide into the map pocket of the door and hide behind a few papers. The authorities would have liked to have everyone believe that outlawing handguns centuries ago had "fixed" the handgun problem, but all it had done was stop Mr. and Mrs. Average from being able to find one. The criminals would always have their sources, and this man was nothing but a really pretty bad guy.

"You could be," he said now. "They come in all shapes and sizes."

"True enough," she agreed. She tilted her head, trying to go for the innocent look. "But I'm not. I'm just looking to score." To add to the effect, Violet glanced around nervously.

He relaxed a little, but Violet could tell he was still a little hinky. She was still too far away to grab him before he could jump in the car and take off, and she needed that car desperately.

"Score what?" He had light brown hair, very clean-cut—that lawyer image again—and was dressed in very expensive, stylish clothes. Brown eyes, like his hair, but they were narrow and suspicious. He was probably a pretty successful drug dealer; at the very least he was smart enough to do his business elsewhere. The car was probably custom—it might even have reinforced doors to stop bullets. The thought made her want it even more.

"Look," Violet said and pulled her hand out of her pocket. The yellow card she held up was pretty standard issue, another one of those single use credit cards recognized by everyone. The bracelet she'd given Six back at the vending machines was small time, a little thing meant for incidentals like groceries and fast food. This yellow piece of plastic was serious business; like her coat, it changed colors, darkening as the balance got lower. That cheerful yellow color said she was toting an available balance of somewhere between ten and twelve thousand credits. It was a nice chunk of change, and if he was thinking about robbing her, he'd wait, because the card would require her to press a pre-coded PIN number onto the micro-keypad built into the back of it. On the other hand, if he thought he was gaining a new customer who was on the rich side, he wouldn't try for the thief route at all—it was much better to have a live one on the line than a dead one on the ground.

The dealer's eyes lit up unmistakably—greed was guaranteed to do that. "All right," he said. "I might be able to point you in the right direction."

Violet's grin got wider. She was only a few feet away from him now, and she stretched out her hand, offering the card in that universal *Charge it!* body language. "Maybe your direction includes Hot Ice?"

She was very close to him now, within a few feet. So close, in fact, that she saw his eyebrow shoot up. "Hot ice?" His gaze cut to the credit card still in her hand. "Not generally a pricey item."

"I know, and I appreciate your honesty," Violet said smoothly. "I'm looking to outfit a party."

"Ah." He nodded, then glanced back toward the trunk of his car. "Let me open—"

He never got to finish his sentence.

Violet despised drug dealers—next to Daxus, she thought they were the scum of the earth. Still, it wasn't in her nature to kill a man for his car, even a nice ride like this. Instead, she left him lying in an unconscious puddle back on the bad side of the invisible line that divided the 'hood part of the city from the better part. So much for street smarts—how smart could he have been to lay it all down for a pretty face and a brightly-colored credit card? He'd been so easy to pick up on, and even easier to take down—the overconfident criminals always were.

This car . . . now it was something. The automobile had fabulous speed and pickup—especially once she'd lightened the car's load by opening the trunk and dumping the twelve cases of various pills and sweets plus six hundred pounds of Chicago Black into an industrial Dumpster. Speed notwithstanding, Violet couldn't help but wish for something a little less conspicuous. In the end, though, it didn't matter what she was driving, because Violet had no intention of letting anyone, or anything, stop her.

The Viper's souped-up engine thrummed with power, and although she was already racing through the streets at eighty-plus miles per hour, the vehicle jumped eagerly every time she tapped the accelerator. It was so responsive that it reminded Violet of a big, nervous cat being held back by a trainer, a creature that wanted nothing more than to be let loose and *go*. Too bad she wasn't around a superhighway where she could enjoy it—there were too many people and too much traffic in front of her, and the city streets weren't built for hammering on the speed. She was already leaving a trail of accidents and angry drivers behind her, and no doubt more than a few furious pedestrians had called in photo complaints on their cells. That poor—*not*—unconscious lawyer turned drug dealer would eventually have to sort it all out. What a pity.

Violet glanced over at Six to make sure he was all right, leaving the navigation to the car's computer system. "All right" was a relative term—she'd leaned the seat back for him and he was splayed against its back like a limp, ill-used bundle of rags, a small, skinny scarecrow that had lost its infrastructure and was only a hair's-breadth away from completely falling apart. It hadn't helped to have him sitting on the chilly, damp sidewalk while she'd taken care of the dealer and done the car coup, despite the fact that it had only taken her five or six minutes, at the most, to pull it off. He was in such bad shape that the cold had settled into his flesh and turned his lips practically blue.

Her gaze checked the road needlessly, then dropped momentarily to where her phone was plugged into the dashboard jack so it could auto-plot the car's route to Daxus using the Viper's GPS computer. She could see their progress on the tracking grid screen, and it wouldn't be long before their arrival. Now, then, was the time to check the weapons inventory in her flat space arsenal . . . not that she had any doubt she'd have enough. A wonderful thing, flatspace: weightless and spaceless, able to provide her with a nearly inexhaustible array of killing implements at her fingertips.

"You can't make it in."

She jerked slightly at the sound of Six's weak voice, barely audible above the hungry growl of the engine. When she looked over at him, it seemed like his eyes were the only thing left alive in his small body; they glittered hot and cold as the lights from the passing street-lamps and never-ending neon signs flashed through the window, glittering even in the last gray shades of daylight. Nothing else on his body moved—just those eyes. Watching and judging. *Knowing.*

She scowled. "Thanks for the vote of confidence." She didn't say anything else for a long moment, then she added, "Haven't you been paying attention? Killing is what I *do*. It's what I'm good at. I'm a titan—a *monolith*. Nothing can stop me." Violet wanted to soften her expression when she looked over at him, but she didn't know how.

The boy only stared at her. Finally, he said, "I know. I can see it in your eyes."

She swallowed, hating herself. Hating the world. "Well . . . what fucking choice do I *have?*"

Six's eyes widened, as if he couldn't believe she didn't already know. "A very clear one," he said with a tiny nod. "To watch me die, or . . ." He nodded again. "Make me watch you do the same."

≫

The main entry gate to the ArchMinistry was open, a circumstance that was nearly unheard of. Violet could see why—on the other side of the square, Daxus was standing at the top of the stairs and waiting for her, heading a ridiculous mini-army of what had to be nearly a thousand soldiers. If it hadn't been for the smell of gun oil in the air and the dull gray of the countless weapons held at the ready, it might have been a beautiful sight, like something out of the history archives she had studied in school as a teenager. The ArchMinistry of Medical Policy itself was like a palace of lights and metal, seated dead center in a square that very much resembled the ancient palaces in the now disintegrated Soviet Union—Leningrad, perhaps. Like the dead royalty who had occupied such long-gone places, the people in power at the ArchMinistry had turned the buildings and grounds into something like a country unto itself, lording it over all who came within its purview.

But all that was about to end.

Violet would see to that.

The Viper hurtled through the front gate without incident, then went into a controlled power slide that stopped it some twenty yards in front of the waiting front lines. From her position, Violet could see that Daxus had placed himself where he would look like he was the head of everything, but he could still escape without incident should the battle go badly. Again, it was just like the battles of the ancients, where the king sits above everything and watches his men die before him, royal sword at the ready should he need to go in and personally save the day. In Daxus's case, his "sword" was cradled comfortably in the crook of his left arm in the form of a machine pistol, while his right hand curled around the grip of a smaller pistol. He might see it as ancient tactics—*if* the long-ago veterinarian was actually that well read—but Violet found it rather amusing that he had so little faith in his small army that he felt he couldn't just go on about his business and leave them to deal with a single female vampire—a sick one, at that.

She yanked up her phone and dialed him, and when the Viper had barely stopped its movement, the driver's door slid open and Violet catapulted out of her seat and faced the men a mere sixty feet away. On the surface they saw her armed with only a standard-grade machine pistol and a sword, but each and every soldier in front of her knew she was capable of much, much more. Daxus might not see it from his oh-so-lofty position, but from here . . .

Violet grinned as they stepped back, just a bit.

Despite the reassuring presence of his troops, Daxus sent her a look that made it clear he thought she was insane, then pulled a mouth-mic from his collar and snapped it into place. "Are you mental?" His voice rang clearly into her ear from the headset. "I—"

"The antidote," she interrupted rigidly. Her face was expressionless.

"I *told* you," he insisted and jerked one hand impatiently. "There is *no cure!*"

"Bullshit," Violet said crudely. "You wouldn't create a human-lethal antigen that didn't have an antidote you could administer to yourself and your people."

Daxus stared at Violet for a long moment, then a smile reluctantly played across his mouth. "Very nice, Violet. Well . . . yes. There *is* an antidote." He lifted his chin and looked at her disdainfully. "And yes, when I get the boy, isolate the antigen, and release it into the atmosphere, yes—anyone who wants to live will queue up daily at this door to get it."

Violet's mouth dropped open in amazement, but at least she finally understood why the man had taken her call rather than shouted his words over the heads of his soldiers. It'd be pretty poor policy to announce to your people you were about to dose them with something that was guaranteed to kill them, and then make them pay for the privilege of staying alive. But . . . his own race? "I thought we were the ones you hated," she finally marveled. "I thought *we* were the ones you wanted to wipe out."

From where she stood, she could still clearly see the hunger in his eyes, the *greed.* "What's the problem, Violet? You *were* . . . past tense. But now you and those like you are all but extinct." He lifted his shoulders and tried unsuccessfully to seem sad. "What's someone like me— a man with a job to do—going to use to keep order? This is a society that left to itself would sprint toward chaos like an Olympic event." He shook his head. "Oh, we did our job too well. Now we must make amends."

The muscles in Violet's jaw ticked with the effort it took for her to speak, but she was still able to get the words out. They sounded more like a hiss than actually talking. "You disgust me."

He shrugged. "It's a relative term. Just give me what I want."

Her mouth twisted into a sneer of anticipation. "Come and *get* it."

He glared at her for a moment, then suddenly jerked his arm above his head. The troops staggered in upward rows on the steps below him homed in on her position and fired as one, sending tens of thousands of rounds into her and the Viper parked behind her. Without a word, Violet dropped to one knee and used her sword to brace herself, leaning forward as though she were facing the vicious winds of an onrushing hurricane. The barrage of bullets seemed to last forever, thundering through the air with a roar loud enough to shatter unaccustomed eardrums and make the ground tremble. When it finally ended, when the last shell casing had fallen to the ground and the atmosphere was filled with smoke and the smell of gunpowder, the soldiers lowered their weapons and stared at Violet in amazement.

A few feet behind Violet there was almost nothing left of the Viper but shredded, smoking metal and shattered glass. Long ribbons of fiberglass, twisted beyond recognition by the firepower, swayed in the artificially hot breeze, while the countless bullet holes in the iron and aluminum parts of the engine ticked as the metal cooled and expanded.

Even so, Violet still knelt there, head down and unmoving.

Untouched.

Uninjured.

And smiling sadly.

Daxus stared at her, disbelieving, then his features twisted into a mask of hatred. Up to this point, he had simply stood back and watched the assault, trusting in the art of ammunition and the training of his soldiers, not to mention the completely mismatched proportion—one to a thousand—to eliminate the annoying little problem of Violet. Now that his plan had been foiled, he realized he would have to take care of it himself.

The lines of his soldiers parted instinctively as Daxus raised his own machine pistol and lunged forward, sprinting down the steps and holding his finger on the full autotrigger. His bullets razored through Violet's form and sent a thousand shining blots of firework sparks into the air as they pinged into what little was left of the car to her rear; with its tires long reduced to shreds of hot rubber, it rocked on its rims, bouncing back and forth with each burst of machine pistol fire.

At ten feet Daxus was convinced he had her. Flatspace technology was one thing, but force fields were still nothing but movie-based wishful thinking—it would take several more decades to get that engineering to work. Then he was five feet away, then three, and finally he was right on top of her and glaring at her as he made his machine pistol hammer another few dozen rounds into her head.

But Violet only looked up at him. "You won't have him, Daxus," she said softly. He had to lean down to hear Violet's words, and this close to her, Daxus finally realized he could see the faintest of shimmies in Violet's image.

His mouth worked, then his gaze cut to the car. The driver's window had been obliterated, of course, but when he sprinted over to it and waved away the gun smoke, he saw it.

Violet's phone, lying undamaged on the front seat. It was quite literally a miracle that it hadn't been blown into little more than plastic vapor and bits of wire.

Damn her. She had made him into the supreme fool in front of practically his entire regime.

"You *bitch!*" Daxus howled, then for no good reason he pointed the pistol at the device and fired. It blew into a thousand pieces and the image of Violet a few feet away winked out. All Daxus could do was spin helplessly in front of the car's pathetic remains—

And wonder where the hell Violet had gone.

TWENTY

Violet watched Daxus from her carefully concealed position in the lush, wet bushes just outside the front entrance, then pulled off her mouth-mic and disabled it. Nothing more than habit, actually—with the phone now obliterated, it wasn't likely he or his security forces could track her anymore. And really, had she expected anything other than attempted death from Daxus anyway? Anything *better*? No, of course not. Well . . . maybe. Hope was such a tricky thing—it could spring up unbidden in even the most cynical of people. Like her, for instance, a woman who had once had everything she'd ever dreamed of, past, present, and future, and then had it yanked away forever by a sick, panicked man wielding an organism so tiny she couldn't even see it. Funny how that organism— the Hemophage virus—killed not just people, but hope itself. Or maybe, like the vampires in the ridiculous old legends, hope wasn't dead, just *un*dead, springing back to life at the most unexpected of moments.

After a few more seconds, Violet finally found the

courage to meet Six's eyes. She immediately wished she hadn't. In those clear blue irises, she saw everything she didn't want to admit—fear, defeat, helplessness. *Hopelessness.*

"There's just too many of them, V." The boy said the words gently, as though he were bringing the worst of news to someone who might break under its weight. "Just too many."

It was a crushing thing to give in to, but all Violet could do was nod.

⚡

Finally, the dismal sky had cleared up. Most of the clouds from earlier had been blown away by a brisk, chilly wind, but that, too, had faded; what was left in the sky looked like layers of thin cotton, cheesecloth worked apart by a baker's fingers. To the west, the rays of the setting sun peeked through the tall buildings and washed the sky in rare shades of pink and purple, making the clouds look like pastel-colored strips of fabric. Violet had never seen such a sunset except in coffee-table books, those oversized, expensive tomes full of magnificent photographs of a part of the western United States that she had never visited. Did places like that even exist anymore? Or had they been overrun by people and compounds headed by madmen like Daxus? She would never know. Even where Violet and Six were, in one of the concrete and metal playgrounds at Grant Park and the lakefront— about as far away from the western sun a person could get in Chicago without actually getting doused with Lake Michigan water—the ground and grass were tinged with pale color; Violet wished she could see the water of Lake

Michigan on the other side of the Outer Drive, wished she could take Six to watch how the sunlight sparkled on the ceaselessly moving waves. But no—he was too fragile, too tired. Even if she could carry him without being obvious, the sun would disappear for the day before she could get him over there. At least she'd gotten him this far, to the real-life equivalent of the picture he'd once handed her beneath the dazzle of a late-night fireworks display.

Balancing herself, Violet gave the merry-go-round another spin, making Six scream with breathless laughter as he whirled around. At first she'd been afraid to put him on it, terrified that he couldn't hold on. Rather than see him tumble, a little improvising with her jacket and a couple of knots had saved the day. Now the boy was enjoying himself, and she was enjoying watching him . . . as much as she could, anyway, knowing that she had failed him in that most important part. He was going to die—there was nothing she could do to prevent it. But, damn it, at least he would have had a little bit of the boyhood that Daxus and the circumstances of his own existence had denied him.

She let the merry-go-round slow enough so that Six could catch his breath—the boy was laughing so much that he was nearly delirious. When it came almost to a stop, she saw Six pull on the knot she'd tied around his chest so he could slip off and lie on the grass. She went over to be with him, and for a couple of minutes, the child just sprawled there with Violet right next to him. His chest still hitched with giggles as he looked up at the color-splashed sky, the patches of pink and purple interspersed with that special, brilliant shade of blue that precedes sunset only on the rarest of days when the air is

heavy with the perfect amount of moisture from an earlier drizzle. Eventually, Six's laughter faded and he made
no sound, just stared into the blue nothingness as if he
could see something she couldn't.

The silence made Violet look over nervously. "Are
you okay?"

He blinked. "No," he said quietly.

Violet jerked and sat up. His honesty was startling and
carried a reminder she hadn't really wanted. She had
monitored it now and then, of course, but sometime during the last hour or so the meta-crystal on Six's chest had
slid away from the ominous dark gray that the stone had
been holding all day and gone fully into undeniable, irreversible black.

But Six only turned his head to look at her and smiled
faintly. "No—it's all that spinning. I think it made me
sick."

Violet relaxed again, returning his smile as she let herself lean sideways onto the cool, soft grass. Her stance
was a lie, of course—she knew full well that Six's time
was heartbreakingly short. But she wouldn't show it,
wouldn't ruin the last bit of time he had, especially when
he was so obviously enjoying himself. She propped herself on one elbow and locked away her emotions as she
watched Six fold his hands behind his head, savoring
the way he was immersing himself in this mini-slice of
the world. She could see the deepening blue of the dusk
sky reflected in his eyes as he watched the sun go down.

"Sunset," he said suddenly, as though he could read
her thoughts. "My first." She started to agree with him,
then realized that for all her efforts, she couldn't speak
around the lump that had blossomed in her throat. His
first, yes . . . also his last. Even though she'd known all

along that it was coming, the realization was a brutal one, crushing in its implications, in the way it highlighted her failure to help him. His next whispered words chased away the thoughts of self-recrimination and brought her mind back to completely focus on him. "But it's so . . . dark."

Violet pressed her lips together, fighting for enough control to speak without having her voice shake. "Six—"

"So dark," the boy repeated, and this time she could barely hear his voice. He sighed.

"Six?" She yanked herself upright, then pulled the child into her arms. His body came up and onto her lap without resistence. Still warm, but little more than a rag doll covered in human skin. "Six?"

His eyes were looking right at her, but there was no . . . focus in them. No *seeing.* "Smaller," he breathed.

"Six!" she cried.

"Violet?" His blinded eyes fluttered. "Are you there, Violet?"

Abruptly the breeze picked up again, chilling the tears that were suddenly sliding down her cheeks. "Yes, Six." She brushed a tiny, wayward lock of his hair off his forehead, a small clump of hairs that had somehow escaped the barber's scissors. "Yes, Six, I'm here. I won't leave. I'll never leave."

The breeze churned up another notch, turning into a surprising, sudden wind. The quickest of glances gave Violet the reason—human Security Enforcers, dropping from half a dozen sleek, black Whisperjet helicopters that had lowered to a hover position over their small spot in the park. She wasn't surprised and she hadn't forgotten; so much had happened since Six had come into her life, and she'd had so many plans, but she'd never found a way to get that damnable tracking device out of his body. She turned her gaze back to Six's face and saw his brow furrow at the noise of the copters. She stroked his cheek, wishing she could do something, *anything,* to bring him more comfort than her sad and helpless presence. "Violet? What's that sound?"

"Nothing," she said as reassuringly as she could. The skin of his face was cold and clammy, chilled almost blue by his dropping body temperature and the roar of the helicopters around them. It was obvious that he didn't feel it, and that made her heart crack a little more. She was forcing herself to stay outwardly calm, to keep anything but serenity from coming through in her voice. It was all so much—the boy dying in her arms, Daxus, her own impending death, the soldiers about to descend on her. She could no longer tell if the high-pitched whine in her ears was her own nerves or the scream of the helicopters' engines. "It's nothing—just the wind."

One by one, the shadows of the Security Enforcers fell over her and the boy, like overlapping waves of impending doom edging closer and closer. Violet was glad Six couldn't see them, that even though his eyes were open, his vision of anything in this world had already been obliterated. He was so innocent. He shouldn't have to spend his last coherent moments in this world full of terror.

Six's small hand moved up and waved in the air for a moment, the fingers fumbling until he found the top of Violet's hand and covered it. "It's okay, Violet." She felt a sob rise in her chest and barely ground it away as Six's eyes fluttered and closed. Now she could barely hear him. "It's okay," he repeated.

And then he was still.

Violet hadn't even realized she'd started crying until a teardrop ran from her eye to hang on the end of her nose, then slipped off and dropped onto the child's nose. It was too late—he was beyond knowing how wretched she felt to lose him. Instinct made Violet want to wail Six's name, scream it as loud as she could, but the commonsense part of her logic reminded her that it was useless, a wasted expenditure of energy that her body simply no longer had. No amount of calling out or grief would make this small boy see her face or hear her voice anymore, and it certainly wouldn't bring him back.

Now she and Six were surrounded so tightly by the soldiers that she couldn't see past the ring of bodies. They pressed forward, stupidly unaware of just how quickly she could kill them. A lightning-fast jump to her feet, a faster unsheathing of her sword, and the first two rows would fall over like a house of cards.

Or maybe . . . these assassins had more awareness than that which she credited to them. Kill them? She didn't want to kill anything, or anyone. This boy . . . he was *it,* the last of everything that had been worth fighting for in her miserably short life. If it had all come down to him, and if she really had given everything she could to help him and failed . . . well, then why bother with any of it?

In her peripheral vision, Violet saw a sudden break in the circle of soldiers pressing on her, then Daxus pushed his way inside. Although he loomed over her like some kind of silhouetted vision of destruction, Violet felt oddly unaffected by his presence, completely unafraid. After all, what could he now do to her that would hurt her more than Six's death? She had endured so much, but the end of this child . . . well, it was the end of her.

At Daxus's side were a couple of Hazmat-outfitted paramedics. When they saw the child lying limply on Violet's lap, they surged past the Vice-Cardinal and bent over him. It only took a moment for both of them to lean back and look up at their boss. "It's too late," one of them said. Behind his breather mask, his voice sounded foggy and cold, like a subdued underwater echo. "The boy's gone."

It was getting darker by the moment but Violet could still see Daxus's face fold into a scowl and his cheeks as they flushed nearly crimson. "Damn it!" He jerked his head up, then swept his gaze over the park area. "Quarantine the corpse and get it back to the ArchMinistry as soon as possible. Maybe we can salvage something out of it."

Violet tried to hang on to Six, but she didn't seem to have any strength left—she was so *tired*. Her hands were pushed aside by the gloved Enforcers, then Six's body was lifted off her lap and whisked away. She was through fighting, through trying. She just sat there, silently marveling at how strange it felt to have the warm weight of the child gone from her lap. It brought to mind memories, old and indescribably painful, from many years ago. So many hellish things that she'd rather leave unremembered, especially when she had so much more in the present than she could handle.

One of the Security Enforcers stepped forward. The patch on his uniform marked him as the unit's leader and his long weapon gleamed in the dusk. "And her, sir?"

Daxus whirled so quickly that the heel of one boot sent up a clot of dirt and grass. He glared at Violet, so furious that for a few seconds he couldn't even speak. Then, without bothering to say anything, he leaned over and reached around the soldier's main weapon, yanking the sidearm out of the leader's leg holster. Without hesitating, he turned back and delivered a vicious kick to Violet's ribs, a blow hard enough to send her toppling sideways onto the grass.

But Violet was still done with the fighting, with the struggling. Now she just lay at Daxus's feet, her body curled in a fetal position. The grass was cool and prickly against her cheek; she could smell the greenness of it, the undercurrent of earth, and that made her think of the passage from the old Christian Bible.

Dust to dust, ashes to ashes.

As Daxus stared down at her, Violet turned her head just enough so that she could catch a last glimpse of the setting sun. It looked like a bloody red ball as it finally dropped below the top of the last building blocking it from view. The only thing between her and it was a single, crumpled piece of paper.

Not surprisingly, Violet's disinterest just made Daxus all the more angry, and he leaned over and pointed his borrowed gun at Violet's head.

Nothing.

He pushed the barrel against her scalp, hard enough to be painful, wanting to see a reaction from her, *needing* to see her fear. But to Violet's eyes and mind, that was just what she felt . . . nothing. Her world and emotions and everything that she was had finally been narrowed down to this single, defining moment. In another two seconds her life would be over and the last thing she'd ever see was that sad scrap of paper lying just a few inches away from her face on the ground—Six's drawing of his mythical playground. It rocked in the wind, but she could enjoy her last, satisfied smile. At least in that she hadn't failed him.

"You've outlived your usefulness," Daxus ground out. And shot Violet in the head.

≷

Daxus turned his back on Violet's body and stepped toward the Security Enforcer whose gun he'd taken. He tossed the weapon back to him, then distastefully stripped off the gloves he was wearing—they were splattered with Violet's infected blood—and dropped them on top of her body with a grimace. "Have an Incendiary Team sanitize this area immediately," he ordered. He sent a last, withering look in the direction of Violet's corpse, then strode away, heading for his waiting vehicle. There was a lightness to his step that he hadn't felt in months—Violet had been the sharp thorn in his lion's paw for longer than he cared to admit, and at last, *at last*, he was rid of her for good. At this rate, it wouldn't be long until he was rid of *all* the damned vampires.

Behind him, the paramedics were spraying Six's body with safety preservation foam; the fluffy white material began to harden almost instantly around the child's form and ultimately took on a shape like a gigantic cocoon. When the sterile foam had solidified enough, they pushed handles into the sides of the mass and lifted it, hustling toward another larger wagon.

Standing outside his armored limousine as the white-suited Incendiary Team took their places around the playground, Daxus let them set up to do their dirty business while he carefully sanitized his hands—twice. Then he directed his attention to his waiting security and medical staff. "Get the boy's body on ice and prepped for disassembly," he instructed. "We'll go in for salvage at daybreak." The other members of the sanitation team didn't need supervision or specific orders to know what to do, so without another word, Daxus climbed into the vehicle and shut the door firmly behind him.

As he and his team members pulled away, a wall of blue and orange flames surged high into the air behind them and separated them from the view of Violet's body.

TWENTY-ONE

*A*bove *the mouth that Violet knew and loved so well,*
her husband's black eyes flashed with indignation and
anger. Furious color rode high in his cheeks and his dark
hair was wild and standing in unevenly cut tufts—once
such a fastidious and appearance-conscious man, since
they had locked her away, Song jat had put little thought
into what others thought of him or how he looked. In-
stead, the doctor had devoted himself to two things: his
career—the thing that had always both distracted and
upheld him—and trying to find a way to get his wife back.
His job kept him from going completely crazy, gave him
something on which to focus so much of the frustrated en-
ergy that was generated by their situation. That was
probably a good thing, but this battle in which they were
entangled didn't look to be getting any better.

Ever.

Right now Song jat was again at the detainee hospital
and well into another of the seemingly endless arguments
he'd been having on a daily basis with everyone from

physicians to nurses to orderlies, all of whom seemed to have unlimited amounts of that one thing he wanted so badly: time with his wife, Violet. If he could have found someone on the custodial staff with the right set of keys, he would have tried buying his way into the isolation ward . . . or maybe he would have simply hit the man over the head and taken the damned things.

"But she's my wife!" The last word came out at nearly a bellow, and other people—staff, patients, he didn't care who—turned to look in his direction. The woman in front of him—he didn't have a clue what her name was because there had been so many and he'd stopped bothering with the damned name tags months ago—looked appropriately aghast at the volume level of his voice. Her response was immediate and full of righteousness, the tone of someone who believes to their bones that the person with whom they're having a confrontation is dead wrong, even when they have nothing on which to base their own position but the statements of someone else "in charge." "Dr. Song jat Sharif, you need to restrain yourself!"

"I'm a fucking medical professional," he snarled. "I don't need to restrain myself. You haven't let me see my wife in four months!"

The other doctor drew herself up stiffly and still refused to move out of his way. Her face was like stone and she kept moving from left to right across the floor, continually managing to keep her body squarely in his path so that he couldn't duck around her. "Doctor, we are at the early stages of what appears to be an epidemic of potentially staggering proportions." She waved her arm vaguely in the direction of the quarantine area, and Sharif's gaze cut again—as it so often did—to the heavy locking system across the double doors just behind her. "As one of the ground zero victims, your wife needs to be studied. Seeing you could cause an emotional reaction that could adversely affect her condition."

Song glared at the woman, then he lost patience and bodily pushed her aside so he could press the front of his chest and face against the unbreakable one-way viewing glass that separated him from Violet. He could see her right there—so damned close—but he couldn't touch her, couldn't talk to her. God, he needed her so badly, and he could see she needed him. His pleasantly plump wife had disappeared; now Violet's form had thinned out and her eyes were open, but she clearly wasn't aware of him or anyone else; her pupils were half-dilated and glassy, heavy with drugs. Her arms lay limply at her sides and her waist, the bulge of pregnancy gone and covered by a sheet. Even so, he could still make out the lines that showed through the fabric, those of thick leather restraining straps around her wrists. Why did they have to do that? Unless—

"What about the baby?" he demanded suddenly.

"I'm sorry, Dr. Sharif," the woman said. Her voice was bland, as though she were reciting a well-rehearsed litany, one she had practiced many times in her head in case the need arose. A well-rehearsed lie. "Your son was lost due to complications shortly after birth." She didn't blink, but he thought he saw her hold on the clipboard she was hugging tighten. It was a nearly imperceptible movement, a barely noticeable whiteness in her knuckles, but he had been a doctor for too long to miss that oh-sorapid bit of body language.

He stared at her as the weight of her words rolled over him. Son? He and Violet had had a son? God—he'd never even been told, never even known that Violet had gone into labor. He should have been there with her, to hold her hand through the pain, to see the child come into the world, to hold him. If the boy had died, he and Violet should have been given the right to bury him, to name him and lay him to rest. They had plots, for God's sake, a family mausoleum. And Violet had been so healthy—what kind of complications?

Without warning, Song Jat yanked the clipboard out of the doctor's stiff grasp and riffled through the medical charts on it, turning his back and shouldering her aside when she tried to grab at it from around his back. "Dr. Sharif—that is confidential medical information!" The tone of her voice had changed to desperation.

Confidential? Bullshit—this was his wife's chart. And Song Jat had been in the medical profession for decades anyway. He was very good at what he did, and he only needed a few seconds to scan the charts and find the information he wanted. When his gaze stopped on the words, it took another second, a strange sort of fast eternity, for their meaning to sink into his brain. Then he gasped.

"Fentanyl?" For a long, terrible moment, the stress of the truth he'd discovered made it impossible for him to make the connection between this one particular word and its consequences. He couldn't recall what exactly the drug did, why they would give it to . . .

Of course he couldn't remember. He didn't want to.

But he knew.

Oh, God, he knew.

"Fentanyl," he repeated. He felt like he was moving through ice as he turned to face the other physician. She seemed to be paralyzed with fear as she stared at him

with wide eyes. Her throat worked but no sound came out of her mouth. Where the skin on his face had previously been red from anger, now Song jat felt the blood drain away. His flesh went cold and he took a step toward her.

"Security!" she finally squawked. She stumbled backward, trying to stay out of his reach as he brought up the clipboard and shook it at her.

"You euthanized my son with Fentanyl!" Song jat was more than bellowing now, he was screaming, his lungs and body feeding the rage and hate he'd bottled up for so long.

"It's not our policy!" the doctor shouted back at him. While she might have just been trying to be heard over his fury, raising her voice only fueled the fire in Violet's husband. "It's that new Office of Medicine and Politics! He was born with the disease—what kind of life would that have been?" Her voice rose another notch, climbing into screech range. "Security!"

"Violet!" Dr. Sharif yelled suddenly. Still hanging on to the medical clipboard, he shoved the doctor aside when she tried again to take it from him, this time knocking her sideways hard enough to make her stagger against the wall. Then he was there, at the glass window, and using the clipboard to hammer wildly on its surface. "Violet—VIOLET!" In another five seconds, two burly security guards were grabbing him painfully by each of his arms and hauling him backward. The clipboard clattered to the floor and he still kept shouting—

"Violet! VIOLET!"

—but she didn't hear him, she didn't see him, she didn't do anything. He kept his gaze pinned on her face as they pulled him away, trying to wait, trying to hope for some response, but there was nothing—

"Violet! Violet!"

She heard the voice from far away—farther away than anyone, human *or* vampire, had a right to hear, in fact, as though someone had implanted hearing aid amplifiers deep into her eardrums.

The voice was annoying, and she tried to ignore it. After all, she was cool and comfortable, and it was dark; it had been a long time since she hadn't woken with a hundred nagging aches and pains from the constant physical battles, with the sting of God's good sunlight trying to blister her oversensitive eyes. Such a very, very long time since she had been . . . *content.*

But . . .

"Violet?"

. . . that voice, that damnable *noise.* It would not be ignored. It just kept nagging at her, on and on, worrying at her consciousness like one of those nasty, yappy little old-woman dogs that chews at the ankles of visitors. Against her will, her eyelids fluttered and tried to open, but she squeezed them tightly against the irritating noise.

"Violet!"

But that movement—the one, stupidly simple little act of using the muscles in her eyes and face—was the worst possible thing she could have done. It was her undoing, that dreaded straw that broke her iron will. It was the thing that forced blood to circulate and muscles to wake, that made sensation spread through the surface and subsurface of her skin until awareness crawled across her nerve endings edge to edge as though she were a giant spiderweb.

"Violet!"

There was no fighting it, no resisting. At last, she surrendered to her body and let her eyelids slowly open.

There was a shadow across her vision, someone standing over her—a hazy figure who seemed vaguely familiar. That face . . .

"G-Garth . . ."

Her voice was a raspy whisper, like air being forced through a grate clogged with old debris. He stared down at her, his eyes wide and eager as he scanned her face and examined her pupils. He looked absurdly pleased. "Your recuperative powers are nothing short of amazing," he said with a wide grin.

Violet blinked back at him. The edges of her eyelids and her lashes were crusty and slightly sticky, as though she'd been sleeping for a very long time. Her body felt stiff and cold, unwilling to move. None of it felt good, none of it felt like she would have expected. "Is this . . .?"

"Heaven?" Garth's grin faded into a small, sad smile, but his eyes were bright and victorious. "No." He inclined his head toward something to his left and Violet forced her own head to turn so she could see. The movement was grating, like making a wheel turn on ungreased gears, and there was pain in her head, intense enough to border on vicious. Still, her vision was finally clearing and she could just make out two wriggling forms on the floor—humans, bound and gagged and wearing Incendiary Team uniforms. The avenues of thought were stuck on foggy in her brain, but things were grudgingly beginning to sort themselves out . . . and she wasn't very pleased with the results. "We very thoughtfully subbed in for the Incendiary Team," Garth told her, then shrugged. Now his expression had morphed into an obviously pleased-with-himself grin.

"But . . ." Violet's voice was still raspy, more like a

croak; she cleared her throat and tried again. "I thought . . ."

"You were," Garth said and nodded energetically. Feeling had returned to all her limbs and for the first time she registered that he was wearing a surgical outfit, full green scrubs and latex gloves that he now peeled off and tossed into a trash can she couldn't see. "Your heart stopped three times," he continued. "But four hours of surgery and . . ." He shrugged and lifted his chin almost arrogantly. "A lot of prayer, and we managed to save your life."

She stared at him and wished vaguely that she could slap that satisfied look off his face only because it was so irritating. Then, as the full realization of what had happened went through her brain, she pushed up on her elbows and made herself sit up. Pain zinged through her scalp like a thousand nasty beestings. "You . . ." It took an immense effort just to swallow. "You *what?*" She managed to swing her legs over the side of the cot on which she was lying. When she found her footing, somehow Violet got herself in an upright position. "You stupid, stupid son of a *bitch!*" Fury rammed through her, but she wasn't sure what was stronger—her rage or the monstrous ache in her head. She reached automatically for her hair and found it covered by a bandage, then she balled up her fists and tried to hit Garth. Surprised, he dodged out of the way. "I was *there!*" she cried. She flailed at him again, but her strength wasn't there yet, she was still in too much pain to be effective; he avoided her next swing, then caught her by the wrists and let her rant. "I was fucking *there,* and you brought me back!"

Garth's expression twisted into something she couldn't read—pain, regret, she didn't know what. He let go of her wrists and she grabbed him by the collar and pushed him backward, using her weight to slam him against the wall. She felt the vibration run through the incision in her scalp, and it was just another ugly, jolting reminder that she was still alive. Garth grunted as the breath got knocked out of his lungs, but he didn't try to defend himself or push her away. "Why?" Violet demanded. "*Why? Explain that to me!*"

His blue eyes were wide and this close, Violet could see that now he was nearly crying. "Isn't it—" he began, then shook his head as his voice choked. His voice was thick with anguish as he tried again. "Isn't it *obvious?*"

She glared at him, eye to eye, then flushed and released her hold on his shirt. Her hands fell to her sides as she stepped back and her gaze on him changed into dismay. Dear God—

He was in love with her.

TWENTY-TWO

She and Garth faced each other outside the truck as she got ready to leave for the last time. He kept trying to meet her eyes, to pin her down with his pain-filled gaze, but Violet wouldn't do it—she knew better. Instead, Violet looked to the left, to the right, at the ground, up at the beautiful, star-filled night sky. Seeing that sky was nearly as painful—it would have been better had it been full of clouds, heavy thunderclouds ready to spit lightning and spill cold, cold rain on them both. To stand beneath a sparkling blanket of heaven with a man, a good one, who loved her, but whose love she could never return—God, Violet would have rather gone through the pain of dying again. And really, that wasn't so far off.

Finally, she gritted her teeth and let her eyes meet his. Instead of holding it, his gaze dropped to the meta-crystal he'd finally convinced her to wear; he reached over and touched it, and when Violet glanced downward, she saw that only the smallest sliver of white remained on one edge. Garth had performed a miracle in bringing her back, but even his miracle had its limitations.

"Violet," Garth said hoarsely, "since you left with the boy, I've been working like crazy. Just like . . . *crazy*." When she tried to glance away again, his fingers reached out and gently steered her face back to look at him. "What that kid wrote down . . . there's something *there*. I can *see* it, and maybe if you just stuck around—"

She shook her head and looked away again, staring at the ground. She didn't have to say the words for him to know that she would not be talked out of leaving. Not this time, not anytime. She'd lost too much, and she couldn't rebuild this time. If she did . . . well, it was nothing but a never-ending cycle of loss. She couldn't go through that again, even if she were able to survive. *Especially* if she could.

Garth's fingers had been resting on her forearm, and now he let them slide down so he could grasp her hand. His fingers squeezed hers gently and she could feel the desperation in them, the *want*. "In all the time I've known you," he said mournfully, "why won't you ever let anyone *in?*"

This time Violet did meet his gaze, didn't look away or try to downplay anything. "Because," she said simply, "these moments, as beautiful as they are? They're fucking evil when they're *gone*." She inhaled deeply, feeling the chilly air seep into her lungs and spread outward from there, like energy radiating from a power cell into a machine. She nodded at him, then eased her hand out of his and turned her back.

Without saying good-bye, Violet disappeared into the night.

≩

It was a stupid, stupid thing, but it had never occurred to Violet that they would have told her husband she was dead.

In retrospect, she'd been an idiot. Of course they would have done that—he was like a bulldog when he set his mind to something, and it would have been the only thing that could have stopped him from hounding them about releasing her. It would have also, at least in his mind, if not justified that made him accept the reason they had killed their son. She could almost hear the lies they would have made up, perhaps about how she had been one of the alpha victims and the virus hadn't strengthened itself fully yet, and so she had succumbed more easily, more quickly than the Hemophage victims who came later. He would have never dreamed that she could not only recover but escape the clutches of the ArchMinistry—

Just as she had never considered he might move on.

Time had been . . . different for her back then, a blur of faceless people and vaguely colored images, the stream of overhead fluorescent lights that looked like the white and colored ribbons of light in time-lapse photographs taken of congested city highways. Somewhere in that mental muddle she had gained strength and started struggling against it on her own, managing to avoid her medication just enough so that awareness could creep back in, then more and more. Not swallowing her pills, honing her acting skills so that even the experienced nurses couldn't tell that the slack-faced, dull-witted patient really hadn't been taking the medicine like an obedient

*little zombie. As time returned to normal, the waiting be-
came agony, the time spent lying in absolute stillness beneath the stark white hospital sheets a form of torture she
wouldn't have wished on anyone. Hers was a world of
white anonymity, where no one—doctors, nurses, aides—
talked about anything other than medications and the
virus, where nothing was decorated to denote the passing
of seasons or holidays and windows were a long-ago fantasy. It wasn't until later, much later, that Violet would
discover that it hadn't been months since her incarcera-
tion and her son's murder, but years, and that the rest of
the world, her uninfected husband included, had accepted her "death" and gone on about their business.*

*Their old apartment was empty, and the only indicator
that the building hadn't been simply abandoned was a
faded yellow real estate sign that hung askew in the bottom corner of the living-room window—*

FOR SALE! PRIME LOCATION!

*While that should have been a major clue, back then—
especially because she'd just regained her freedom—Violet had still been full of that crazy stuff called hope and
belief and love. Undaunted, she'd headed back to the
medical center, careful to stay camouflaged and away
from the security teams and police. She wasn't going to
go inside—never that—but if she had learned nothing
else from her imprisonment at the ArchMinistry, she had
learned patience. So Violet waited, seated in the shade of
one of the ancient, massive oak trees that lined the walkway outside the main entrance. It was actually nice, just
to sit there and enjoy the smells of the leaves and bushes,
of the recently mowed grass, to take in the sight of people
dressed in something other than hospital whites and isolation suits. It didn't take long—not going by what most*

people would have called that anyway—but Song jat had come out with too many other people, several other doctors and nurses. It had been impossible for Violet to approach because they'd moved to the parking area in a cluster and to follow would have forced her to walk past the parking lot's security checkpoint; there was nothing she could do but watch as her husband got into a black Mercedes-Benz and drove away . . . but not before Violet had a chance to jot down the license plate number.

With a little research—automobile license information was public, if you knew where to find it—Violet had her husband's current address. She didn't wait around or dwell on whether she should or shouldn't try to contact him. There was no question involved here: Song jat was her husband, her partner, her soul mate—the man with whom she'd once stood before God and their family and friends and pledged to spend eternity. The companion she'd breakfasted with each morning, the lover with whom she'd conceived a child. She'd meant forever back then, and she still did.

The address led her to a house in an upper-class neighborhood, an area a lot more ritzy than she and Song had been able to afford when they were together—that was good, because it meant his career was going well. The new house, which was second in from the cross street, was a little older, one of the classier ones around and built in the style of a Swiss chalet in a white and chocolate color scheme. Three stories and probably a basement, one of those tri-century dwellings of the reproduction period that had been refurbished with solar power to meet the modern energy and environmental requirements. It stood on a large lot but property was still a precious commodity, so it was fairly close to the side-

walk, probably to save yard room for the back, where it really counted. Violet couldn't help grinning as she imagined a patio with repro-Adirondack furniture and a fancy gas grill—he'd always loved to cook out.

The familiar kind of oak trees made a wall on either side of the lot and separated the property, throwing shade onto the sides of the house but leaving the front open to the cooler northern exposure. That meant the backyard would be bright and splashed with sun in the afternoons, and the thought made Violet's stomach twist a bit as she realized this was something she would never be able to truly share with Song. Had he put in a covered patio? It didn't matter; they would still have plenty of other good things in their life together. It might take a little effort to keep her hidden, but he was intelligent, well connected, and affluent, so Song would find ways to do it. After all, he loved her.

Violet made sure her sunglasses were in place, then turned onto the walk that led to the front door. She'd taken no more than four steps when the front door swung open and Song stepped outside. Her heart skipped a beat—he looked so handsome, just as he had the last time she remembered seeing him! His hair was still dark, free of the silver that had peppered his father's hair at a much younger age, and he'd clearly worked to keep himself fit and strong while she'd been in the hospital. She'd almost been afraid to see him for the first time, worried that he'd let himself go as so many people often did when a family member had a serious illness and they spent all their time at the hospital—she'd seen it hundreds of times back when she'd been a nurse.

He stopped on the porch and he was already smiling. Violet lifted her arm to wave but the return smile forming on her lips froze as he turned back toward the still-open door and ushered more people out of the house. Her hand wavered in the air and dropped back to her side as two small girls ran out on the porch. An instant later they were followed by a pretty young woman whose blond hair was cut in a short, expensive style that framed her face and accented her large eyes. Even from her position at the end of the walkway, Violet could see they were a startling bright green.

Everything in the world was abruptly blotted out except for the four people on that front porch. It was the perfect family picture—husband, wife, two beautiful children, framed by painted white posts on either side of a small front porch. Rosebushes bloomed on each side of the porch, the grass was green and lush, the heavily leafed oak trees rustled in the breeze. It was all so right.

Except it was also so very, very wrong.

Violet was paralyzed, trapped in place by her sudden inability to think, or breathe, or do anything. She wanted to run forward and shove the woman aside but she couldn't; she wanted to backtrack, erase her steps and what she was seeing, pretend it had never happened at all and that she had decided to let Song jat Sharif go on about his life and the business of believing she was dead. But she couldn't do that either, she couldn't undo. She couldn't do anything but stand there and stare stupidly forward with her mouth open as everything she had looked forward to—everything she had hoped—since her escape from the hospital disintegrated and burned away in the bright light of real life.

The girls, who were perhaps ages three and four, were laughing and dancing around their grinning father, then one of them glanced over and saw her. She stopped and tilted her head quizzically, and that movement, that tiny gesture, was enough to catch her father's attention and make him follow her gaze.

Oh no.

Too late—her eyes met Song's and his widened in astonishment and the realization of what—who—he was seeing made him jerk. His face drained of color and his mouth worked, and finally Violet managed to break her paralysis and start backing away.

"My God . . ." The slight breeze carried his shocked voice on the air currents and she heard it all the way out on the walkway, even though she was already nearly back on the sidewalk. "Vi?"

The woman on the porch had grabbed the two girls and was staring not at Violet but at Song, her expression a tortured mix of disbelief and pain. As Violet's had done years earlier, her life and everything in it was crumbling right in front of her eyes, destroyed in a single instant by the appearance of someone who, at least to her, was a complete stranger.

Violet could not let that happen.

"Violet!" Song screamed and bolted down the porch steps.

She turned and broke into a run.

"VIOLET!"

And that last bellowing of her name would be her final memory of the marriage between her and Song jat Sharif.

TWENTY-THREE

Violet had been in cruddier places, although at this particular moment, she really couldn't recall when.

This one was called the Contemplation Motel, which was an interesting name considering her state of mind. She hadn't realized that when she'd checked in—the stuttering LED sign on the corner just said M TEL, and it was obvious that the O hadn't worked in years. The tiny set of rooms was in a bad pocket of old housing just to the southwest of Chicago's downtown area, an eight-block square that the city's aldermen either hadn't gotten around to cleaning up or had used the funds appropriated for it to spend on other items of, shall we say, "significant" need. Those things probably included nice little powerboats on which to cruise Lake Michigan in the summertime, memberships in the exclusive Standard Club, or dinners at Tru's Restaurant or Spiaggia, where two hundred bucks was barely enough to get two people started on the way to the main course. Maybe the Contemplation Motel had once been an okay joint—it had sure never been as much as a two-star—but now it was a second home for synthetic drug traffickers, the streetwise ones who were at the midstep level, past the rookies who were getting started but proudly driving their first high-end automobile. The parking lot was a moving picturama of Mercedes, Jags, and the occasional Lexus, but at this point, the dealers still had to ferry themselves around; add three more years—if they didn't get gunned down by another dealer or the drug force—and everybody in the lot would have a driver and a bullet-resistant limo. And, of course, they'd be plying their trade a long way from the Contemplation.

Violet's room was . . . well, nasty. The sheets were gray and clearly not washed, and it stank of cigarette smoke and old sex. She found a couple of clean towels hanging in the bathroom and spread those on top of the bedspread before she sprawled onto it, flipped on her back, and stared at the ceiling. Like the walls, it was dirty and cracked, with black spots of mildew along the edges and old, dust-filled spiderwebs clumped in the corners. Cockroaches had been wiped out before she was born, but Violet had no doubt that this was exactly the sort of room in which they'd bred and fed in abundance. She'd seen pictures of them back in medical school because of the diseases they'd spread, and she could imagine them scuttling along the baseboards and searching for water in the tiny, greasy bathroom. She'd gone in there and caught a hazy glimpse of herself in the spotted mirror—tangled hair that barely covered Garth's stitchery, bleary, shadowed eyes—but she hadn't cared enough to clean herself up.

Next to Violet on the bedspread, which was made of some kind of coarse, unidentifiable material in a horribly outdated and dark pattern, was her cell phone, and for at least the fifth or sixth time, the damned thing began ringing. It made a tinny, insistent *ding*, but Violet didn't move—she kept her gaze on the ceiling and ignored the phone, too tired to even reach for it to shut off the oh-so-annoying sound. She could feel her hair—unwashed for several days now, it was dirty and tangled and matted with blood on the bottom layer—tickling the back of her neck, but the sensation wasn't at all pleasing. As she thought about *that* on top of everything else, the phone finally stopped ringing, and once more a sweet, extremely calm silence moved in to take its place. Oddly enough, the noise of the traffic was muffled in here . . . or maybe that wasn't strange at all, given the extra-insulated dark curtains and the heavy-duty steel door installed. Rah-rah for the hotel management—clearly they were up on protecting their chosen clientele from unwanted visitors . . . or at least giving them time to hightail it out the tiny bathroom window. After all, the motel's clientele was clearly important to them—who else but people who didn't want to be found would stay in a place like this?

Her cell phone began ringing again and Violet sighed but still made no move to answer it. She thought about breaking the thing, then dismissed the idea—that would take energy, and will, and she had precious little of either. There was, perhaps, just enough left of each to do what she had to do, that one thing that was irreversible—provided Garth didn't know where she was—and which would give her what she desired the most.

Release.

Ignoring the cell phone, Violet's fingers crawled over the bedspread until they brushed against the object she sought—a single bullet. It was a .357 hollow point—

outlawed years ago because of the danger to the police, but of course certain "organizations" still made them— and she picked it up and examined it for a moment, considering its smooth, deadly power, its simplicity. Loaded into the waiting gun and fired, the point would spread and by the time it hit its target—a millisecond later—the bullet's tip would be nearly a half inch wide. The entry hole from this would do what Daxus's standard-issue ammunition had failed to accomplish, and even Garth wouldn't be able to undo the damage.

Sweet, sweet *release*.

The cell phone stopped ringing—again—and Violet rolled the bullet through her fingers like a card dealer playing with a card, skipping it from one to the next, then the next. Finally, she picked up her chrome-plated .357, popped open the chamber, and loaded it. She spun the cylinder, then grinned darkly. Maybe she should make a game of it, play a little ancient Russian roulette—

The cell phone started ringing again.

The sound made her jerk. "*Damn* it," Violet hissed. She glared at it, but of course that didn't make it shut up. All she wanted was some peace, some *quiet*—

She yanked up the phone and snapped it open. Before she could say anything, Garth's voice shot through the earpiece. "*Violet, where have you been?*" he demanded. "*I've been calling and calling you.*" She didn't bother to answer, just stared at the wall and gritted her teeth while she waited to hear what else he had to say. Didn't it ever stop? "*Did you know you were famous?*" he finally asked. "*Check the box.*"

For a long few seconds, she did nothing, then she sighed and reached for the remote on the dusty nightstand. She found the power button and flicked it to ON, then steered it around and finally found a spot on the dirty ceiling where the screen image would show and she didn't have to put any effort into watching it. The quality was crappy—why wasn't she surprised?—but it still wasn't hard to make out the newscast. A couple of pushes on the volume button and she could hear a male reporter's voice commenting on the picture unfolding over her head.

"This footage was taken earlier of a Hemophage with what is reportedly a human child."

Violet dropped the remote and blinked as the image of a familiar playground came into view, faraway and obviously taken from an overhead position—a news helicopter, one of those roving things that people derisively called "flying ambulance chasers." The camera's high-powered viewpoint began to zoom in on the playground, closer and closer, until Violet could clearly recognize herself, sitting on the ground with Six draped across her lap. Her hands squeezed into fists as the scene in front of her widening eyes forced her to relive the heartache of Six dying in her arms. You had to appreciate the miracles of modern technology as, despite the distance, the camera still picked up the tears spilling down her cheeks, the moisture sparkling in the morning sunrise as it dripped onto Six's unmoving face.

The camera view panned out a bit and Violet saw the wall of Security Enforcers that had surrounded her and Six—funny, she hadn't even noticed they were there at the time, or if she had, she hadn't cared. The three-deep circle of men parted suddenly, and Violet recognized Daxus as he pushed through and stared down at her. There was no mistaking his glittering eyes or the unadulterated hatred on his face as he turned and pulled a gun from the holster of the Security Enforcer nearest him. The reporter's voice—Violet hadn't been listening so she had no idea what he was saying—rose with excitement as Daxus pushed the muzzle of the gun against the side of her head, then the camera abruptly cut away to the reporter himself, blathering on at full speed about unnecessary violence and who were the real victims and God knew what else. In the hotel room, Violet just lay there with the cell phone pressed into one ear, staring but not really seeing the image, realizing she had just vicariously relived her own death . . . as had the millions of people watching the six o'clock news broadcast.

Garth's voice yanked her back to reality. *"What do you think? Poster girl for a new era in human-vampire relations?"* He sounded ridiculously pleased with the whole thing.

Violet just kept staring at the ceiling, her mind working now, finally, going over and over what she had just seen, trying—again—to process everything that had happened over the last couple of days. Something wasn't meshing about Six, about the way he'd been born and raised, about the way Daxus had insisted on getting him back after allowing the child to be moved in the first place.

"Violet, listen," Garth said. *"Listen, I think I've found something. Something very interesting."*

I'll just bet you did, she thought suddenly. She yanked herself upright and swept the remote onto the floor, then glanced around the ratty motel room and curled her lip. "Where are you?" she demanded.

"Uh . . . northbound on the Kennedy."

She could hear the surprise in his voice at her unexpected interest. Weakness suddenly spilled over her and she wobbled on the bed, nastily sick to her stomach for a few seconds. When it passed, Violet swung her legs over the side and found a steady enough footing to stand. She knew where he was headed; random travel was rare for the Hemophage trucks—at least as far as any of the human security forces knew—and Garth's route on the Kennedy Expressway meant the secret docking area in Lincoln Park just to the south of the Lagoon. "Stay on course," she said as she pulled on her coat and shoved the .357 into a flat-space holster. She ran a hand over her hair to smooth it down, winced as she skimmed the incision, then inhaled deeply. It took an immense effort to make her voice stay crisp and strong, but she damned well did it. "I'll meet you."

⚡

Garth stood to the side and watched as Violet loaded up from the truck's arsenal, shoving weapon after weapon into the bottomless storage areas of the flat-space holsters on her hips. He kept trying to meet her eyes, but Violet wouldn't allow that—she didn't need emotion right now, or the bindings that would go with it. What she would see there would be too painful, especially given that he'd probably told himself he would never see her again.

The driver glanced back at them. "ArchMinistry coming up," he called. Garth scrubbed at his face but Violet just nodded her acknowledgment.

"V," Garth said, "when I said I'd found something interesting, this is *not* what I was talking about."

"I'm aware of that," Violet said shortly. She kept on stockpiling, gun after gun, lasers, everything and anything she could think of that might come in handy. She was going to need it *all*.

"Violet, you *can't* go in there," Garth said desperately. "It's impossible—why do you think we went through so much trouble to have you intercept the case *before* it got back to the ArchMinistry from the L.L.D.D.?"

"He's got Six in there."

Garth spread his hands. "For God's sake, V—the boy is *dead*. What's the point?" When she didn't answer, he paced back and forth in front of her, short, sharp steps that betrayed his frustration. "Retribution?" He jabbed a finger at her and she resisted the urge to slap it out of the way. "You're throwing yourself away for *nothing*."

Violet pressed her lips together tightly but still said nothing. What good would it do to remind him that there wasn't much left of her life to begin with? Stepping directly into her path, Garth reached out and flipped over the meta-crystal hanging from her neck; now it was almost entirely, frighteningly black. Despite his efforts— the substitute Incendiary Team, the surgery, the transfusions—he still couldn't stop the Hemophage virus. She was dying.

Violet ignored the anguished look he gave her and pushed him out of the way. They were pulling to a stop outside the main gate of the ArchMinistry now. "He's not dead," she said flatly.

Garth's eyes widened, then his expression slid into a scowl. "What? What do you mean?"

There was a jerk and the air brakes hissed as their momentum slowed. Violet pushed open the back door a couple of inches, then paused and turned back to face him. "I mean Six is alive."

Before he could respond, she opened the door the rest

of the way, then jumped down from the back and headed around to the front of the truck and the gate. But if she'd thought that would be the end of the conversation, she was wrong. An instant later, Garth leaped out and followed. "How can he be alive?" When she kept going rather than answer, he lunged forward and grabbed her arm roughly enough to make her wince. "Violet, *wait!*"

Finally Violet paused and met his eyes. He knew even before he spoke that there was no changing her mind, but he had to try anyway. "Look, Violet. What the boy wrote on that paper—it's the chemical foundation of what I'm certain is a cure for Hemophagia. Daxus's researchers probably developed it years ago in that same lab in which he was bred. I'm not certain how he got hold of it, but just give me a little time. I can cure you. I *know* it."

Violet stared at him. After a moment her granite expression softened and Garth actually thought she was going to relent. But no . . . she only reached out and gently placed her forefinger against his lips, silencing him.

Then she left him there and strode purposefully across the square toward the main entrance into the huge Arch-Ministry building.

And there was nothing Garth could do but watch her go.

TWENTY-FOUR

There was little that could be said about the cold lab other than just that—it was cold and sterile, a harsh, white environment that was never meant for anything alive. Six's small body lay on an alcohol-washed white granite slab under a bank of high-powered surgical lamps, and his skin was covered with a fine, sparkling sheen of ice crystals. There were already a half-dozen doctors and technicians waiting as Daxus, dressed in a surgical thermal-liquid hazard suit and wearing a breathing mask, approached the slab bearing the boy's body. He gave the other members of the medical team a calculating, deprecatory glance, then stared down at the child's body.

"The antigen can't survive without a living host," he finally told them, even though all of the men and women in the room already knew this. "But we may still be able to salvage some viable basic protein analogs that will save us time in reculturing the antigen in another clone." What they didn't know, of course, was the true nature of the antigen Daxus was talking about—few people did—but that was as it should be. Few people were willing to take part in creating something that could kill them.

He nodded at the lead surgeon, who in turn began barking orders to the other techs and doctors. They scurried around the laboratory like the well-trained rats they were, each performing a specific function to prepare for the coming dissection. It was only a matter of minutes before the elder medical member of the team stood at the head of the slab ready to unwrap the sterile steel bone saw he held in his left hand.

Daxus smiled. He always found it so interesting to see what the inside of a human body looked like.

Especially the brain.

≯

Standing silently behind the guard, Violet had had more than enough time to examine him. The man's body was silhouetted by the rising sun, and he was probably squinting out at his post, worrying more about the sting of the light in his watering eyes than the unlikely notion that someone might come up behind him. No doubt he took for granted being able to stand in the sunlight each day and thought himself capable and highly trained. Having a position guarding the perimeter probably made him think highly of himself, although it was likely he had no more than a high school diploma.

Foolish human, Violet thought derisively. This is the price you will pay for your overconfidence.

She decapitated him.

He never knew it was coming, so at least in that his death at her hands was merciful—no pain, no anticipation of the killing or dread of the unknown. Just a simple, clean swipe of her sword and his soul—if there was such a thing—was on its way to the hereafter . . . if there was such a thing as *that,* either.

As the sentry's body slumped sideways and went down, Violet reached forward and caught him by the arm, stopping his machine pistol before it could clatter to the ground and draw anyone else's attention. She let the corpse fall the rest of the way and regarded the weapon for a moment, then shrugged and tucked it under one arm—as long as it was loaded, there was never such a thing as a useless weapon. She glanced around but there was no one else with whom she'd have to deal, at least on a one-to-one basis. And let's face it: the only way in was the front door. Everything else—windows, doors, even the delivery areas—were covered with titanium bars or alloy mesh, all heavily wired and laser-sensored. Not only would she never make it undetected, nothing short of a bomb would get her through one of those entrances to begin with.

So . . . the front door it was.

No one could say that the entrance to the ArchMinistry wasn't heavily guarded—the dozen men standing at the ready as she approached were proof that it was. But even the largest army has its failings, and usually in communication—either they were so startled that Violet walked right up to them or Daxus hadn't bothered to circulate her identity down the ranks. And why should he? He believed to his bones that he had put the fatal shot into her skull.

In any event, that's all they did—watch—as she approached the archway of the high-tech weapons scanner, then stepped into it. The man assigned to reading the scan glanced at her with a bored expression on his face, then looked over at the screen a few inches in front of him. The blue and white display hesitated as the software tried to figure out what to do about the flat space it was reading, then it began cycling rapidly through the weaponry Violet had loaded into her flat-space holsters. The text ticked rapidly across the screen like wild digital confetti. The guard's jaw dropped.

"I'm here to see the Vice-Cardinal," Violet said simply, right before the alarms blared.

≉

In the cold lab, Daxus watched as the lead surgeon pressed the ON button on the bone saw and carefully lowered it to Six's forehead. He would start with a thin cut down the center line, then follow it across—

Through the speakers hidden in the ceiling tiles, the alarms began shrieking. The surgeon jerked the saw up and looked around, not sure what to do. The rest of the people in the room shuffled like nervous lemmings, looking anxiously to Daxus for guidance.

The Vice-Cardinal spun as the double doors at the far end of the lab burst open and a Security Tech barreled into the room, completely forgetting that it was supposed to stay a sterile environment. "It's her!" he cried breathlessly. His eyes were wide and panicked.

Daxus ripped off the hood of his hazard suit and stared at him. "But she's *dead!*"

The other man sputtered and couldn't find the words, so instead he yanked a mini Flex-Screen out of his side pocket and shoved it in front of Daxus's face. Daxus squinted at it, then jerked it out of the guard's hands and held it up higher so he could see . . . because he couldn't possibly be seeing what he thought he was. He just *couldn't*.

The lobby area, just behind the weapons scanner at the main entrance, was saturated with blood and layered with the dead bodies of his entry security forces.

"My God," Daxus breathed. This couldn't be happening, he wouldn't *let* it. He'd put the gun to Violet's head himself and squeezed the trigger—for God's sake, the damnable evening news had even put footage of it, which should never have existed in the first place, on the evening news for the entire city of Chicago to see. Now the local and national newspapers were buzzing about it, and of course the Internet had taken it to all parts global in a matter of minutes. The underground sites had even uploaded the more gory film of the actual shooting, although the camera had stopped filming right after the execution itself when the security forces had noticed the helicopter and begun firing at it.

If he was catching hell for killing her, what the hell was Violet doing *alive?*

But there she was, staring forward with an expression that was like stone as she stepped over the corpses and headed deeper into the building, completely unconcerned at the fresh security forces that were flowing into place behind her. She just kept coming.

Heading toward *him.*

Daxus tossed the Flex-Screen back at the guard, then gestured at the others to follow him as he raced out of the lab and into the corridor. After the sealed, sterile whiteness of the operating area, it was disconcerting to see dawn starting to spill through the narrow glass block windows that were set into the line of the ceiling along the hallway—sometimes it amazed him how deeply he could get immersed into this Hemophage thing, and just how quickly his life was passing. He really needed to get this Violet problem solved so he could move on with the bigger and better things—and there were so *many*—that he had planned for himself and the ArchMinistry of Medical Policy. He was going to be the next best thing to an American King, and he simply didn't need this Violet issue following him into his upcoming reign.

With his team streaming behind him like good little mice, Daxus hurried to the end of the corridor and turned into another, this one lined with his most elite force, the heavily armed ArchMinistry Sentinels. He should have been comforted, but . . . damn it. There it was—that nagging voice at the back of his skull, the memory of all the unfortunates who had already fallen at Violet's hand. God, the thought just made him absolutely *furious*. "The boy is *dead*," he snapped at no one in particular. "This is pure suicide!"

"Maybe someone should tell *her* that, sir."

Daxus blinked when he realized the Security Tech was still rushing alongside him, then sent the man a murderous look that made him wisely shut up. Another turn, and then he, the team, and the elite force were piling into a stairway and climbing—they didn't dare take the elevators with Violet somewhere in the building. The risk of being trapped by her was far too great. "I want the Gravity Shifters released from the armory," Daxus ordered.

The Security Tech gaped at him. "But, sir, they're still experimental!"

"Now, damn it!" Daxus nearly screamed. "I am going to *level* that bitch!"

TWENTY-FIVE

Without so much as blinking, Violet left a path of blood and destruction behind her, and with the sunrise at her back she slammed through the double doors and into the corridor not far behind Daxus. He was so close—her heightened vampire senses made her able to literally *smell* him, the cloying scent of too much expensive after-shave and the more earthly, sweaty *fear* that was spilling from his pores as he ran like the coward he was. When the doors banged shut behind her, Violet jerked up short and faced the waiting security forces, line after line of densely packed soldiers, and every one of them with a gun aimed directly at her. She stared at them for a long moment, and they stared back . . .

Then fired.

But she'd known it was coming—the anticipation was in the air, just like Daxus's terror. She dived right at them the instant before the front-line men squeezed their triggers, and the arc of her body took her down and made her roll into their legs, where she cut a blood-soaked swath through flesh and bone using a pair of swords pulled from the flat-space sheaths hanging on her hip belt. She swung and cut, swung and cut, and she lost track of time as she fought her way through the crush of bodies, *beneath* them, using the men's own fear of friendly fire to her own advantage.

Sometime later—a few minutes or perhaps a lifetime—Violet burst into the ArchMinistry Library, a two-story circular room lined with black and silver volumes, the culmination of centuries of the so-called wisdom that had resulted in the segregation and genocide of millions of other people just like her. She felt like she was living the same quarter hour over and over—charge into an area, find it full of soldiers, kill anything and everyone in sight, then do it all over again. Her hands were burning from the gunfire, nerves tingling and trembling from the never-ceasing firing from her left side, the constant back and forth sweep of her right. Draw, fire until empty, toss away, draw again. Draw, fire until empty, toss away, draw again. It became a litany running through her mind, undercutting the basic autopilot that kept her alive, moving her constantly forward and ahead of the soldiers' bullets, making sure she wove back and forth in patterns too random for any one person to follow.

And finally, it was just her, standing in the midst of a sea of carnage and stench and death.

Violet lifted her chin and looked around the room, careful to keep up the appearance of strength and fearlessness, determined not to show how tired she was. A room like this, Violet knew, would have a half-dozen cameras hidden away, just to make sure no one filched any of the nearly priceless books. Daxus was probably watching her on a bank of computer screens, planning his next move, thinking he was going to kill her all over again. Or maybe he wasn't doing that at all. Maybe he was sweating instead, trembling. She hoped so—she hoped his skin was gray with panic, that his hands were clammy and cold and shaking, his voice hoarse with anxiety as he ordered his men around.

While none of that seemed too far-fetched, it was more likely that he was conferring with his assistants and security managers, wondering how much she had left in the way of weapons and ammunition. Violet grinned as she recalled the expressions on the faces of the scanner techs back at the entrance, at the pure shock on their faces when their scanners revealed the practically bottomless flat-space arsenal she'd brought to help defend herself. If his security leaders had an ounce of courage in them, they'd be telling Daxus about those scans right now, as well as reminding him that everything they'd thrown at her so far had been virtually useless.

But there was no more time to dwell on her accomplishments, real or imagined. Violet scrambled over the corpses and made her way across the library, aiming for the exit on the other side of the room. Pushing through it, ready for another battle, she found herself entering instead an internal corridor. She was surprised to find it empty, silent, and well lit. That told her it was clearly a private exit meant for only the most precious among the ArchMinistry's inner circle. It was a good guess that Daxus was following it, and since she could see a dead end at the far side, that also meant he'd had only one route to take.

Up.

She leaned against the wall, panting and betting that there were no hidden cameras in this private corridor. She could feel her body tiring, wanting to give out, but she mustn't let the physical side of herself take control right now. There were more important things in the world than herself—Six, for instance. She *knew* the boy was alive, just as she knew Daxus had come through this corridor. She would find Daxus, and when she did, she would find Six.

Violet wiped at her face, then realized her hand was wet—she was covered in blood. Was it hers? Or that of the men she had killed? She had no idea. She hurt in dozens of places, everything from beestinglike annoyances to bone-deep aches, but she honestly didn't know if she had any openly bleeding wounds. She didn't feel anything major and right now, she didn't have time to be concerned about it.

She took a deep breath, tuned out the pain, and began to climb the stairwell at the end of the corridor.

⚡

He was sweating.

Daxus pulled an expensive silk handkerchief from his jacket pocket and pressed it under his chin, trying to look unaffected in front of the elite Sentinel soldiers waiting for his orders. He wished he could see their faces, but their dark visors hid everything. Were they laughing at his fear? If they were, they were fools—they should be just as afraid. His gaze darted across them, searching for holes, searching for weakness, anything that Violet might find and exploit. He saw nothing, but then he'd believed that about the literally hundreds of men before these, all of whom had fallen before the blade of her swords and the blaze of her guns.

Daxus paced in front of them like an Army Drill Sergeant, trying to mask his nervousness behind a commanding, merciless demeanor. Did it show anyway? Of course it did, in every bead of perspiration that rolled down his neck and soaked into his collar, and he wasn't stupid enough to think that any one of these men would miss something like that. They were too highly trained and there was nothing to be done to hide it. If they silently ridiculed him because of it, that was fine—Daxus was willing to bet that every man in this room would start sweating just like him once they faced off with Violet in the flesh.

"Excellent work," he said, because he had to say *something*, he couldn't just keep walking silently back and forth. "Everyone's doing excellent work. Keep it up." The words sounded inane even to his own ears, but he couldn't seem to think of anything better. Finally, he just turned his back and ducked inside the door to the Mortal Sciences Lab.

In here, he felt a bit—but only that—safer. The men waiting inside the lab were the very best the ArchMinistry had to offer in the way of protection . . . no, the best of the best. They were the Praetorian Guard, named after the soldiers who had once helped rule ancient Rome. But were they going to be good enough? God, he hoped so.

They looked at him expectantly and he said, "Everything's good," automatically. "Everything's under control. We're just going to . . ." He glanced toward the closed door and was helpless to stop himself from visibly swallowing. "Wait here for a little while."

⚡

It didn't take long for Violet to reach the rooftop, and if she had previously been surprised about the emptiness of the path in front of her, this situation fell right into the realm of her expectations—the place was crawling with Security Commandos, a miniature army clearly positioned between her and her goal. That would never do, and she waded into them like the blade of a lawnmower, moving with precision and speed, with every move calculated to expend the least amount of energy necessary. She was past the point of feeling pain or exhaustion, of feeling anything but the need to keep going. If she'd been a regular person, or a human soldier, she might have been proud of herself when she reduced the assault force to nothing more than moaning puddles of destroyed flesh, but she wasn't a regular person, and she was dying on top of that. She was just . . .

Tired.

At the end of the battle, she slumped against the entrance to the skybridge on the far side—toward which she had been struggling the entire time—and let herself rest, but only for a moment. There was something odd about her sword hand, something . . . *cold,* and when she glanced down at it, her eyes widened at the double spurt of blood—too much to lose. Two fingers and part of the hand were just . . . *gone,* shot off by one of the Commando's bullets. She hadn't even felt it.

Violet clamped her other hand over it to slow the bleeding and her face twisted. She was losing steam, losing blood, losing *herself*—could she even do this? She wasn't afraid of dying—she'd done that once and wanted to do it a hundred times more—but she *was* afraid of failing, of being killed and losing Six forever, leaving him in the hands of a cold and heartless man whose only goals in life were power and greed.

No, damn it—she would *not* fail, she would *not!* Violet let go of her wound and wiped her sodden hand on the side of her coat, then spun her machine pistol around to face the roof's surface and fired it. Two seconds later, without even hesitating, she swung the gun over and pressed the stubs of her missing fingers against the red-hot barrel, searing the wound—most of it, anyway—shut. Even for her, this time there was no suppressing a scream.

It took a precious half minute for the grayness to clear from her vision, then Violet pushed off from the wall and steadied herself. Her hand was still oozing blood but at least it wasn't pouring out of her anymore—she'd bought herself a little more time, although at this rate her time left was going to be shortened considerably. If she was going to find Six and get him to safety, she needed to get on with it.

Straightening her shoulders, Violet stepped onto the skybridge that led to the Mortal Sciences Lab. That's where Daxus would have Six, she was sure of it. Heading toward her from the other end were more soldiers, and more after that, but she would not be stopped.

She would *not*.

⚡

Violet was coming.

Only a fool would miss the signs, or misread them and stupidly believe in the wrong outcome. Daxus could hear the screams and shouting of men, a barrage of seemingly never-ending gunfire—even a few small explosions as various pieces of equipment got in the way of the ammunitions fire meant for human flesh. If he'd been a man with a conscience, the screaming would have weighed heavily on him, but he hadn't the time to be concerned about the lost lives of others. He was the most important thing here, and he could only be concerned about that. This woman, this *vampire,* was like a juggernaut, a huge, unstoppable force that was going to crush everything in its hunger to get to him . . .

Fine.

He still had a few surprises for her.

Daxus found the gaze of the head of his Praetorian Guard and nodded curtly at him. "Why don't you and your men go out there and see what's going on," he suggested. His voice was mild but the man was smart enough to read between the lines. Daxus was pleased to see that just below the line of the leader's diamond-black helmet, a cruel smile flashed briefly across the craggy face. Without making a sound, the leader made a series of sharp gestures in the air; his men snapped to action—no doubt each hand movement meant something well beyond Daxus's understanding. They moved together like a precision machine, streaming out the door in eerie, deadly silence and leaving Daxus alone in the lab.

Well, not quite.

There was the body of the boy.

With one ear following the sounds outside, Daxus moved over to stand next to the cold granite slab and stared down at Six's corpse. All this fuss, and for what? A cadaver. What the hell did Violet plan to do with the kid's body when—*if*—she got it, anyway? The antigen served no purpose for her, and she had to realize that whatever was in the child could be recultured. It might take time, but there was no deadline.

No limitations, either.

Daxus smiled as he heard the whine of small machinery on the other side of the lab door. Experimental? Oh, no . . . the Gravity Shifters had been operational for months.

Just ask Violet.

⚡

The last corridor.

The last of the soldiers . . . she hoped.

These men were . . . different, silent and clearly more cunning. They didn't scare her, but they did make her more wary—you never knew what kinds of tricks Daxus had up his sleeve, what was next in the nastiness that might come out of that man's brain. There were only eight of them, dressed completely in black and surrounding her without a sound, measuring her movements, assessing her strength. That was all right—others had tried the same thing and failed.

She drew her sword but the fancy spin-work of previous times was gone forever, lost with the two fingers. The wound on her hand throbbed in time to her rapid heartbeat, giving her an ugly jolt with every pulse. That was all right, too—the pain helped keep her head clear when the loss of blood might have made her sluggish or slowed her reflexes. There was nothing like a couple of bundles of raw nerve endings to make you sit up and take notice of the situation around you, to keep you aware of your own painful flesh.

They circled her warily and she let them, moving in

one-half time to their steps, gaze flicking back and forth. She was ready to dive in, ready for blood, when a hand signal from the one who was apparently the commander made them all move at once—

Onto the walls and ceilings.

Gravity Shifters.

Damn it!

She crouched in the midst of them, feeling like a fly caught in the middle of a three-dimensional spiderweb filled with black widows. The soldiers scuttled over her head, around and behind her back, everywhere . . . but at least they were smart enough to know that guns were a danger here; they would end up as easily shooting one another as they would her. Swords were smarter, and so each man wielded at least one, a few others, those more proficient, had a weapon for each hand. The metal edges sparkled overhead, bouncing light back and forth and making it difficult for Violet to keep track of who was where—it was like trying to monitor the stars sparkling in a lightening sky.

Violet ground her teeth and waited. She should have anticipated this—if the Hemophages had Gravity Shifters, it stood to reason that the humans did, too. They were always a little behind in technology because they didn't have desperation fueling them like the vampires, but they eventually caught up. Hemophages had gotten the Gravity Shifters operational months ago, so it was certainly about time. But damn it . . . it wasn't *fair.* She'd had so little to her advantage—yeah, speed and strength—but she was outnumbered by the hundreds and with a shortened life span to boot. There should be *something* to even the damned odds. It just wasn't fucking *fair.*

But it wasn't going to make a damned bit of difference.

"You're all going to die," she said flatly, and went to work to prove it.

TWENTY-SIX

Daxus had heard it all.

The screams, the gunfire, the silence.

More screams, the clash of swords, the second silence.

Daxus was alone now in the Mortal Sciences Lab—well, except for the body of the kid who had started all of this. When it was finally quiet, he had some time, about twenty seconds actually, to let his imagination go to work. It was amazing how quickly the mind could function, and his brain managed to cover both ends of the spectrum; in the first circumstance, the last two or three of his brave and strong Praetorian Guard triumphantly pushed open the door, hauled Violet's dead body into the lab, and tossed it at his feet. Daxus looked down at it and prodded it disdainfully with one foot, then lifted his chin and gave it a little dismissive wave of his hand—the signal for his soldiers to drag it away and get it out of his life for good. He went back to dissecting the boy's body, culturing the antigen and, essentially, becoming the most important man in the entire world.

The second version, however, was not so kind to his psyche. His mind gave him the disturbing image of Violet storming through the lab door and gunning him down in his tracks, before he even had a chance to say a word or defend himself. He felt each imaginary bullet rip through his skin and put liquid trails of fire into his body, felt his ribs shatter and his sternum explode, experienced the sensation of his own heartbeat stuttering and slowing until a terrifying, inescapable blackness overwhelmed him.

Neither one happened, but the second illusion was a whole lot closer to the truth.

≷

She'd had enough surprises for one day, so Violet pushed the door to the Mortal Sciences Lab open carefully, standing off to the side and letting the metal-reinforced wall be her shield. Everything about her body was in high gear and silently screaming—her pulse was racing, her blood was singing, her nerve endings were throbbing, especially the ugly remaining nubs on her sword hand. She had so much adrenaline in her system right now that she had a constant, high-pitched whine in her ears. She still had plenty of guns in her flat-space holsters, but for now she was going to hang on to her sword—funny, but that long, sharp blade had always turned out to be the best backup that a girl had.

She snapped a quick look past the threshold and yanked herself backward again, but that glance had given Violet the comfort zone she needed. Still being cautious, she inched around the edge of the door and finally stepped into the room. Lo and behold, there was Daxus,

and all by his lonesome, too. Wouldn't you know it—
he'd run out of guards. Apparently she'd worked her way
through his entire inventory.

Her mouth twisted. "Is that all you've got, you son of
a bitch?"

Daxus opened his mouth to answer, but for a long moment he couldn't—he was literally trembling so much
that his lips didn't want to work. Finally he managed to
swallow, then speak. "For God's sake, Violet—the child's
dead."

She could hear the desperation in his voice, the puz-
zlement. But Violet only sneered back at him. "You obviously don't have a clear grasp of what 'dead' really is."
She took a step in his direction and pulled her lips back
in a sinister smile. "Allow me to demonstrate."

Daxus scrambled backward, knocking aside a cart
covered in medical implements. It crashed to the floor,
but he didn't notice, even when his feet nearly tangled in
the metal pieces. "Violet, for God's sake!" he said again.
"I'm unarmed!"

But she only gave him another hideously dark grin and
stared pointedly at each of his arms. "No," she said
mockingly. She'd switched her weapon to her other hand,
and a jerk of her uninjured wrist made her sword blade
vibrate in the air between them. "Not yet, you're not."

"Wait!" Daxus held up a hand, then hastily yanked it
back and shoved it behind him, trying to steady himself.
He looked at her with naked curiosity. He just *had* to ask.
"What happened?"

She gazed back at him and knew exactly what he
meant. "I found a way back," she said simply. He stared
at her but it was clear he didn't understand. That was all
right, because neither did she, and she certainly wasn't

going to tell him about Garth. In fact, she didn't care to tell him about anything else at all.

But before she could move, Daxus's hand snapped forward again, and this time it held a flame-throwing pistol, one of those unpleasant little surprises that Violet had tried her best to avoid by coming into this lab so cautiously. Clearly she hadn't been careful *enough*.

"Oh, no," Daxus said when she started to step to the side. He smiled, quite pleased with himself and the way things had shifted in his favor. He waggled it in the air between them, always making sure its barrel was aimed at her face.

She shrugged, then suddenly flicked her injured hand at him. With an almost slow-motion beauty, she—and Daxus—watched a thin spray of blood droplets sail across the distance separating them, flowing like a small crimson shower. He opened his mouth to scream, then gasped and reeled backward instead, scrubbing frantically at his face with his left hand. "Blood!" he cried. "You got your *blood* on me!" Rage suffused his face, making his skin go purple. The flame pistol's muzzle had wandered upward, and now he jerked it back in Violet's direction and squeezed the trigger—

—but Violet was faster.

She snapped her sword up in front of her and turned the blade so that the flat of it faced Daxus's weapon. The stream of thickened petroleum fuel that shot out of the flame pistol's barrel hit dead center on the blade, then sprayed harmlessly to either side.

Daxus growled in frustration and yanked the gun to eye level as he backed up—there, splattered over the pilot light on the ignition switch, was a dime-sized drop of Violet's blood.

If he expected her to comment, he was going to wait a long time—she only looked calmly back at him. Furious, Daxus threw the weapon aside and with a murderous look in her direction, he dived to the other side of the cold granite slab holding Six's covered body. Before Violet could go after him, he reappeared; held triumphantly—and expertly—in his right hand was a long and wickedly sharp Turkish sword.

Another one of Daxus's ugly secrets, but that was okay—she was always up for a good sword fight. He lunged at her but Violet parried his attack easily, and each used the first few moments of swordplay to measure the skill of the other. Again and again, in and out, and as they circled the slab, Violet's gaze flicked to something on his arm—blood. He was cut. A corner of her mouth lifted.

Daxus took a half second to follow her gaze, but he only shrugged. "Yes," he agreed. "No doubt in a fair fight you would beat me." He shook his head and gave her a tooth-filled grin. "But that's not how I got where I am today."

Before she could retort, he smacked the top of the diamond biohazard ring he wore on one hand with the hilt of his sword. Violet jerked as one by one the high windows around the top of the lab began to black out—that damned ring must have had a remote built into it. In only a few seconds, the room was plunged into darkness.

Damn.

Violet's head snapped to the right as a sudden, faint whirring sound split the silence. She identified the noise instantly: Starlight Goggles adjusting to what little light there was in the room. The amount certainly wasn't enough to do *her* any good but the goggles would amplify it to give the wearer—Daxus—a pretty damned clear picture of the interior of the room.

And whoever was in it.

"Can you see me, Violet?" Daxus's voice was full of contempt and . . . *entertainment*. The bastard was actually having *fun*. "Because I can see *you*. Too bad you're the freak who converted with only mild photokemia."

He was right about that—her brethren were able to see in the dark much better than she. But answering would only give her position away that much sooner—at least if she was quiet she could try to hide, to duck down behind the body slab and work her way around it or under it. Desperately, Violet tried to build a mental picture that would remind her of what else was in the lab—if Daxus had been directly in front of her on the other side of the slab, the cart that he had overturned should be slightly to her left. She needed to try to avoid it, as well as the implements that had spilled on the floor. Not only were they sharp, they would be noisy against the tile floor and—

Violet spun in the darkness as she heard Daxus break into a run, but she couldn't tell from which direction he was coming—

Until he put a long strip of fire along her left back shoulder blade.

Violet cried out and instinctively ducked away, then heard Daxus's blade whistle over her head as she rolled on the floor—a second too late and she'd probably be dead. Something sharp and wrapped in plastic poked at the rear of her thighs—one of the scalpels that had hit the floor from the fallen cart. She snatched it up as she kept rolling, then crawling, trying to find her way around the granite slab that had suddenly become a barrier to the path of safety rather than something behind which she could hide.

Desperate to distract him, she tossed the scalpel into the darkness, hoping he would follow its sound. No such luck—he ignored it completely.

"Oooh," Daxus said complacently. "Bet that stung."

As much as she wanted to snipe back at him, Violet didn't dare answer. Did he know where she was? Of course he did, but she still couldn't see a damned thing. There was a hiss in the air, the unmistakable sound of a blade, and reflex made her jerk backward. Too late, and she gave another outraged cry as Daxus's sword parted leather, fabric, and skin across her rib cage—if she hadn't backed up, the bastard would have easily eviscerated her. She wasn't doing so hot in this confrontation.

"Don't worry," Daxus said smugly. "I didn't hit anything vital . . . *yet*. We're saving that—" Instead of finishing his sentence, he managed to cut her again, this time catching her down the side of one leg. The pain was too much, unexpected, and Violet couldn't stop another scream from escaping her lips.

Damn it, she would *not* be filleted by a lowly veterinarian turned homicidal maniac—it was a vulgar, embarrassing way to die and she would *not* have him standing and gloating over her corpse again the way he had back in the playground. She had seen that on video and she didn't need to imagine the things he might do to her here, where he was positive there were no cameras to record his atrocities.

She strained her eyes again, but it was useless. She simply could *not* see in here, not without some kind of light. Her hands scrabbled across the floor, the cold stone tiles that were easy to clean of blood and body fluids—

Oh, yeah.

With her mouth pulled into a rictus grin, Violet brought up the sword she was still holding on to, then whacked its edge against the floor, hard. A fistful of sparks flew from the blade where it kissed the stone beneath her knees. She heard Daxus grunt in surprise from the other side of the room as the flare of unexpected light stung his eyes before the super-sensitive goggles could adjust to it. He couldn't make it to her position in time to stop her from doing it again, slightly to the right of the first hit. This time the sparks bounced onto what she needed, a splattering off the main puddle of petroleum fuel.

Whoooosh.

Fire blossomed along her blade, rich and red-orange, fed by the fuel still coating the steel. It was more than enough light for Violet to see by, and when Daxus charged toward her, her weapon was already raised and on the offense. She met him strike for strike, instantly igniting his blade as the fuel jumped from one metal to the other. With his advantage gone, after the first strike Daxus tore off the cumbersome Starlight Goggles and tossed them angrily aside. He flailed at Violet with an intensity that she suddenly couldn't match—her energy and strength were waning, being sucked away by the ever-present disease and the nonstop battles she had fought over the last several days. Violet could see the blood-covered parts of her own body every time Daxus swiped at her, every time his blade connected and made a wound that was instantly cauterized by the flames. All the flash-views did was remind her of the pain, and her exhaustion. Had she even hurt him in return? Cut him even once?

Tchiiiiing!

And then her sword was suddenly *gone*.

She dived into the darkness without hesitating, knowing it was her only refuge. Daxus's Starlight Goggles were down here somewhere, but they wouldn't do any good while there was firelight. All she had going for her right now was the darkness itself—the flaming sword that Daxus was using as a torch would hinder his eyesight more than help it. Even so, it was only a matter of time until he found her.

"Do you hope God's merciful, Violet?" he asked in a taunting voice. He sounded outright gleeful. "Do you think He'll welcome you into His arms, like the so very many you've sent His way?"

Violet's bruised fingers brushed lightly against something on the floor. Her fingers closed around the object instinctively, then she lifted it, careful to stay silent. She let him ramble on but didn't bother to follow the words as she smiled and rose in the darkness behind him. "I know He will," she said calmly. Daxus jerked around, trying to squint past his burning blade so he could see her. "Do you know why?" Before he could answer, Violet brought her hand around from where she'd been holding it behind her back. "Because God's a girl."

Daxus moved his sword to the side, then his eyes bulged as he realized she was pointing the flame pistol right at him. It wouldn't light, of course, but who needed a light when there was already fire?

"Let there be light," Violet said softly, and squeezed the trigger.

Petroleum fuel arced out of the muzzle and past his sword, catching Daxus full in the face and chest. He screamed but he didn't even have enough time to take a breath for a second cry—his lungs fried and he went up in flames instantly as the fuel streamed past the fire on his weapon. Mouth wide in agony, flesh already blackening and blistering, he reached for Violet one final time—

Her sword snapped forward and she sliced off the fingers of Daxus's hand.

His biohazard ring slid free and sailed upward. Violet snatched it out of the air, and when Daxus's flaming body would have fallen toward her, Violet's well-timed kick pushed it backward and away from her and the granite slab on which Six lay. Daxus crashed against the wall, then curled up and sank to the ground. The stench of cooked flesh spun in the air but Violet ignored it, letting only enough time pass to make sure he wasn't going to somehow rise again. When she was certain that he was finally, *finally* dead, she turned and pressed the surface of the ring. "Let there be *life*," she said softly.

And one by one the windows faded from black to transparent, and let the dawn shine into the Mortal Sciences Lab.

AT THE END . . .

Taking Six off the dissection slab had been harder than Violet had imagined it would be. She had convinced herself that the child was alive, and while she still believed that was true, even her rock-solid faith started to falter when she lifted his ice-covered flesh from the unyielding surface and cradled him in her arms. There was something about deadweight that was . . . *undeniable,* and if there was ever a time when the religious people of the world could have preached about the meaning of believing in something mankind couldn't see, about *faith,* this was sure it. The boy's neck stretched out and his head hung straight back and down, while his body stayed limp and completely unresponsive—he had all the appeal and warmth of a cold fish taken out of the refrigerator.

But one thing kept Violet going, and that was the still-remembered knowledge that was rooted in her old medical background. By now, if Six was truly dead, his body should have been stiff and exhibiting full rigor mortis. Most laypeople thought that once a body got that way, that's how it stayed. But that wasn't true. There was a certain timetable that death followed, a predictable one that had helped both doctors and the police calculate the time of death for centuries: a dead body was pliable for so long, it was stiff for so much longer, and then it was forever limp, amen. By now Six's "corpse" should be well into the proverbial stiff as a board realm. He should look a lot like the cadavers generally seen in the funeral home caskets, except without the makeup and dress-up duds for burial. But he didn't, and to Violet that meant he wasn't dead, that what she had seen on that video of her and the child in the park was true. He wasn't dead at all.

He was just . . . *waiting*.

She had to admit that she had no idea how or when to bring him out of this state of . . . whatever it was. Coma? Suspended animation? She knew only that she was positive he was *in* it. Daxus had no doubt gone by the seemingly inescapable evidence of the meta-crystal that had hung around the child's neck. It was gone now, probably disposed of by his medical team, but Violet clearly remembered its solid black color as the last seeming spark of life had left Six's body—Daxus would have taken that visual evidence as nothing short of biblical truth. And under normal circumstances, he would have been right. But these were anything but normal circumstances, weren't they? Now the normal was abnormal, and based on that, all that was left was for Violet to help Six somehow find a way back as Garth had helped her.

No one tried to stop her as she carried Six up to the rooftop. Had she really killed Daxus's entire army? She doubted it, but she could picture him ordering all those men to their deaths without explaining his motives to his higher-ups—and there were, of course, others who were superior to him. They might be silent and out of sight, but they were there—they always were. If that was the case, Daxus's death—he likely had a life monitor embedded in the base of his brain and tied into the ArchMinistry's main motherboard—would have brought to a halt any and all of his ugly, secret little enterprises . . . such as the plan to virtually enslave mankind. In any case, here she was—a vampire—standing on the roof of the ArchMinistry in the light of the morning sun, like some kind of a goddess offering up the body of a child in return for untold favors.

Behind her sunglasses, Violet could see across most of the city's sprawl from her position. It was so quiet in the morning light, so blissfully serene—full of foolish people ignorant of the evil residing within its seemingly peaceful boundaries. She knelt facing the east, feeling the rays of the sun on her own skin at the same time that they touched Six's flesh, warming the skin and melting the thin layer of ice crystals still covering parts of his body. The droplets crawled toward the ground, wetting his hair and soaking into her leather coat. Like the city, he looked so peaceful, so quiet . . . but she knew he was in there. She *knew.*

Violet smiled and brushed his cheek tenderly with her fingertips. "Six," she whispered. "Six. Wake up, Six."

For a long, painful moment, there was nothing. Had she been wrong about this? Had she done so much, and killed so many, just to get to this point only to discover Garth was right?

Then, without actually opening his eyelids, Six blinked.

Another blink, and another, like he was stranded in REM sleep and fighting to get out, just as she had when

Garth had brought her back from Daxus's fatal shot. It seemed to take forever, but finally the boy opened his eyes and focused on her. She'd been the last thing he'd seen back at the playground, and it was only fitting that she be the first thing he saw now. Her smile widened.

"V-Violet?" Six's voice was hoarse, barely audible. He swallowed with effort. "I t-thought I was dead."

Violet shook her head and pulled him into a half-sitting position so she could rock him like a baby. "No, no," she assured him. He felt good in her arms, like he belonged there. "No, my dear."

Yes, she'd been right about what she'd glimpsed on that news footage. God love the freedom of the press and their ability to broadcast the evil of the world. Even they hadn't realized what they had filmed, and amid all the excitement and fervor in the playground, Daxus, for all his phobias and sterility, had missed that one tiny thing—

A tear, one of Violet's, that had fallen onto Six's nose and slid unnoticed into the boy's half-open eye.

Without realizing it, without *intending* it, Violet had done the one thing that would, at least for the next decade, give Six the strength and stamina he would need to fight off the deadly antigen his barely human father had embedded in his blood: the Hemophage virus.

His eyes started to clear. When Six looked up at her quizzically, Violet smiled again. "You've just been reborn," she told him firmly. After a moment he returned her smile, then she released her hold and stood. She held out a hand and he took it, giving himself a few seconds to climb to his feet. He was unsteady at first, but it wasn't long before his balance returned and he could stand on his own and gaze out at the lightening cityscape with undisguised wonder. There was, Violet suddenly realized, an entire world out there that he had never even known about. Playgrounds? They were the least of it. There were schools and museums and stores and movies and countless other avenues of knowledge and entertainment. This was a child who'd been fed only food substitute and a few vending machine items—wait until he tasted fresh fruit, pizza, and popcorn. There were so many things waiting for him. She might not be here to share them with him, or she might, but in either case she refused to think of what was waiting since he had only ten years to experience it. If she could take Garth's words to heart, that ten-year period might hold a miracle for Six and the rest of her kind.

Violet let Six look for a few more moments, then put a hand on his shoulder and tugged on him until he turned to face her. "I've been meaning to give you something," she told him. She knelt in front of him, then reached into a pocket with her uninjured hand. His gaze followed the movement, then he squinted as he realized there was something . . . *funny* about that spot on her jacket. Was it moving?

She grinned and pulled her hand from her pocket, then held it up. Six's mouth dropped open in astonishment. He gave a very childlike squeal and reached for the tiny object on her palm, and Violet willingly handed over the rat she'd rescued from a corner of the Mortal Sciences Lab right before she'd gathered up Six's body. With its cage—labeled "Aurora Six"—crushed in a corner, the creature had nearly been another one of the mortalities of her battle with Daxus. She'd seen the soft white creature cowering in the corner, terrified by the flames and the fight, by the hideous smell of burning human flesh. Aurora Six had been used to human touch, and when she'd cooed at it, the rat had come to her, more than willing to hide in the safe darkness of her jacket pocket. Violet had decided it would make the perfect beginning pet for a gentle child just learning to explore the world.

Six stroked the rat's shining white fur carefully and it chittered up at him and sat up, rubbing its whiskers with its paws and looking as if it had never been more comfortable. "It's beautiful," he said simply.

Violet looked back at Six, seeing not the rat, but the boy, and the world, and the future.

"Yes," she said, and smiled. "It is."

ABOUT THE AUTHOR

Yvonne Navarro has been a waitress, a nurse's aide, a bookkeeper and gift shop cashier, an accounting clerk, and a secretary in everything from office furniture stores to a journalism society. Her first novel, *AfterAge*, was published in 1993 and was a finalist for the Bram Stoker Award for Superior Achievement in a First Novel. In 1995 her second novel, *deadrush*, was published, and it also was a finalist for the Bram Stoker Award, this time in the category of Superior Achievement in a novel. *Final Impact*, her third solo novel, was published in 1997, and won both the *Chicago Women in Publishing*'s Award for Excellence in Adult Fiction and the "Unreal Worlds" Award for Best Horror Paperback of 1997 from the *Rocky Mountain News*. She's also written a number of media tie-in novels such as *Hellboy*, *Elektra*, and *Species*, and several *Buffy the Vampire Slayer* novels. She is currently an Operations Officer for a military contractor at historic Fort Huachuca in southern Arizona. She has written nineteen novels and has one nonfiction book, and still has those never-ending plans for more. She lives in southern Arizona with her husband, author Weston Ochse, and two Great Danes, Lily and The Goblin.